Reign II:

A Story Of The Seventh Millennium

David J. Keyser

By The Author Of *We See Him As He Is*.

ISBN: 978-0-6151-5764-1

Dedication:

To The King.

Foreword

"We say that when the King returns it will be wonderful. But why don't we dream of it? If it will be real, it should be the subject of our fondest dreams. Even if we can not be sure now what it will be like, dreams can sometimes glimpse the truth."

The author does not pretend to actually describe in this book what the millennial reign will be like or to predict the time for the beginning of those 1,000 years. This is all fictional speculation, a sort of "What if . . ." story based on one historic position that there will be a literal reign for a thousand years from Jerusalem which still lies in our future.

Dais - a platform raised above the floor of a room, or a raised out-door terrace for people of importance to use.

In a moment, in the twinkling of an eye, at
the last trump: for the trumpet shall sound,
and the dead shall be raised incorruptible,
and we shall be changed.
I Cor. 15:52

Do ye not know that the saints shall judge
the world?
I Cor. 6:2

They lived and reigned with Christ a
thousand years.
Rev. 20:4

The Contents Of This Volume

1. Carl   17

2. Orin   63

3. Patricia   95

4. Andrew   143

5. Mandie   175

6. Ken   203

7. Kathryn   247

The Annatic Line

1. *Anna was the mother of Mark.
2. *Mark was the father of Carl.
3. **Carl was the father of Alice.
4. Alice was the mother of May.
5. *May was the aunt of Orin and Eric.
6. **Orin was the father of James.
7. James was the father or Patricia.
8. **Patricia was the mother of Andrew.
9. **Andrew was the father of Joan and Marie.
10. *Joan was the sister of Marie. Marie was the mother of Mandie.
11. **Mandie was the mother of Ken.
12. **Ken was the father of Merle.
13. *Merle was the mother of Kathryn.
14. **Kathryn was the mother of Sarah and Elizabeth.
15. *Tim is the son of Elizabeth who died in childbirth. Tim was raised by Sarah.

*As found in the 1st Volume, *We See Him As He Is*

** As Found in the 2nd Volume, this volume.

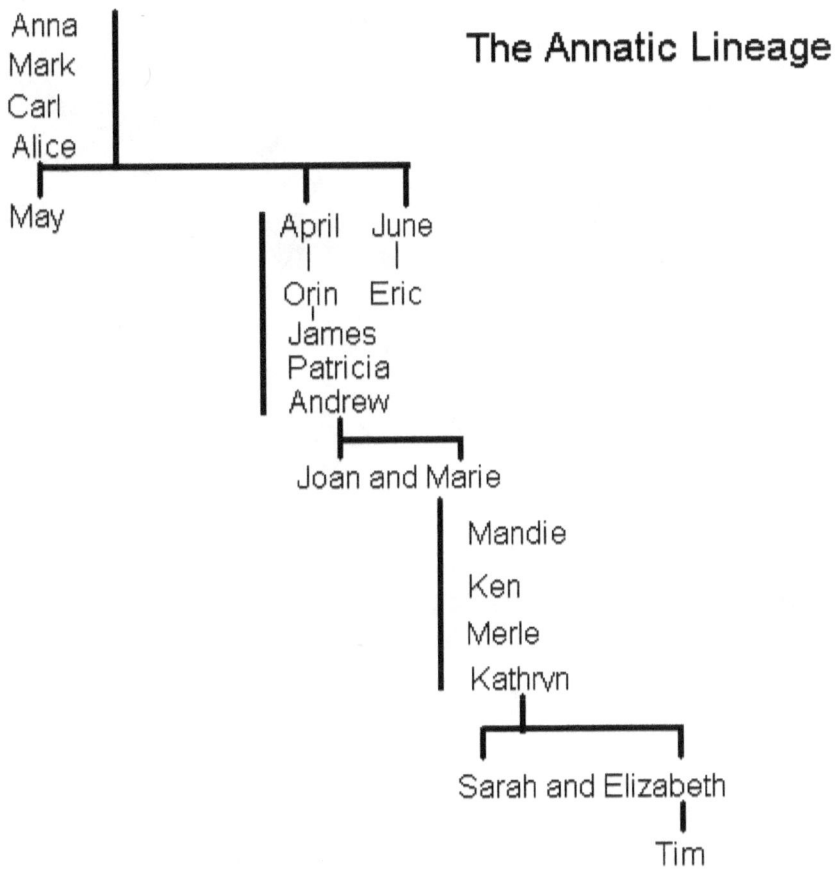

The Annatic Lineage

Introduction

WHEN the Emperor returned after his long absence in the other realm, he immediately subdued the entire earth by his glorious power. He established his capital at the ancient city of Jerusalem and appointed rulers over the earth. The earth was divided into two halves, the eastern and the western. Over each of these was appointed a Viceroy who reported directly to the Emperor Himself. The Viceroy of the Eastern half of the world is John the Beloved who rules from the Isle of Patmos where he was martyred in the 1st century of the Emperor's absence and which has been entirely rebuilt to hold his palace and his court. The Western half of the world is under the rule of Viceroy Luis Cepata. He rules from his palace in Montevideo where he was martyred in the 21st century of the Emperor's absence. The Viceroys, like all other Immortals were resurrected at the Emperor's Glorious Return. Under the Viceroys are Territorial Governors or Over-Lords who are over large portions of the world. Under these Over-Lords are Metropolitans who rule over large cities and their surrounding areas. Under the Metropolitans are various local governors. These rulers are all Immortals who won their places by faithful service and often martyrdom for the Emperor during their mortal lives when the Emperor was not seen in this world.

The angels of the Emperor are numerous and many are now visible in the world. They have their own hierarchy and they serve the Emperor and his Governors throughout the earth. The Immortals are often not found in this world but are with the Emperor on "the other side" or "beyond the veil" where mortals are not able to go. They fellowship and feast with Him there and come and go as they please. The Immortals and angels travel by means known only to them and appear and disappear throughout the earth at will. They are able to take a mortal with them to any place in this world, on this side of the "great veil." One special Immortal is the Governor Elaine, a sub-governor of the Metropolitan Henry Sawyer of Atlanta. Elaine is also the Imperial Legate in charge of the house of Anna where Anna and her descendants have been designated the Keepers of the Sacred records of the Empire. The Keeper is the only mortal with an angel assistant, his name is Lucius and he serves each generation of Keepers.

All mortals including the Keepers are born and live and die just as the Immortals did during their mortality when the Emperor was not seen on the earth.

This is the second volume of the journals of the children of Anna which were written during the now nearly one thousand years of the reign of the Emperor who rules from Jerusalem. Our family was chosen to be the Keepers of the records of all that went before and all that happened during the Glorious Reign. Eventually, after the Keeper May, our full titles became: the Keeper of the Ancient Books, the Primary Interpreter of the books of Anna, the Chronicler of Imperial truth, and the Spiritual Primate of the mortals on the earth.

I am the Keeper Tim, probably the last of the line. I am the 15th generation from Mother Anna by direct succession. It is the year 997 C.R. In this volume I have compiled excerpts from the journals of my ancestors Carl, Orin, Patricia, Andrew, Mandie, Ken, and Kathryn. Not everything has been reproduced here; that would require many hundreds of volumes. Each entry is either dated in the glorious year Christus Regnus (C.R.), or where my ancestor left no date it is marked No Date [N.D.]. I have also added the dates of office for each.

Carl

214 –280 C.R.

04.14.214 C.R.   My name is Carl. I am now the Keeper. Mark was my father, Anna my grandmother. I take up my pen to tell you something of my time in this unique family office that began with Anna. The first memory that I wish to relate happened when I was about 7 years old.

I was always excited when I got to see my father. This was very seldom as he was almost always busy with his many duties. I would frequent my father's study often in the hopes of finding him there, but I was usually disappointed. When I did find him, there was always time for a hug. He would stop his work and hold out his arms to me. I would run into them and we would make many hugging noises. Then he would put me back down and turn back to his work. Usually, my mother Martha would discover me by that time and come to fetch me away.

"Come now, Carl, leave your father to his duties," she would say. "He has a lot of important work to do." At that I would leave the room.

On one occasion my mother was busy elsewhere for some reason. Father's angel, Lucius, was usually in the same room with father, but today father had a visitor and most mortals are somewhat afraid of angels in the Empire as they often carry out the discipline of the Immortals and the Emperor. I knew that when Lucius was standing in the hall with his back to the wall, that he had been expelled from the study because father was meeting with another mortal who would have been inhibited by Lucius' presence. I got up from my nap and passed Lucius as I headed for the study. I peeked in very slowly and father saw me. He asked his guest to wait and came out.

"Now Carl, I have to finish speaking with this man and your mother is on an errand so Lucius is going to watch you for a while."

I nodded thinking, 'now this will be fun.' Lucius had never been my baby sitter before, but I knew that he would do whatever father told him to do and that he would not hurt me. I knew that father was the only mortal to have a helping angel. Many had angels watching them, but no one else had one serving them.

On father's order the angel floated down beside me and with outstretched palms shepherded me to the back garden. Then he gently patted a section of grass and seemed to smile at me, at least I sensed a smile. I quickly sat down where he had indicated. He then began to audibly count to ten in my language. Then ten fingers seemed to form on his hands as he held up a finger for each number. I repeated these numbers a couple of times. Then he showed me a picture of some foreign looking people and said,

"Germany."

Then he began to count again, "Ein, Zwei, Drei, . ." As he counted, one of the figures in the picture would jump to the count. I watched the people in the picture which seemed to stay just before my eyes and counted in that language. After I did this three times in a row correctly, Lucius would swoop around behind me and grasping me by the waist would take me on a low altitude flight around the garden. I squealed in delight. What a wonderful reward! Then Lucius would show me another group of strange people and we would start all over again.

"Africa."

"Moja, mbili, tatu, . . ."

Then, "Spain."

"Uno, duo, tres, . . . "

Each time I got all ten right for three times in a row, I would get my free ride around the garden. Each time was better than the last. I learned to count in many languages that day. I thought it was wonderful that the family of Anna should have their own personal angel. I had hoped that this would happen often, but it never happened again. Once, when I discovered Lucius in the hallway, I walked up and boldly said,

"Spain."

He motioned with his hand to stop and I gave it up quickly. Father had to instruct him. Later when he began serving me, we did not play games at all. He was always obedient and helpful but in adulthood I actually find him to be quit boring. He is, after all, rather dull, efficient but dull. Come to think of it every angel that I have ever seen is rather efficient but dull. No sense of humor, even though they know how to care for children. Lucius was the governor Elaine's invisible guardian when she was a mortal.

[No Date] Although my mother did not command Lucius, we were both protected by him on many occasions. Once we were in a town in the mountains of Spain and my father had gone aside to meet with some officials there. I must have been about 11 by then. I thought of myself as quite a young man and was very protective of mother. The people of the village were having a street festival. There were many colorful costumes and a lot of dancing in the streets. Normally, we are not concerned about safety in our surroundings because of the Great Peace of the Glorious Reign which provides safety for everyone. In this situation mother and I were very relaxed. Father was at the 'proceedings' and we presumed that Lucius was with him. As all of the colorful costumes passed before us in the parade, I pressed further and further out into the street. Mother kept a firm grip on the back of my coat and I strained against the pull. Suddenly a man dressed as a clown snatched me from my mother's grasp and ran very quickly through the crowd heading for the opening of a side street just ahead. Lucius appeared suddenly directly in front of the man hovering about 6 feet in the air. He had made himself very large and very bright. The man caught his breath and screamed. I was actually frightened by the scream. The man dropped me right away and soon my breathless mother arrived and I was back in her arms. Three other angels arrived almost immediately behind Lucius, also appearing very large. The entire celebration halted for several blocks until a local Immortal arrived to judge the situation. As I talked to mother and father several times thereafter, this is how I remember the details.

It seems that there was a secret dark cult operating in the area which had been there for years, even generations. When they found out through a mortal government informer that we were there, they quickly put together a plan to kidnap the son of the son of Anna. This was the first time I really understood how important our family is. As usual these types of wrong doers underestimated the power of the angelic patrol and perhaps even of the Emperor Himself. These cultists were under the observation of the local patrol who instantly signaled Lucius to come. He took the forefront in the confrontation and soon the local Immortal Judge arrived and my father was with her. Father came and put his arms around mother and me.

The Immortal, the local governor named Juanita Rodriguez, immediately took authority. Her angels moved to the front and Lucius fell back to be with us. Several of my abductor's partners were brought forward. Governor Juanita asked them a few questions which they did not answer well. Then she passed sentence against them and they died on the spot. Their crime, as are all crimes, was a crime against the Emperor. The Imperial Code is very clear. These rebels were descendents of an ancient hate group who have existed since before the return of the Emperor. Almost strangely, the entire parade and celebration continued as soon as the bodies of these offenders were removed. It is clear that the mortals of the earth accept and appreciate the Imperial rule. It gives us all peace and safety.

[N.D.] As I grew older, I developed an interest in studying the Imperial Code and the various mortal laws and regulations that had developed from it.

I present the articles of the Imperial Code here. It is very simple.

The Imperial Code

1. All crimes are against the Emperor Himself personally.
2. All peoples will live in peace and harmony throughout the earth.
3. All of creation is to be respected.
4. Any disrespect for the Emperor, any Immortal governor or the Imperial government is a crime.
5. Lying to an Immortal is a crime.
6. All crimes will be judged by the Emperor or one of his Immortal governors.
7. All mortals are to honor authority, Immortal and mortal, civil and familiar.
8. Punishment for all crimes shall be either death or continual supervision by an angel at the judges' discretion.
9. Any physical harm by one mortal to another is a

crime.

10. Illicit sexual actions towards any mortal or animal, or any other perverted action is a crime.
11. The taking of another's goods is a crime.
12. The Imperial Code takes precedence and guidance over all mortal laws or ordinances.

05.20.217 C.R.   My research and my journaling have been halted by the death of my dear wife, Toni. I will write more later as I am able.

06.18.217 C.R.   I am doing a little better today. It has been almost a month. I still dread waking in the morning. I wish I could sleep forever.

08.01.217 C.R.   I write because Elaine has urged me to get back to work. First, I feel that I must give an account of Toni's passing. Of course, it was a great shock to me as it was totally unexpected. We had been married for five years of which I have been Keeper for three. One morning almost three months ago now I left Toni in the library at the residence to visit some mortal friends in a nearby town. I had been in school with them and we have continued our friendships as time has allowed. After a few hours Lucius placed himself directly in front of me, so I immediately gave him my attention. My first thought was that there was something of importance happening at a Dais somewhere and that I would have to go.

"Keeper, you must return home at once," he said. He took me there right away. We arrived in the library. Toni was lying on a daybed there that we use for short rests. I thought she was asleep or perhaps ill. Elaine arrived with me. It almost seemed that we collided in transit; at the end of the transit there seemed to be a jolt and we both arrived in the library simultaneously. I resolved mentally to follow up on this but when I saw Toni this thought left my mind.

"I am so sorry, Carl," Elaine said immediately. She took my arm. Of course, at first I could not believe it. I spoke to Toni and then shook her. When the reality of it hit me, I started to cry. Elaine put her arm around me.

"Elaine," I said. "Do something, please!" I cried out.

"I can not," she answered. "There is a block against it. I am so sorry, my dear Carl."

"The Emperor wills it?" I asked in unbelief.

"For some reason. It can not be appealed," she said softly.

She took me to the parlor and told me to lie down. She stroked my forehead and I slept for a long time. I know that this sleep was of her doing. It was not a natural sleep, but it was long and relatively peaceful.

[N.D.] The funeral was small and quiet. Toni was buried in our private plot near the residence. I started crying again and cried for days. It has gone from pain to numbness. Now I believe that the numbness is starting to fade. Elaine has given me that wonderful gift of sleep several times. It has helped a lot. I have not asked for an audience with the Emperor over this; I don't think I want to know the reasons.

07.12.218 C.R. As a part of my continuing grief therapy I have started an informal study based on the vast resources of my father's office. I am still fascinated with the Imperial Code and other laws, both Immortal and mortal which are based on it. After about 4 months of my studying Elaine appeared at the residence and I put down the book I was reading on the top of a great pile of books to greet her. She hugged me.

"Reading?" she asked.

"Yes, law actually. I find it very interesting."

She sat down.

"Carl, dear, ..." she began. I knew that this was moderately serious.

"Yes, Ma'am." I responded with a smile.

She made a fake pass at my nose. She had always been playful with me. Father said that she had never been this way with him. I enjoyed it but I also understood that since I am a mortal, it can never amount to anything romantic. It is just that she is always so young and beautiful. Then again, the Immortals do not involve themselves with romance. They say that they have something better.

"You'll not distract me with that 'Ma'am' talk," she said smiling.

I put on a more serious look.

"Carl, the point that I want to make is this: your duties are far more, shall we say 'lofty,' than the law."

I looked her squarely in the eye.

"Your duties are inspirational. You need to inspire love and admiration for the Emperor. Your knowledge of things both before and after His return will enable you to do this. Anna's descendents have a great honor in doing this. The Imperial law will be enforced by Immortals and angels and the mortal code is barely a shadow of the Imperial law. To be totally frank with you, Carl, the mortal law is only allowed because it inspires some additional loyalty to the Imperial Code. Do you understand?"

I sat quiet for a minute. "Yes, Elaine, I understand."

"Good," she patted my hand. "Then don't spend too much time in the law, all right?'

"Yes, Elaine. Of course." She rose to leave. We hugged and she was gone.

Reign II

01.11.219 C.R.   I am reviewing that incident in Spain when I was a child that I wrote about earlier. As I have grown older, I have developed a fuller understanding of such matters and what lies behind them. In the end it always comes down to the time before the Great Reign. The mortals lived back then under other governments and certain regional traits developed along with certain beliefs and habits and patterns of living. The people of one area would often think that they were better than those of another area and they often felt that they had been wronged by another area and sought to get revenge. Invisible dark princes held sway over the hearts and minds of mortals and mortal groups. When the Emperor returned, these dark princes were imprisoned somewhere away from our world so that they no longer hold this influence to cause hatred and harm and death among mortals. However, these hatreds were often pushed deep into the group consciousness of various peoples and they can still express themselves even today during the Reign. In this particular case where I was briefly abducted, a certain border people in the mountains had always held certain hateful views. The Emperor has ordered everyone to live in peace. But they could not obey this order. People are allowed to continue their cultural customs and traditions so long as they did not conflict with Imperial law. Those who disobey are punished.

Some groups, like this one, actually believe that they can somehow gain some leverage with the Emperor which will cause Him to allow them to be self governing. They say that they have 'an historical right.' That is why they seized me as a boy. They thought that by threatening my life they could gain a concession from the Emperor. They were wrong. Imperial rule is absolute; it is benign and giving, but it is absolute and total. People must learn to accept this. These people had been observed from the beginning. They were only allowed to proceed as far as they did to make a point. That point being that all is seen by

25

the angelic patrols and by the Presence, and that all crimes are immediately judged and punished. When their rebellion became ripe, their treason was ripe. They were executed but not for my kidnapping. They were executed for treason against the Emperor. As the first Imperial law says, all crimes are against the Emperor personally. Even before the Reign this was true, but then the Emperor waited to pass judgment. Mortal law did its best to keep order during that time. But at His Return all crimes against the Emperor were judged.

I once asked Elaine why the dark princes persevered in causing hatred and hurt among mortals before the return. Surely they knew that they could not get away with it in the end.

"They knew, " she said. "They always knew that their days were numbered. But you see, Carl, the dark princes actually feed on human pain and misery. They do it to feed their own twisted appetite. All they hoped to do was to delay the inevitable end."

I understood.

"During this Reign," Elaine continued. "you have the Immortals and the angels to watch and the Immortals to judge. This is their reward for being faithful to the Emperor when he could not be seen. Governor Juanita Rodriguez was exercising her right to act for the Emperor which she earned during her mortal lifetime."

I wondered what was to become of mortals of my day. That was not talked about much and I was hesitant to ask even Elaine about this. I guess all that we can do is serve faithfully and trust the Emperor to do the right thing. Perhaps one of my descendents can further explore the heart of the Emperor in this regard.

04.19.228 C.R. I remember reading in my grandmother's crude journals about her impression of the Emperor. She was absolutely caught up in her enthusiasm for Him. From that first time on the lawn at the Dais of Metropolitan Henry Sawyer when she was so surprised and terrified at the appearance of the Emperor until her death, she thought about the Emperor daily. Grandfather did not seem to be quite as involved, but we have no journals from him to read. My father Mark had a healthy respect and awe for the Emperor but nothing like that which his mother had. Anna would go on and on in her private journal about being "lost in the Emperor's eyes" and about the peace and sweet smell that accompanied his person. She also talked a lot about his invisible Presence. I am now thirty five years old and I have never met the Emperor. I think that it is high time that I did.

01.18.229 C.R   Today I called on Elaine at her residence without an appointment. There is no rule against this; it is just that you run the risk of her not being there since she is gone so much of the time. Lucius deposited me in her reception room. No one was there except her receiving angel, they rotate so I did not know the name of this one.

"I am called Kobiel by mortals, Keeper," he said immediately. By now I have become accustomed to being recognized by angels as the Keeper. I have also become accustomed, perhaps I should say spoiled, to being transported at my will to any place on this earth by Lucius which is a great luxury afforded only to the Keeper.

"Where is your mistress, Kobiel?" I asked somewhat bluntly. In truth I was so expectant about the possibility of meeting the Emperor that I surprised myself with my impatience. Fortunately, angels do not suffer from moods or pride so Kobiel answered quickly without offense.

"She is at the Capital, Keeper. May I send a message for you?" he asked obligingly.

"Yes, please tell her that I would, er . . like to see her at her earliest convenience," I said.

"May I tell her why?" he asked.

"Yes, of course, I would like to meet,...have an audience with the Emperor." There, it was out.

"Which one, sir?" the angel continued.

"I don't understand," I replied. "There is only one Emperor."

"No, Keeper. Please forgive. I meant do you want to meet him or do you want an audience?" he asked.

"Uh,... either," I answered. I did not know there was a difference. Sensing my ignorance the angel continued. "You can meet him at any time, Keeper. At least you yourself can as the Keeper. Most any time, that is, if He is not otherwise involved. However, formal audiences are scheduled by the Lord Chancellor, King David of Israel, and you have to wait for them."

"I see. Then I guess that I just want to meet him," I said.

The angel nodded and stood there for a minute or so. At least it seemed like several minutes to me. Then he spoke again.

"My Mistress instructs me to bring you and your angel to the Capital immediately."

"Well, I am not quite dressed," I started to say.

"Is that better?" the angel asked.

I looked down and found that I was dressed in a beautiful blue satin robe and that my father's medallion was hanging around my neck. I kept it in a safe and secret place at my residence. I caught my breath but said nothing for a few seconds. I thought about how I would respond. Both Kobiel and Lucius waited patiently without a trace of humor or superiority on their faces.

"Yes, well then, let's be off," I said softly.

They opened a portal for me, they don't need one, and we were instantly at the Capital. We stood in a small but elegant room with large open windows overlooking the city of Jerusalem as it was now rebuilt for the Victorious Emperor. After a few moments I sat on a seat by the window and looked out. I could see the magnificent Canopy of angels over the Capital. It dwarfed the canopy of Metropolitan Henry Sawyer of Atlanta and even that of the Over-Lord Janice Holland of the East Coast. I have seen the Canopy of Luis Cepata in Montevideo and it is almost as grand as this one at the Capital. The choruses seemed to be humming a haunting melody which blended easily into the background if you wanted it to. After a while Elaine entered the room by herself. I was startled because I thought that the Emperor might be with her.

"Carl, my dear, I am so glad that you are here. I thought you would never ask," she said as she stood on her tiptoes to kiss my forehead. I bent down to help as I was used to this ritual from childhood. Elaine is a dear and so human for an Immortal. But then again she was once mortal like me.

"I did not know that you were waiting for me to ask," I answered.

"We are always thrilled when a mortal wants to meet the Emperor. Most are afraid of him, but some have learned to love him like we do."

"Grandmother loved him," I added.

"That she did, Carl. And I am so proud of her." Elaine always spoke of grandmother in the present even though she has been dead for years.

"Now," Elaine began, she sat down on a large divan and motioned for me to sit next to her. I obeyed her as a child. I now looked older that she does, but she has looked that way since my first childhood memory of her. I must admit that I do not really understand Immortals and now I am about the meet the most Immortal One of all. I sensed a little fear. "No need for fear, Carl," she patted my hand.

'How does she do that?' I thought.

Elaine continued, "The Emperor is out walking in the Palace parklands," she said. "Come here." She motioned to the window and waved her hand at the surrounding city and countryside.

"You see the Palace parklands now extend out about 300 kilometers in all directions. All the Emperor's favorite places and boyhood haunts are included, places like Bethany, Nazareth, Bethlehem, and the others, and a good deal of water," she said.

"Right now he is just over there, near Bethany. Do you want to go now?" she asked.

"Yes, of course," I said taking a deep breath.

"Let's see," Elaine continued, "I think that Kobiel overdressed you for hiking. So hiking gear please, Kobiel." I was now dressed in a nice hiking suit. That made twice today that I was dressed by an angel. I wondered if Lucius will do this for me from now on.

"Lucius can do that for you if you want," Elaine said. I would have to think about it. I have always kept my own clothes.

We appeared alongside a group of about 15 men who were walking up the road to Bethany. The angels were not with us. This was a very informal meeting. All around things were blooming. The path consisted of a fine smooth gravel. I had thought that this area would be dry and dusty but then, of course, it had been changed at the Emperor's wishes. I wondered which one was His Majesty.

One of the men spoke to Elaine. "Sister Elaine, I have not seen you since the last feast," he said. "And this is the mortal Keeper?"

"You know that it is, Nathanael," Elaine answered smiling. "I thought you were the one with no guile," she teased.

"He still is, Elaine," one of them said. Then they all stopped and cleared a path between me and the speaker. I thought, this must be him. I walked towards him but I did not meet his eyes. He looked little different from the others in height and coloring and dress. I knew that I would have to meet his gaze so I did. It was Him. It is Him. The God-Man Himself. The eyes never lie. His eyes are incapable of it. I was flooded by the peace that grandmother Anna described but I was not overwhelmed, no doubt, because he did not wish it. Very deliberately I got down on one knee. "Your Majesty," was all I could say. He motioned for me to stand.

"Carl, it is good to see you," he said.

"And I you, Sire." I just looked at him. I got up the courage to glance at his hands. He held them out for me to see. Yes, the scars were still there. He wore them like a prize. The same for His feet. I could not see His side.

"Come, let us walk," he said.

We walked to Bethany and had some sweet wine and then we all walked some more. He liked to walk. I listened to them talk and finally asked some questions of my own. Not every answer was as complete as I hoped it would be but it was enough. Each answer was perfect. Before long I got the impression that I was asking questions that were, shall we say, too big. The others seemed to chat about small things. I seemed to want answers to the meaning of life and things like that. Finally, as I fell back for a time to think, Nathanael said softly to me, "You see, Carl, He Is the meaning of life." I dared not think too loudly around these Immortals. If they know what they know, how much does the Emperor know. I settled into the group, just enjoying His company. Elaine was still with us. Overall my impressions were not anything like I had expected. There was little of the grand or showy here. Perhaps that was reserved for an audience or, worse still, a judgment. I can not say that I actually saw Him sweat. But I could hear Him breathe. He touched me on the shoulder once and I nearly passed out. But he is really human, human and then a whole lot more. That walk that afternoon was fantastic. He walked casually, as if He had nothing else to do. That night there was an audience and it was, as I suspected, quite different. Lucius re-dressed me in the blue robe that I arrived in for the audience. It was a general audience and I went with Elaine.

The Palace Throne Room was packed. There must have been ten thousand people there. Most of them were Immortals but there were some mortals. I could tell the difference but I can not explain how. The mortals, like myself, seemed less confident somehow although we all looked a lot like the Immortals who were all dressed in simple but handsome attire here. Some of the angelic Canopy had moved inside so the ceiling was covered with them. Their harmonizing was exquisitely beautiful and profound. When they all stood, I did too. The Emperor entered from behind the throne from the 'other side.' Mortals can't go there, but this is a permanent sort of portal to the throne on the other side. He was simply dressed in a white robe and he walked casually to the throne on this side.

For a long time we all just sang praises to the Emperor, Immortals, angels and mortals together. It was unbelievable. The sound was fantastic and the Presence in the Throne room was overwhelming. The Emperor sat calmly on the throne and smiled. It was as if we were all singing out our love to Him at once. I shall never be the same again and I will want to come to an Imperial audience as often as possible. I intend to tell Lucius not to let me miss even one.

09.10.240 C.R. This morning at the Dais of Henry Sawyer, Metropolitan of Atlanta, I saw a young mortal woman that looked so much like Toni that I found myself staring. Her name is Eva.

Eva and her family are in trouble. They have been caught stealing and someone has been hurt in the process.

Reign II

The family seems to consist of Eva and her three brothers, two sisters, her mother and father, two married uncles on her mother's side, a single uncle and three married uncles on her father's side, and eight cousins. Her father seems to be the leader of the group. He is actually no more than a highwayman. They post detour signs for the large transport vehicles on the roads to lure them into a remote area where the road is blocked. Then they force the driver from the vehicle and steal all the goods which they sell to various people who can resell them. They were allowed to do this several times in order to expose the entire ring. The driver in the last incident was injured as they pulled him out of the vehicle and hit him. At this point the patrol intervened. Immortals arrived and healed the driver's wounds on the spot. And the entire ring was taken into custody. The distributors had been dealt with before I arrived at the Dais. Eva helped handle and transport the goods. She said that she did only as her father instructed her. This alone is not a sufficient defense. I am fascinated with this woman. She is about six years younger than I am.

Prince Henry sentenced Eva's entire family to supervision and they were each attached to an angel. Some of them pulled against the attachment. This attachment can not be seen. The one used here acts like a belt around the waist with an invisible cord about 10 feet long attached to the angel. They can not move any further away at any time. Their sentence can last for years depending on how fast their attitude changes. The angels will not harm them, but neither will they allow them to harm anyone else. The angel can move closer and completely subdue the mortal at any time and there is no privacy in the life of the mortal until the supervision is lifted. This punishment is, of course, much lighter than a death penalty, so many are thankful to receive it. They will have work assignments which may not be too pleasant, like working at garbage removal. And although their housing will be clean and they will have good clothing and enough to eat, it will not be luxurious.

When Eva was attached to her supervisor, such a sad look came over her face. I could not help myself. I approached the Metropolitan. Elaine was present at the time but I did not check with her first.

"Excellency," I blurted.

Henry Sawyer turned to look at me. His expression was kindly.

"Sir," I said as I walked quickly to his side.

"Yes, Keeper Carl. What do you want?" he asked softly.

"Sir, can that one," I pointed to Eva, "can she be appointed to my staff? I will watch her carefully and treat her with the utmost respect," I said.

It seemed like a long time to me before he answered, but it probably was not so long.

"What is it about her," the Metropolitan asked still speaking softly as if to me alone.

"I am not sure, sir." I answered. "Perhaps it just seems like she is more of a victim here under her father's wrongdoing. I know that she has no excuse before the law. But she seems less malicious than the rest. Less . . ." I stopped because the Metropolitan's look seemed to indicate that I was not being completely honest.

"Yes, sir," I continued. "I am attracted to her. She is so beautiful and seems to be so gentle. But I will not use my position to unfair advantage. I promise."

A quick smile passed between Henry Sawyer and Elaine. He thought for a minute.

"What position would she hold in your house?" he asked.

"I don't know yet. I would have to talk to her first, I guess." I did not sound very sure.

"You, girl, young Eva," the Metropolitan said. She looked straight at him terrified. "Don't be afraid girl, come up here," he commanded.

She came carefully up the steps of the Dais. Her supervisor followed quietly; the connection between them seemed to stretch this time. When she arrived at the top, she knelt before the Metropolitan. He put two fingers under her chin and raised her face so he could look into her eyes which he did for some time. "Um, hmm," he said. "This is the Keeper, Carl," he said motioning to me.

"Sir," she replied softly.

"He is willing to let you work for him, under his supervision and this angel here," he pointed to Lucius nearby. "What can you do? Ah, can you cook? Can you read and write? Garden? Anything else?"

She answered slowly, deliberately. "I can read and write well. I have helped others in my family that way. I can cook fairly well. I have grown flowers, but I could learn to grow food. I can speak in front of people. I am a quick learner." She finished and lowered her eyes again.

"Good," the Metropolitan responded.

He looked at me. She glanced up at me. She was still on her knees. I wanted desperately to help her up. She was even beautiful on her knees. She has large luminous dark eyes, a fine shape and small hands and feet. Her hair is jet black and falls just below her shoulder blades. I was in love again. How many men get such a second chance? The Metropolitan leaned forward and I moved in closer.

"Are you a virgin?" he asked her very softly. I was certain that only he and I and possibly the female under-governor to his left were the only ones who heard the question.

"Yes, my lord," she answered. She blushed as she glanced at me. "On that my father has been very insistent. He is not all bad, my lord."

"I know." Then Henry Sawyer smiled gently at her. "Do you accept this assignment in lieu of the other punishment? The Keeper will treat you with respect."

"Yes, my lord," she answered. She looked only at the Metropolitan.

"Fine, then. Off with you," he said.

I extended a hand to help her up. She took it and looked directly at me with a questioning look on her face which seemed to ask why I was doing this. I smiled in return. I fear that smile gave away too much. So I will proceed slowly.

She walked behind me back to my residence. Her sandals are worn and her long skirt and shirt are shabby. But to me she still looks like a queen. She carries herself with self respect although she is not presuming. Once near the residence she stumbled over a root in the path and I almost leaped to help her but I restrained myself. I wanted so to touch her. I must be very careful. When we got to the residence, I introduced her to one of my librarians, an older woman named Doreen, who is very kind. I told Eva to do as Doreen said and then I introduced her to our cook, Lorice.

"She may help you as well, Lorice," I said. "I trust that between you she will not be idle," I said sounding very official.

"We'll take care of her, Keeper," Lorice said.

"Put her in the room next to yours, Lorice. And get her some more clothes," I said. They nodded and went off.

I sat down and took a deep breath. What a morning! I had arisen wondering if anything interesting would happen today. Now I realized that I had challenged the Metropolitan, made an unprecedented request, fallen in love, and actually brought this woman to my home. Then a terrible thought crossed my mind. What if she does not fall in love with me? I ate some lunch and got busy with some research.

[N.D.]   For the next few weeks I saw Eva around the residence. She was always polite and I tried not to act too interested. I told Doreen to include her in the weekly staff meetings which we held in the garden. With the three librarians, Lorice and her assistant, two gardeners and three security men and Eva and myself we number twelve mortals. Lorice is married to Jon the head gardener, has been as long as I can remember.

[N.D.]   For the first two weeks Eva didn't say anything at the meetings. I asked Doreen and Lorice how she was doing and they said that she was cooperative and helpful and that she had a positive attitude.

"I think the attitude is real, Keeper," Doreen said. "I mean not just to satisfy her sentence." I nodded.

At the third meeting Eva asked permission to reorganize the newspaper section. Doreen recommended it. So I agreed. I felt like I was about to go insane. How could I proceed with her? I did not feel like I could go to Elaine for advice as somehow I felt that this was as big a test for me as it was for Eva. After all, I had started it.

The next week everyone except Doreen and Eva left the meeting quickly. I summoned up my courage.

"Doreen, can you leave Eva here at the table with me for a few minutes? I would like to talk to her about how she is settling in, " I said.

"Certainly, Keeper," she said. She left quietly.

Then I could not think of anything to say. Eva sat two seats away looking into her tea cup.

"So, are you comfortable? I asked.

"Yes, Keeper. I am very comfortable. Everyone has been so kind to me. They do not treat me as a lawbreaker. I am most thankful for your kindness." She looked up from her tea cup and looked me directly in the eyes. I felt my pulse quicken.

"Fine, good," I said. "I want you to be comfortable. I do not think of you as a lawbreaker, not at all."

"You are kind." She was still looking into my eyes. It took all my strength not to declare myself then. But it was too soon.

"I have one request, sir," she said looking down again.

"Yes, er, I mean. What is it?" I managed to answer.

"I wonder, . . . I wonder if it would be possible, once in a while, for me to see my family. I know they are a rascally lot, but I do love them and I miss them. We have always been together, you see?" She looked at me pleadingly.

"I will look into it," I responded.

"Thank you, sir," she said. When she looked away, I told her that we were pleased with her work and that she could get back to whatever she had to do. I watched her as she got up and got in a few glimpses as she walked away. What a woman! I am hopelessly in love.

[N.D.] For the past several weeks the entire staff seemed to leave us alone after the staff meeting. I had gotten permission from Elaine for Eva to visit her family for a couple of hours under Lucius' watchful eye and she came back grateful but sad. I told her that she could see them monthly if she wanted to. At first we talked about her duties and then we branched off onto other subjects. She was very interested in my travels as Keeper. And she told me a few funny stories about her family. One story was about her cousin Juan who is a very clumsy and unsuccessful thief. I knew that soon I would have to tell her how I feel.

[N.D.] At today's staff meeting many issues came up and I found myself meeting afterwards with Doreen for a long time.

[N.D.] I have waited another long week. The day before this meeting I was checking with Doreen on some research. She had come to my office. She gathered up her papers to leave and paused.

"Keeper," she said. "Carl." I looked up. She sometimes called me Carl, she is much older. "She loves you. You know that don't you?" Doreen said. I was awestruck.

"Really"

"Yes. I don't know if I will ever understand men," she said.

"I have been being, . . . careful," I said.

"Then you do care for her?"

"Care for her? I adore her, Doreen."

"Good," she smiled. "Then find a way to tell her," she answered.

[N.D.] After the next staff meeting they all vanished quickly. I looked at Eva and she looked at me. She was still two seats away. I hoped that Doreen had been as candid with her as she had been with me.

"May I?" I asked moving over to sit next to her.

"Sure," she answered.

I casually rested my elbow in the table and propped my chin on my hand. I decided to jump.

"I'm in love with you, Eva," I said quietly and deliberately. I was relieved even if she did not respond like I wanted her to. I had held it in so long. She answered right away.

"I have loved you since the first day," she said looking deep into my eyes as tears came to hers. I didn't know what to do next. I knew what I wanted to do. But I felt like I needed to remember my place. Finally, I kissed her gently on the mouth. She received it with great tenderness. When I pulled away, I saw a smile I have never seen before. We had made a good beginning. Now I must talk to Elaine.

[N.D.] "Overall, it's no problem," Elaine said. "So far nothing more than a kiss?"

"So far," I responded.

"You want to marry her?"

"Of course I want to marry her."

"When?"

"Yesterday," I answered.

"It may take a little longer than that," Elaine said. "Henry will have to set aside her sentence. That is a technicality. And the Emperor will have to pardon her if she is to marry the Keeper."

"How difficult is that?" I asked.

"I will take care of that," Elaine said. "Meanwhile, take it easy at the residence"

"O.K. Get back to me soon, please," I asked.

"A day or so, Carl. Just a day or so," she said.

[N.D.] Lucius brought word that Henry Sawyer had dropped the charges against Eva that afternoon. Eva was relieved by this but it was nothing compared to what was to follow.

[N.D.] My meeting with Elaine was on a Wednesday; she returned to my front door on Friday after luncheon. Eva and I had just finished eating in the back garden and we were sitting together quietly. I had my arm around her and she had just snuggled in. Lucius appeared in front of us so I got to my feet. I don't know why Elaine appears at the front door of my residence and then walks through to the garden; she could just appear in the garden.

"Just wanted to give you two lovebirds a few seconds to compose yourselves," she said as she entered.

She was waving some sort of a document. She extended it to me. So I took it and read it immediately.

Jerusalem
The Imperial Palace

Imperial Pardon 12.23.240 C.R.

Know all by this document that one Eva Conception Gonzales, a mortal, is hereby pardoned of all past crimes and misdemeanors against the Emperor as of this date. Any and all such crimes or misdemeanors that she has committed or participated in are charged to the Emperor's own account. All records pertaining to this have been removed from every place, both mortal and Imperial. It is as if they never existed. Her crimes are forgotten by the Emperor Himself as He chooses to exercise His Power Of Forgetfulness in her regard. She is, therefore, found to be in favor with His Majesty and will be considered innocent if she stands before Him.

  Signed in the name of the Emperor and for the Imperial High Court by:
David, The Lord Chancellor
Peter, The Master Of The Feast
John, Viceroy, Eastern Hemisphere
Luis, Viceroy, Western Hemisphere

I had never seen such a document although there may be some among my archives. It was personally signed in the Emperor's name by the Chancellor, the Master Of The Feast and both Viceroys. I read it aloud to Eva in Elaine's presence. The more I read the bigger her beautiful luminous dark brown eyes seemed to become. Then tears came to them. After I finished reading the names at the bottom, she burst into tears. I dropped the pardon on the stones and rushed to hold her just as she sank to the floor. Sitting on the stones she thanked the Emperor again and again to Elaine. I held her and it occurred to me how significant this was to a person convicted of crimes against the Emperor.

Elaine stroked Eva's hair, "There, there little one, I know how you feel. It is a wonderful thing," she said.

I looked at Elaine; my looked said exactly 'what do you mean, I know how you feel?'

Elaine answered, "In our mortality we were all forgiven by the Emperor. That was when we began our new lives. We are now Immortal because of that."

I have read enough of the sacred writings and the journals to understand, at least to some extent, what Elaine was saying.

[N.D.] The very next day I gave Eva a ring to signify our engagement. This is not universally done among us but some choose to practice it. The ring originally belonged to my grandmother Anna. It is gold and rather large with a large blood-red ruby in the center. No one knows just where Anna got the ring. She does not mention it in her journals; it was just found by father among her possessions. Eva never takes it off.

Elaine noticed the ring the other day. "Judah's ring," Elaine said. "Yes, Anna received it the year before she passed. It was a great honor."

I did not ask her to explain.

[N.D.] I have showered Eva with every gift I can think of. Her response is always the same: she does not deserve it, she does not deserve me, she is so thankful, and so on. But she seems to be genuinely happy. And when she is happy, I am happy. Our wedding date has been set. Since I am a widower, a quiet wedding is in order, but Elaine has insisted that it will be held in the Metropolitan's garden. These Immortals never tire of weddings.

03.02.241 C.R. The Metropolitan performed our wedding ceremony today. Janice was there and the Emperor was represented by the Chancellor himself who brought the Lady Abigail who had been one of his mortal wives. I was very happy with it all and Eva seemed to be content.

[N.D.] We took our wedding trip to the Bahamas. The Metropolitan there has been very kind to us. We will return to the Residence in fourteen days.

[N.D.] This entry is for my private journal only. I have a younger sister named Anna, most people call her "little Anna" to distinguish her from my grandmother Anna, the founder of the line. I was eleven years old when Anna was born so she has always been my baby sister. She does not take to this much anymore as she is a grown woman with, I am afraid, considerable experience. Being the granddaughter of the Keeper Anna has not been easy for little Anna. While I take joy in my duties and my office, she complains that she really does not have enough to do. She went off to school when she was sixteen and my poor father Mark had to repeatedly intervene because she could not stay out of trouble. I remember him saying more than once 'this girl is going to be the death of me yet.' When he did die, I am afraid that she remembered this and blamed herself. This did not, however, cause her to act more prudently. She has had an endless line of men, three husbands to date, she is now single again, and the only time I see her is when she needs money or some other favor that she thinks the Keeper can provide. I am convinced that she intends to live on her reputation as the daughter and the sister of the Keeper. Many people, men and women, seek her favor because she is my sister and I do not think she can tell when their motives are not pure. Or maybe she does not care.

Lucius woke me gently at 3 A.M. Atlanta time. He was careful not to wake Eva. I followed him into my private study off the bedroom and sat down rubbing my eyes. After I appeared ready, Lucius began.

"Keeper, I am sorry to inform you that your sister Anna is in poor condition," he said softly with almost a hint of non-angelic pity and remorse.

"What is it this time?" I asked wearily.

"She is at this moment lying unconscious in a filthy room in Barcelona. Her breathing is shallow and her pulse is weak."

I was sufficiently startled and I looked up and asked, "Who is with her now, Lucius?"

"One of my kind. She was discovered by the patrol which has been alerted to send word to you if she ever seemed to be in mortal harm."

"They think she might die?" I asked.

"Most certainly and that right soon if something is not done right away."

"Is Elaine in this world right now?" I asked.

"Yes, right here in Atlanta."

"Then please tell her that I beg her company in this situation, while I dress," I said.

Lucius disappeared. I dressed quickly and gently woke Eva to tell her where I was going.

"Do you want me to go with you, sweetheart?" she asked.

"No, dearest," I kissed her goodbye. "You rest. If I can not return today, I will send Lucius with a message."

Lucius returned with Elaine and her minimum escort.

"Mistress, thank you so much for coming. I simply do not know what to do with my sister," I said.

"No trouble, Carl. I will do anything that I can," she said. In a second we appeared in a disgusting little hotel room in Barcelona looking down on my poor sister Anna.

"I think she's almost dead," I said.

"Nearly," Elaine answered.

"Can you, will you, er, fix her," I asked plaintively

"Yes, of course," Elaine answered. She put one hand on Anna's chest and one on her forehead. "Anna, Anna darling, wake up," Elaine said very softly and lovingly.

"Uh." Anna began to come to. "Where, what, who are you? Oh, Carl, where did you come from?" She started to sit up and then laid back down again as if in pain.

"Just lay there another few minutes," Elaine said.

"Uh, Elaine, er, Mistress!" Anna's eyes opened wide and she tried to sit up again.

"I said, just wait, child," Elaine said firmly. "You are not quite mended yet."

Anna laid back and in a few minutes she seemed completely restored. Elaine took her hands off Anna and told Lucius to find some clean water and some food. He disappeared and reappeared with the food and water in no time.

Anna drank and ate heartedly as we watched her in disgust. She was filthy and acted like she didn't even know it.

"I have left some scars," Elaine said. Anna looked at her quizzically. Elaine turned her and pulled up her blouse to show me the scars. "There are more on the front and on her legs," Elaine said. "They now appear as they normally would after six months of healing."

Anna pulled up her blouse and then her skirt and examined the scars on her stomach and legs. "What? Who? Mistress, make them go away. They are really ugly!" my sister exclaimed.

"I will do nothing of the sort, young lady," Elaine said. "They will not hurt you. I left them to remind you. If I had not come, you would have surely died. You have been beaten severely and more than once recently."

"Maybe you should just let me die," Anna said ashamed to look either one of us in the face.

"Maybe we should. But your loving brother here cares very much for you and your parents and Anna herself would be ashamed," Elaine said.

"I know, I know." Was all that Anna could say. "I don't know. When I am intoxicated, it all seems like fun. When they start to hurt me, I still like it. By the time I am really hurt, it is too late and I am ashamed to admit to you, brother, the kind of life I lead. I don't know. I really don't."

I looked at Elaine. This had happened before and each time I had hoped that she would do better. But she does not.

"Sit here, Anna." Elaine commanded. She motioned for me to follow her outside into a dilapidated garden attached to that pitiful hotel. We walked for a while in silence. Then she stopped.

"Carl, I have one recommendation, but it will not be easy for you to follow. I do, however, believe that it is Anna's only hope for change."

"Anything, Mistress," I said. "Anything, I have no ideas at all."

"I have a friend, an Immortal named Magdalena; she was a mortal friend of the Emperor. She runs a special training home in Crete for girls like Anna. Anna is a little older than most of her charges, but I believe that she would take her in."

"A mortal friend of the Emperor, wow," I said. "Of course, that sounds great."

"Now you would have to have her declared your ward and it would then be your choice to put her there and to confine her there if you wish. Not all the girls are there under the same conditions. Some are even volunteers. Some are put there by their parents or another relative."

"My ward?" I asked.

"Yes, she would then be in a relationship to you as a minor child. You would have legal authority over her."

"How is that done?"

"Henry is her prince. She was born is his realm. He can grant it."

"She won't like it," I said.

"I know," Elaine answered. "But I tell you, dear Carl, I will not pull her back from the edge again like I did tonight. It is your only choice, really."

When I saw how serious Elaine was about this, I agreed. We took Anna back to my house and got her a good bath and put her to bed. She slept a long time. By the time Anna awoke, I was back from the Dais with the Metropolitan's certificate of guardianship. I felt a little sneaky and underhanded when I first got back to the residence, but that didn't last long. Anna was sitting in the garden with one leg slung over the arm of her chair guzzling wine.

"Oh, my dear brother. My rescuer," she said sarcastically.

"Anna, would you like your old room back?" Eva asked her.

"My old room? No, dear, there is no need for that. I am not staying long. As a matter of fact I think I will go back to Spain tonight if my dear brother here will tell Lucius to give me a lift." She looked at me like it was a dare. She did not know what I had in store for her and I no longer felt sneaky.

"I have news for you, my baby sister," I said.

"You know I don't like to be called 'baby' sister," Anna scolded.

I waved the guardianship paper in her face. "Read this," I demanded.

"What? Oh, no. I am my own person. No one tells me what to do. You've learned that haven't you, dear brother. Even when you cut off the money I still get by. I do what I want."

"I am afraid that you don't quite understand, Anna," I said as I sat down beside her. "This is like supervision. You know, attached to an angel. You will go to the home of a lady named Magdalena in Crete and she will teach you to be a descent adult."

"Tied to an angel? I am no criminal," she protested.

"No, you are not a criminal. You are a bum. You are my sister and my ward. Your supervisor will not be attached to you but if you give Magdalena any trouble, the angel will restrain you and he will not let you leave."

"You can't do this. Damn you, no!" she shouted.

"I can and I am, for your own sake," I said.

"Look at the seal. Metropolitan Sawyer has decreed it. You have no choice."

"I'll appeal, I'll appeal to the Emperor if necessary," she said.

At that exact moment Elaine appeared and walked directly to Anna. Anna pushed back in her chair as if trying to avoid Elaine.

"There is no appeal to the Emperor without the agreement of a Viceroy," Elaine said. "I have just talked to the Viceroy Luis and he refuses appeal. You must do as you are told."

"I'll go to John, then," Anna said.

"He will not countermand Luis. This is what you must do. Do you understand?"

Anna knew from childhood that this question asked in that tone was final. "Yes, mistress," she mumbled.

Anna's angel supervisor arrived to take Anna to Magdalena's. Elaine explained that this angel was not Lucius; he would not do as she commanded. She said that she understood. Anna cried and I hugged her. Eva hugged her. And then they were gone.

"Elaine, may I visit her and meet this Magdalena?" I asked.

"Anytime, Carl. Lucius will take you. I would give her about two weeks to get settled in. Magdalena runs a severe program." I was not prepared to ask what that meant just now.

[N.D.] Magdalena is wonderful. She is a beautiful Immortal with a face that tells of much experience. But nothing about her face appears worn or haggard. Her smile is fantastic and her resolve is absolute. She cares about all the girls under her charge. She starts by spending three days and nights with each new girl. She tells them her mortal story and how the Emperor transformed her. She tells them of the continuing transforming power of the Presence in her mortal life. Anna was full of enthusiasm when I first visited her two weeks after she was taken to Magdalena's house. She seemed like a different woman. She said that she has to stay with Magdalena until she passes some tests.

"What kind of tests will they be?" I asked.

"She hasn't told us yet. She says that we will not know when they are coming and we will not know how we did on them for a while after they are over."

"Sounds mysterious," I said. "How many tests will there be?"

"She won't tell us that either," Anna answered.

49

"How do you feel about this," I asked.

"O.K., I guess. I mean I wouldn't feel very good about it if it was someone else. But Magdalena is something else, you know what I mean?"

I agreed. All you have to do is meet her and you are sure that there is not another Immortal like her. She has a lot of love for mortals, something that you do not always feel from some of them, and she does not try to hide the fact that as a mortal herself she was quite acquainted with our weaknesses and faults. She seems thankful every day that she is a child of the Emperor. She loves Him dearly and talks of her relationship with Him as a mortal. She spends a lot of time with her charges and when she is not around, you can always guess were she is, at the Capital as close as she can get to the Emperor. Elaine says that although all the Immortals have the freedom to get close to the Emperor, He seems to be particularly happy to have Magdalena around. They are old friends. I was happy to leave Anna with Magdalena and I plan to visit her there often.

[N.D.] I have learned from Anna that Magdalena was the first person to see the Emperor after His Majesty had raised Himself from the dead. She is surely a very special person.

04.22.260 C.R. For many years Eva and I have wanted a child. It is not just because I am expected to produce an heir. We both want very much to have children. We tried for many years to become pregnant. But we have not been successful. I have mentioned it a couple of times to Elaine and she just encouraged me to be patient. I am aware that Elaine can intervene in these matters as she has in the past, but we have never asked her to help. Eva is now getting older and she has been asking me to ask Elaine to help. So today I asked. Elaine simply put her hand on Eva's stomach for a few seconds and then said that if we did our part we would be expecting soon and that both Eva and the baby would be strong and healthy.

02.03.261 C.R.   Today our daughter Alice was born. She is beautiful.

[N.D.]   This morning Lucius approached me suddenly and said, "Keeper, there is an angel from Imperial Security to see you."

I was busy writing so I did not look up again. "Bring him in," I said.

There was a sharp popping noise when the angel appeared and I intentionally did not look up for a few seconds. When I did, I saw a most impressive angel standing before me. I looked down again to finish my paragraph but stole a glance up again. The newly arrived angel was standing patiently before me. Lucius was looking from me to him and back to me repeatedly. If I did not know better, I would say that Lucius was nervous. I put my pen down and leaned back. I do not react well when I think an angel is trying to push me. I have no actual right to take this attitude except that I rely on Elaine's favor a great deal.

"And you are?" I asked.

"I am called Bruel," he answered with a slight trace of an echo in his voice, something that they do when they want to intimidate. I weighed his attitude for a while trying to decide if I would accept the challenge or not. Finally, I decided that I would go along. It was sure to be important or he would not be here. Lucius still looked nervous, but I must have been imagining that as I know very well that they do not have emotions.

"What do you want?" I asked

"The Legate Elaine has instructed me to inform you that your wife's family is again in danger of discipline," he said.

51

I suddenly felt hollow inside. "What this time?" I asked.

"More of the same. Scams to gain wealth."

"Are they all involved?"

"Primarily Hector, her father, and her oldest brother Pedro," the angel answered.

"Does the Legate have any instructions for me?"

"Not through me, Keeper."

"Can we get back to you?" I asked. I needed time.

"This one can," he answered motioning to Lucius.

"Fine. I will not be long. Is there anything else?" I asked.

"No, Keeper," he responded and then popped away.

"Lucius, what is that popping sound? I have never heard it before," I asked.

"Security uses it," Lucius stated.

"I can tell that, but why? Does it do anything? Er,…accomplish something?" "

"Not really."

"Hmm." 'I never cease to be surprised,' I thought.

"Is Eva in the residence?" I asked.

"No, Keeper, she is in the city purchasing some things," he answered. He does not use the term 'shopping' but my Eva is a master at it.

"Do you want me to bring her to you?" Lucius asked.

"No, no, not right now. I need a little time. Ask Mistress Elaine if I may see her."

Lucius vanished and I changed to meet with Elaine.

Eva's family had been released from supervision slowly over the years. First, the women were released and then the younger men. Her father and oldest brother, the ones now again on the edge, were the last to be released. I have dreaded the day that they would get into trouble again for Eva's sake because she being the wife of the Keeper can not help them if they go to far again. They could face more supervision or even the death penalty if they go too far.

Lucius returned and we went immediately to the Dais of Henry Sawyer where Elaine was in charge that day while the Metropolitan was at the Capital for a Governor's meeting that the Chancellor had called. Since they all communicate immediately through angels or the Presence, I have always thought that their meetings were just another excuse to fellowship with one another and perhaps the Emperor, but I am not the one to decide such things as I am still a lowly, if highly favored, mortal.

"We have only allowed it to go this far so that they may judge themselves with the nature of their actions," Elaine told me. "I was hoping that goodness might prevail, but Hector and Pedro are very close to being arrested. They have not kept good company like they did just after they were released from supervision. Eva's mother Juanita and the other females have done alright."

"They have never asked me for help," I interrupted.

"I know, they are ashamed, I think," Elaine answered. "The younger boys are doing well too. They live far away from Hector and Pedro."

"How free am I to intervene, Mistress?" I asked. When I said 'Mistress', that put our talk on an official level.

"I leave it in your hands for 72 hours, Carl. After that, I will have to act. Use Lucius as you want in this. He may get help from the Legions if he needs it."

"Thank you, Mistress. I have to get busy now." I said. As I nodded to Lucius to take me back to the residence, she smiled a very loving smile at me. We are so blessed to be under her authority as well as that of the Metropolitan and the Over-Lord, the Viceroy and the Emperor.

As soon as we got back to the residence, I sent Lucius for Eva. "Do not tell her anything," I instructed.

"Just tell her that I need her right away." He nodded and disappeared. He returned with Eva in less than a minute.

"What is it, dear?" she asked. From the look on my face she guessed. "Oh dear, my family," she said. All of the energy seemed to drain from her and she sat down. I sat beside her and held her and told her what I knew. She started to cry but fought it back and a determined look crossed her face. "What do you think we should do?" she asked.

I called Lucius closer and we formed a plan. Eva was to put on some dirty ragged clothes and Lucius would take her near to her father and brother. Then she would scream for help and Lucius would vanish. She would tell her father that she had had to leave me and that she had been hunting for them. We always believed that her sister Carla kept in touch with her father, so Eva could say that she found him through Carla. After a day, (we only had three,) she hoped that she could learn from her brother what they were doing and implore them to stop and even to turn themselves in. Lucius used his connections to locate them in the Pyrenees mountains. It was a remote location and I was worried for her safety.

"Lucius can stay with me," she said. "I will be fine."

I thought if I sent Lucius with her then how could I travel to help her. "Perhaps I should go to, in disguise," I said.

"They might catch on and run," she added.

Lucius interrupted, "Keeper."

"Yes, Lucius."

"The Mistress Elaine said that I could get help, did she not?"

"Yes."

"Fine. Then this is Lawton," he said and another angel which looked very much like him suddenly appeared.

"Lawton? What kind of a name is that for an angel?" I asked.

"Please don't ask, Keeper," he said.

To me this whole thing was getting more unusual. "Fine then," I said. "What exactly will Lawton do?"

"He will go with your wife and carry out our plan. He will also protect her, remain invisible, and be in constant contact with me," Lucius finished.

That sounded fine to me. It was now dark in Atlanta and in the Pyrenees. Eva left almost immediately after I held her for a while and kissed her goodbye.

I was nervous waiting with Lucius at the residence but he kept me posted and it was not too long before I had to make another decision.

From Lawton to Lucius to me I learned that Eva had been successful in getting her father to take her in. She immediately started to try to talk him into stopping his actions and his association with the people he had fallen in with.

"Keeper," Lucius aroused me. I had let my mind drift to the day I had met Eva.

"Yes, what?"

"Lawton reports that some of father Hector's associates are now holding Hector, Pedro and Eva at knife point. If we do not come now, Lawton will disarm them immediately."

'What had happened so fast?' I wondered. Lucius and I went immediately to Eva's side. Lucius drew the knives to himself and they landed together in his hand with a loud clanking sound. Now the two angels and myself were totally visible. Hector looked surprised at first, then a knowing look crossed his face. Pedro just nodded. Those who had been threatening them were immobilized by the angels, unable to move as if tied up with invisible cords, the same kind of energy cords used in supervision.

"You lied to me, girl. You lied to your father," Hector accused Eva.

"I had to father. I had to try to convince you to stop this way of life. You are about to be judged." Tears came to her eyes.

"Well, I guess there is some advantage to being related to the Keeper by marriage," Hector said glancing my way.

I did not say anything yet. There was a long silence.

"Well," Hector continued. "When does the judge arrive? When do I pay the piper?"

"What has he done so far?" I asked Lucius.

"Nothing so far," Lucius said. "Just guilt by association. Although he and the brother were very close, these men were going to require them to act tonight so that they would be bound together by their guilt. You acted just in time, Keeper."

I knew that this was no happenstance. We had been helped again by Elaine and the others.

"Get Elaine," I said quietly to Lucius. She was on the spot in a few seconds. At her arrival Hector's comrades cowered in fear and Hector and Pedro would not meet her gaze. I held Eva while Elaine spoke.

"You will be taken to your wife, you and your son, under supervision. If she can not help you to rehabilitate yourselves in a year, then you will be removed from her and dealt with severely," Elaine said. "As for these four," she pointed her scepter at the ones the angels were holding, "There is no hope for them." They died on the spot. Hector and Pedro grew very pale.

"Did you ever doubt the power of the Governors?" I asked them in disbelief. "What do you think they are here for? You are fools? I, I just can't believe,…well…" I took a deep breath. "I wash my hands of you and Pedro, Hector. Mistress, I formally request that they be given no more chances because of their relationship to my wife, " I said.

"Very well, Keeper," Elaine answered. She looked at Hector and Pedro. "You are truly on your own now," she said. "It's change or else."

They look genuinely frightened. Eva and Lucius and I returned to the residence. I hope that is the end of it. Relatives are certainly a burden to us, hers and mine.

[N.D.] Lucius awoke us at 3 A.M. Atlanta time. I remembered that father had once said that nothing good ever happens at 3 A.M. This time he would have been correct. We were both in a sound sleep; I on my back while holding Eva with my right arm. She was content with her head on my chest. It was very dark in the room. There was no moon at all. In order to wake us Lucius had to get very bright. Since he was directly in front and above me, I awoke first and shook Eva gently.

"Uh. What darling?" She muttered.

"Wake up sweetheart," I said. "Lucius has something." She rubbed her eyes and looked up at the angel. I was certainly wide awake. Lucius glanced at Eva and motioned for me to come aside. I decided to ignore his preferences. "Just go ahead, Lucius. She is awake now."

"It is her brother Pedro, Keeper."

"Yes, go ahead."

"He is dead," Lucius said.

Eva drew in her breath sharply and then I was sorry that I did not get the information from Lucius first. His statements are always rather blunt, truthful but blunt. I held her tightly.

"I'm alright, Carl," she said in a few seconds. "It was probably inevitable. How did it happen, Lucius?" she asked.

He was caught in a robbery and killed while trying to escape by the mortal investigators near Amsterdam," Lucius answered.

"My father?" she asked.

"Not involved," Lucius answered.

"Thank the Emperor," Eva said.

We dressed and had Lucius bring the body to us.

[N.D.] We gathered Eva's family and buried Pedro on the residence grounds. After the internment we all ate together and Hector asked to speak to me alone. He has been very distraught at the death of his son. Eva seemed excited that her father wanted to talk to me alone.

"What can I do for you, Hector," I asked.

"Sir, Keeper," he said very respectfully. "This was my fault. I did not lead the boy as I should have and now he is gone." He wept bitterly and I kept my hand on his shoulder. Hector seemed genuinely repentant. When he calmed down, he made a request that really caught me off guard.

"Can you arrange, sir, for me to meet the Emperor," he asked. I did not answer for a moment as I tried to recover my composure.

"I can ask the Immortal Elaine," I said.

"I would so much appreciate it, sir."

"Hector . . ."

"Sir?"

"Why? I mean, you must have a reason," I said.

"I have seen Eva's pardon, sir. And I believe that only the Emperor can calm my heart and show me what I can do to attempt to make amends for my miserable life."

"That sounds good to me," I said. "You and the family stay here with us for a while. You can stay in the cottage." I did not want the family under foot. "And I will talk to the Immortal Elaine as soon as I can."

Hector kissed my hands and thanked me profusely.

I got to Elaine the next day and I was a little surprised that she readily agreed to get an audience for Hector.

[N.D.]   After almost a four month wait, today Hector has his audience with the Emperor. I am told by Lucius that many mortals are saying that he would not have gotten this audience if he were not my father-in-law. The Emperor is always very busy when He is on this side and Hector is little more than a common criminal in the Empire, but I do not question anything that Elaine arranges. Hector is as nervous as a new bride today. He has waited patiently these months and has prepared himself to go three times this morning that I know about. I told him months ago that I would allow Lucius to take him to the capital. He is going alone which is fine with the family since the rest of them are honestly afraid of the Emperor. I asked Hector why he is not afraid of the Emperor and he told me that he has nothing to lose. He said that he is a desperate man who can not change himself. He said that the Emperor was his only hope.

Lucius has just returned without Hector. He tells me that he was dismissed by the Chancellor upon arrival. He was not told when Hector would be returned. Hector has now been gone for over six hours. There must have been a wait to see His Majesty.

Another two hours and still no Hector. Eva is not concerned. No one else asks any questions. I have been busy all day in my study preparing several messages with several of my secretaries.

Hector has returned. He was deposited by an angel from the capital in my waiting room. Hector has greeted everyone with generous hugs and now he sits in a chair with a small very satisfied smile on his face. We invited him to supper with the family.

"Now, now I understand," Hector said. "Every mortal should be able to see the Emperor, then all misunderstanding would be gone. His Majesty is our entire reason for living a productive life. Yes. Yes, it is wonderful." He ate a few more bites, the audience did not hamper his appetite.

"The Chancellor himself has put me in touch with a world-wide mortals group, "The Daughters of Anna." They will arrange for me to speak to groups in many places about what it means to be forgiven by His Majesty. I will tell. I will tell everyone I can about the graciousness and generosity of His Majesty. Why, this group even has a small travel allowance which will help me to get around. Now, my family must all go back to my cousins farm in Spain and I must begin my work," he concluded.

I arranged for Lucius to take the family to Spain and Hector to Paris where he said he would begin his work. Eva seems relieved to see them depart. Our happy home has now returned to normal.

[N.D.]   I get reports through regular channels almost weekly about Hector's goodwill work among criminals and near criminals in many cities. He seems to be fearless in the service of the Emperor. He never told us any more details about his audience, but knowing the Emperor I am not surprised about the change in Hector.

[ND.]   Reports of Hector's work continue to pour in. He has nearly been killed twice in his work. The first time some of his own followers rescued him and the second time his entire party was captured by criminals and Imperial Security showed up to rescue them all. Hector is quoted as saying that dying for the Emperor would be his privilege.

[N.D.] Hector and some of his followers visited us today. They have been speaking in the area. Prince Henry has supported their work here. Hector's entourage now includes his entire family. Eva was glad to see them and we were both relieved to see them leave. Eva and I love the quiet life we have when I am at home. I have been trying to be at home more and more as I grow older.

03.12.275 C.R. Our daughter Alice is a fine young woman. She has been helping me and she should do well as Keeper. She sometimes has trouble keeping her mind on her work, but she returns to it with great fervor.

09.22.279 C.R. As I look back over my life, I wonder if it has been or will be considered unusual for someone of my offices. I have traveled and made many public appearances, yet I have not been particularly popular. My father, Mark, was definitely more popular than I am. I have seen the Emperor on many occasions. I also trust the Emperor because of what I know from the sacred writings and the journals. I do not have to see him to trust him. He will invariably do the right thing; he is fair and he is merciful. We have proved that. I have kept mostly to myself. I lost my first wife when I was young. My second wife now of many years, the beautiful and wonderful Eva, is herself a pardoned criminal. I remember this with joy and not regret as I do not have the Emperor's power of forgetfulness.

Elaine has assured me that my daughter Alice will certainly succeed me.

Carl

Orin

358 – 429 C.R.

09.11.359 C.R. Private Journal. My name is Orin. My grandmother, the Keeper Alice, gave birth to my aunt May late in her life. She was enabled to do this through the intervention of the Immortal Elaine who touched her and made her able to conceive. May's father was the husband of Alice for many years. He died when May was four years old. Alice died when May was twelve years old and Elaine kept the office open for May until she was of age at eighteen. During those eight years that Alice lived after the death of her husband Alice met a man while visiting the Dais of the Overlord of the British Isles. This man's name was Neville Harding and he was a clerk in the Overlord's court there. From all accounts, and I am working from the private letters and diary of Alice herself, he was an attractive man somewhat younger than Alice. He seemed to be of considerable value to the court of the Overlord in coordinating the charitable activities of the court in those islands. He charmed Alice who was still quite attractive and they wanted to be married. The Metropolitan of London, the Immortal Thomas Becket, married them there. Alice was still able to have children and soon bore twin girls. One of the twins is my mother, April and the other is Eric's mother, June. It seems that it was Alice's decision to name them thus and no one challenged her in this regard. So then she had three daughters May, April and June.

Alice was told that it was the Emperor's will that May grow up separate from her half sisters. The twins grew up quite happily in London. After Alice died, May decided not to bring them to the court of Henry Sawyer in

Atlanta. Halfway through her term as Keeper May brought Eric and me, then eight years old, to her residence. Aunt May told us that she did this in order to introduce Eric and I to the succession and to enable us to be trained so that one of us could be chosen to succeed her. Our mothers have been treated with the utmost respect and they have lived very quiet lives in London with occasional visits to Atlanta over the years.

So here we are, Eric and myself, at the age of 18 knowing that, in the end, only one of us could be the Keeper. For official purposes the beginning date of service for the one who is chosen will agree with the departure of the Keeper May.

09.14.359 C.R. Public Journal. The mother of May (served 338-358 C.R.) was the Keeper Alice (served 280-332 C.R.). Alice was a competent Keeper and was generally loved. Alice had three daughters, May, April and June. Some scoffed at her choice to name her daughters after the Spring months even suggesting that if she were to have a fourth daughter she would name her Spring. Alice obviously was not struck with the naming idea at first or April would probably have been the name of her first born But that did not bother her. After May she merely backed up to April for one daughter and named the next daughter June. That was the kind of soul that Alice was. She lived in her own world undaunted by popular opinion and served as Keeper for 52 years.

When May was taken beyond the veil, most of the mortal world was in shock for some time and never knew about the controversy that occurred over the succession of the Keeper. This did not cause any alarm since the Keeper's position is not directly involved in any sort of government and the Immortal Elaine was, after all, in charge and had left the post open for some time in the past. Eric and I are full first cousins, each of us the son of one of

May's sisters. Eric is technically the older of us by almost a month. However, my mother April was older than June by a matter of minutes so it could be reasoned that whatever child was her firstborn was the most eligible for the position.

But these argument are of little import since Elaine's decision on this matter will be final no matter what we mortals may think of it. It seems that our judgment of right and wrong is often faulty in the eyes of the Immortals and the Emperor Himself. I have noticed that we tend to think along the lines of a balance scale and they tend to think along the lines of Royal favor, forgiveness and what is the better answer all round for the empire. I often despair that we mortals can not seem to accommodate ourselves to their way of thinking. After all, they must be correct in their reasonings because they are Immortal and we are not. Is not life the actual issue? I shall continue to seek to understand their point of view.

[N.D.] Even as I wrote the announcement that Aunt May had died in the year 358 C.R., things were moving behind the scenes.

Since May departed this life at such a young age, she had not yet designated a successor when she left. It would, of course, fall to the Immortal Elaine to appoint a new Keeper.

"I do not think there should be any doubt," Eric said just hours after the angel had removed May's body. "I am the oldest."

"We were given identical training," I interjected.

"Yes, but I am the oldest," Eric continued.

"I know. And it is all right with me," I said. "If you are chosen, I will be your faithful follower and your assistant if you will allow me.

"You would assist me?" Eric asked.

"I would," I answered.

Eric looked thoughtful, even pensive.

His sentence was interrupted by the appearance of Elaine at the residence. She appeared on the outer courtyard and proceeded immediately into the reception room where Eric and I were talking. She walked with her usual confident stride while looking around at the gardens and the sky and shaking her long hair as she walked. She was always happy.

"Good day, Mistress," we both greeted her.

"Good day, boys," she said. She sounded very firm today. Eric made his usual face when being called a boy by Elaine. May had not spent much private time with us since she was either working or at the Imperial Palace almost every waking moment. As a result we do not have much confidence. I do not particularly mind the appellation of "boy" especially coming from Elaine as we are only eighteen and she is technically by now hundreds of years old.

Elaine read my notice of May's passing. "This will be fine, " she said, handing it to the librarian.

"I am preparing one as well, " Eric said.

"Orin's will do," she answered firmly. "Both of you sit down."

Due to her tone we both obeyed instantly.

Elaine turned and stood in front of us.

"As of this moment," she continued firmly, "there is no keeper. Do you both understand?"

"But..." Eric uttered.

"None for now, Eric. It will probably be one of you, but, as you are certainly aware, I can name anyone that I think best."

That statement was a shock to me as well as to Eric. We had been thinking all along that the next keeper had to be one of us. On the other hand this remark put us on even footing that was for sure.

"But to interrupt the line, Mistress?" Eric said.

"If I see fit."

"Mistress ..." Eric blurted.

Elaine held one finger to her lips. Silence followed.

"And what do you have to say, Orin," Elaine asked.

"Whatever you think is best, Mistress." I felt that I was sincere.

Again silence.

Finally Elaine spoke. I will have some assignments for each of you. You may do them individually or together. Remain here at the residence until I return or send for you. Make no announcements. Understood?" We both nodded.

"Speak," she commanded.

"Yes, yes, Mistress," we said in unison.

[N.D.] *"Henry, of course I'm aware that I can simply make the appointment. But I am concerned about the boys themselves. I want them to be as close as brothers. I want the one who is not the Keeper to actually help the other."*

"Then you do actually see one of them as Keeper?" Henry Sawyer responded.

"Yes, if that is the best for both of them. Sometimes I think it would be better for them if I chose someone else. There are good candidates."

"Except that you would interrupt the line."

"Yes, we have never done that."

Silence

"There is one we could call on for help, Elaine."

Elaine watched Henry Sawyer for the answer.

"James has always had much wisdom. And he loves to help," Henry offered.

"James the Wise," Elaine said.

They both thought for a few seconds and then nodded.

[N.D.] Eric and I soon learned that James the Wise wanted to talk to us. We were terrified at first. James was, after all, the half brother of the Emperor and actually his advisor.

[N.D.] After our interviews, separate and together, James recommended several assignments for us. To accomplish these assignments we were given special privileges to go to places that would not normally be allowed but not the capital. Instead of Lucius for a help and an escort we were each given another angel temporarily. These assignments, these missions, were not merely exercises for me and Eric; they had outcomes, outcomes which would affect the well being of real people. I was loaned an angel named Mario and Eric was loaned an angel named Andros. Wherever I was, Mario was present either visibly or invisibly. The same was true of Eric and Andros. If we were together, both angels were present in whatever manner seemed most appropriate. These angels, like Lucius, could each make themselves larger and more imposing when it was necessary and they could transport us to places where we were allowed to go. If they refused to take us, we could only presume that we were not permitted to go to that place. We were also given titles which were temporary. We were each called "Keeper Apprentice." The only embarrassing thing about this entire arrangement is that the entire world knows that only one of us can become the Keeper and we are on display as apprentices for all to see. Oh well! What's the use? We can not control this so we might as well get on with it. To be honest I would be relieved for Eric to be the Keeper if he would accept me as his researcher and writer. To be the Keeper is a great public responsibility and I tend to be shy.

For our first assignment Eric and I have been instructed by Elaine, but we believe that the instructions are actually written by James the Wise. James is the writer of the Second Testament book which bears his name. The assignment is this: we are to travel the world in any way we choose, together or individually, but some kind of mix is recommended, and question the populace both at the Princes' Dais' and in the streets and public gatherings regarding the Imperial rule and ask for opinions of the world-wide rule itself. We are to reassure all that they can speak their minds without fear of punishment and that we do not require the people to give us their names, only that we interview them personally. Then we are to give our considered opinions as to the validity of these opinions, bearing in mind that we must comment on each one and not just say such things as "whatever seems best to the Emperor" or the like. This is a big assignment and we are given one short year to complete it.

[N.D.] "This is absurd!" Eric shouted at me after almost three months of being into our task. "How am I to know if I am giving the correct answer to these opinions. Look! Just look at them. Why they vary from 'The Emperor is always just' to 'He should be replaced by another Immortal' or 'a mortal electorate should be formed.' How? How I ask you, are we to know?"

"Well, Eric I think ..."

"It is all just too much," he interrupted.

I tried again. "I think we can only do our best. After all, they are aware of our limitations."

"I am not interested in displaying my limitations, dear cousin. Are you?"

"I do not particularly mind."

"There, you see, how can you be the Keeper if you will not be firmer about these matters?"

"Perhaps I should not be," I replied.

"Oh, no! You will not get away with that," Eric roared. "You must at least give me a fair run. I will not have it said that I gained the office by default. You must do your best."

"I am, I am doing my best," I answered.

We both grew quiet for some time.

[N.D.] When we turned in our reports, they both exceeded 1,000 pages each. They were received by Elaine graciously but we were not given any indication of how we did. We were simply given another assignment.

[N.D.] Our next assignment was a real surprise to both of us. We were told to meet with Elaine at her residence bright and early one morning. We arrived very early knowing that Immortals do not require sleep, just one of the many things about them that we no longer try to understand. While we are sleeping, they are apparently either traveling, holding night court, or somewhere on the 'other side.' Elaine joined us in her receiving room within minutes of our arrival.

"I think you boys will like this assignment," she said happily.

We sat very straight waiting for these instructions.

"You are each to proceed individually to anywhere you like and return here to this room in 4 months with your choice of a bride." With this she leaned back, clasped her hands and raised them to her chin as she watched us intently.

"A bride?" I said. "As in a wife? My life partner?"

"Precisely," she responded.

I looked at Eric. He seemed to be taking this quite calmly.

"Where, . . . where do we start looking?" I asked.

"Anywhere, anyway, you like," Elaine said calmly.

"Is our method as important as the final result in this, er . . . test?" I asked.

"You method only need to be honorable," Elaine said.

"Why is this test being put to us," Eric asked.

"Because, as Keeper, which ever one of you becomes the Keeper, your wife, your life partner, will be a very important part of the office. The person you choose will help demonstrate what you think of the office. "And," she hesitated, "after the turn the succession has taken with the Keeper May, we must be sure that you boys are on solid ground in the area of marriage and propagation." She looked very serious.

We nodded. I think Eric liked this assignment better than I. But, we had both had thoughts of marriage and this was the perfect opportunity to take care of this important matter although it leaves little room for romance. In the end, considering how the line has developed from grandmother, I consider it a fair test. We returned to our residence and with our respective angels set out on our individual journeys. Neither of us confided in the other about our destinations. In the end I will hear Eric's report when he returns, so for now I shall just record my actions.

[N.D.] I have a distant cousin named Malcolm who is descended from the Keeper Mark, through his daughter 'little Anna.' This 'little Anna' was the younger sister of the Keeper Carl. Malcolm is a few generations down from Carl. We have a lot of cousins in the family and there are certain mortals who keep exacting records of all the Annatic line, careful to name every cousin so that the succession is well documented. No one has ever had to use these records since decisions regarding the succession are always made by the Immortal Elaine. It seems to give some people something to do to keep track of such things. I know cousin Malcolm because he was a favorite of my mother. He is a professor at a college in the British Isles. He is known there in some circles as 'Malcolm the Wise.' As a mere mortal it is quite an honor to have the reputation for wisdom that Malcolm has. Traveling under my title as 'Keeper Apprentice' I had my temporary angel, Mario, take me to him. I do miss Lucius. I don't know why since angels are pretty much alike. Perhaps it is just because I have grown up around Lucius. In some unexplainable way I feel that Lucius likes me. I don't know why I feel this.

Malcolm's rooms are filled with books, tea leaves, and tobacco smoke. He prefers the pipe and I do not mind the smell that much. When I arrived, it was, as usual, raining. Malcolm was slouching in a huge chair with a book.

"My dear cousin," he said struggling to his feet. He has a large belly. He took several long strides across the room and embraced me warmly. I finally managed to struggle free and look him in the eye so then he took my hand and shook it for a long time.

"So good to see you again, cousin Malcolm," I said.

"And I, you, dear Orin. What brings you to my part of the world?" he asked.

"Great need, cousin, great need. I need your advice and counsel," I responded and proceeded to explain the assignment.

"A bride?!" cousin Malcolm exclaimed. "That is your assignment?"

"Yes," I answered. "They seem to think that my choice is of the utmost importance."

"Were you given any instructions as to how to go about this endeavor?" Malcolm asked.

"No, none."

"Then that is also a part of the test." He sat up straight as if to think clearer. "Yes, it is not only your choice but how you go about it. You said that you have to make a detailed report?"

"Yes, every aspect."

"Well, first of all, you have done the right thing by seeking counsel. No matter what they might think of my counsel, you can never tell about the Immortals, you know. They will respect the fact that you sought counsel. There is safety in a multitude of counselors, you know."

"Yes, well, I do now."

"Good! Now, how shall we proceed?" Malcolm was getting excited about getting into the problem. "First, I should arrange for you to meet some of our finest women," Malcolm continued. "I have some good contacts around here. But it will not do to have it known that the Keeper Apprentice is looking for a life mate. No, that must be our little secret."

"A Keeper Apprentice," I said. "There is another, and I doubt that he will keep it a secret."

"Um-Huum, then we best not waste any time."

"I'm in a hurry?" I asked.

"Only to the extent that when Eric starts blathering this about, you will also become an amorous target for thousands of eligible young maidens," Malcolm replied. He seems to have a way of sounding as old fashioned as possible, but it is a part of his charm.

"In addition to the fine families that I know, it would also be good for you to get some references from a Dais or two or a hundred," Malcolm added.

"Yes, most of the Metropolitans and even the Over-Lords have Immortals who counsel the mortal families in their areas," I said. "They would know who the really nice women are," I added.

"Now, you're thinking, boy," Malcolm said. "Let's do this intelligently and systematically."

I nodded in agreement.

[N.D.] During the next two months I had more dinners, more long walks, more visits to the Dais' of the world and more serious conversations with young women than I could count. I am keeping a private diary of them all. I feel a little insensitive actually rating these women as most of them are fine girls indeed. Malcolm and I have developed a rating system for intelligence, sensitivity, artistic competence, motherly characteristics, and love of the Emperor. So there is a number after each woman's name. Five is the highest rating for all categories and there are five numbers for the categories I have just listed. So, a number of 54534 would mean that she, in my opinion, rates a top number of 5 for intelligence, 4 for sensitivity, 5 for artistic, 3 for motherly and 4 for love of the Emperor. I have also added a star for exceptional good looks as this is also important to me but that part will not be included in my final report. Right now there are 87 entries in my book and 11 of them have at least four 5's and one 4. How to choose? Malcolm has recommended that I ask some Immortal for a special dose of the Presence. I have occasionally thought that I have felt the Presence in my duties as Keeper Apprentice, but it is a new concept to ask for Him in this personal endeavor. However, I have decided that it is important enough to ask for. I do not particularly want to go to Elaine or James the Wise for this. So I have decided to ask the Over-Lord Janice for help. She is sort of like a grandmother or perhaps a great aunt to me. I asked my temporary escort Mario, (I would never have thought that any angel could be less interesting than Lucius until now,) to take me to Janice. I was warmly received.

"Orin, my dear, so glad to see you, my boy. What brings you to visit old Janice?" she asked when I arrived. She likes to think of herself as old although none of them have any age anymore. She put her arm around me and had a seat brought for me next to her. The seat was not of the same construction as her regular Dais seats but it was not a stool so I felt greatly honored; me sitting on a Dais in an actual chair. I remember thinking that if the Emperor should suddenly arrive I would get as far from this chair as possible before I fell on my face before Him. But the Emperor did not come that day.

"Where have you been keeping yourself?" Janice asked.

"Mostly with my cousin, Malcolm, near Cambridge," I answered.

"Yes, Malcolm, Malcolm the Wise, quite a man for a mortal," she said. "And Eric, where is he?" she added.

"I don't know. You haven't seen him?" I asked.

"No, not for many months," she said.

I thought that maybe he would ask her help, but apparently he had not. I explained my challenge and made my request.

"Orin, you dear boy," she said. "Of course I will intervene to get you a special portion of the Presence for this very important task," she said. "That you should ask recommends you highly. Here, kneel before me," she said. I obeyed quickly.

She touched me and simply said, "A special portion of the Presence for this young man, please."

I waited expectantly. In a few seconds I felt it. It was wonderful. Why one would not even need a challenge or a reason for this. The Presence is so gentle and peaceful. He came over me like a warm spring rain after a long dry spell. I felt loved. I felt complete. I felt that I would never be lonely again. I felt mildly drunk. I just sat there cross legged in front of Janice and enjoyed it.

She left me there and walked to the front of the Dais to deal with some wrongdoer. As she returned to me, I heard her say, "Now that supervision need not last very long if you will cooperate." I heard some male mortal respond, "Yes, Highness, I will cooperate fully!"

"So, are you ready to get up," Janice asked me.

"Yes, I, . . .I feel fine," I said.

"You should, you should indeed," she said.

"Now, Orin, just present each of your candidates to the Presence one at a time and very slowly. Be aware of His reaction to each and before long you will know who she is.

"Yes, thank you," I answered.

"And stay here as my guest for a while," she said.

[N.D.] I stayed at Janice's court for two weeks. I stayed in private contemplation and presented my top choices to the Presence very slowly. I felt no change in the Presence for any particular woman. So I went back in my notes and presented some of the others thinking that perhaps I had been wrong in my ratings. When I brought up the name Carin that I had met at the Dais of the Metropolitan of Copenhagen, the Presence stirred Himself. He is not inside me, but he seems very near. I reviewed my notes and tried to recall this woman. I had rated her 43345 with a star; actually not very high. But her highest score was for love of the Emperor although I had several others with a 5 in that area. I decided that either I was misreading the Presence or my evaluation of this woman was not correct. I started all over again. Near the end when I got to Carin, again the Presence stirred Himself strongly. I told Mario to take me to the Dais of the Metropolitan of Copenhagen immediately. We arrived in the middle of the night there. It so happened that the Metropolitan was holding night court himself. He greeted me warmly. I tried to act very proper and not to rush, but it was difficult for me to do.

"You have something on your mind, Orin," finally the Metropolitan said.

"Yes, Excellency," I said. Being of European descent he did not mind the title. "I would like to see, again, a young woman named Carin."

"Carin, Horst Mueller's daughter?" he said.

"Yes, yes, that's the one."

"Why my dear boy, that is no problem. She lives only a few miles from here. But would you just as soon wait until dawn?" he asked.

"Yes, that would be better," I said. No use making this any bigger than it already is.

"Good. Fine. Then feel free to join my mortal staff for a little breakfast," he said. Peter Coop was a genial host and a great ruler. He hardly ever left the Dais. Therefore most of his under rulers spent a lot of time on the other side.

[N.D.] About an hour after dawn Carin arrived at the Dais. I took her into the Metropolitan's garden to talk. The weather was rather brisk so the Metropolitan ordered the garden warmed. I don't know how they do this, but it works well. We walked for a while and then sat down on a bench. I was looking at her very intently since the Presence seemed to be so strong on her. His stirring was very obvious from the moment she arrived. It was obviously His will that I marry her. So I looked all the harder.

"Sir," she said in the universal language. She speaks it well. "You stare." She lowered her eyes.

"I'm, I'm so sorry," I said. "I do not mean to be impolite."

She did not respond. I was asking myself, 'who is this woman that I apparently am destined to spend the rest of my life with? She is slightly built but sort of willowy and attractive. She has light skin and chestnut hair, large brown eyes, and a nice face overall. I find no fault with her, but I still do not see what is so special.'

She looked at me and spoke softly, "Are my fondest dreams coming true?"

"Maybe. What are your fondest dreams?" I asked.

"That you should want me," she answered.

My time with her before began to become clearer. We had walked in this very garden and I had gone home with her to supper. I had seen her two other times before I left her right here in this garden. She is very sweet.

"Yes, I believe they are; I believe I do," I heard myself saying. "Perhaps we can spend a week together, in the daytime and evening, I mean."

"I am at your call," she said.

"I might not become Keeper," I said.

"You could be a street cleaner, Orin," she said. Then she did not divert her eyes.

[N.D.] In the next week I came to understand the wisdom of the Presence and I begged him not to depart from me. So far he has not. I am very happy. I now have the Presence and Carin. She is my perfect partner. She is attentive and affectionate. She is intelligent and caring. She adores the Emperor and loves me. My grading system must have been wrong. We will be married here in Copenhagen next month. Elaine has approved of everything and will be here for the wedding.

04.05.361 C.R.   The Over-Lord Janice performed our wedding ceremony. The Emperor was represented by both Viceroys. It was a very festive occasion and Carin and I are very happy.

04.30.361 C.R.   We took our wedding trip to the Greek Islands. It was very beautiful and we did a lot of swimming in the clear waters there.

05.07.361 C.R.   Eric and I are preparing for our next official meeting with Elaine. Eric came to my wedding with his intended. Her name is Lilia. He found her at a festival in California.

05.09.361 C.R.   Eric and I met with Elaine today. We were surprised to find James the Wise there. James is a very impressive Immortal. He does not speak a lot but when he does, it is usually profound so everyone tends to listen to him. We mortals are not sure of what position he holds in the Empire. I heard Elaine refer to him once as a "Signet." I do not know what that means. He is revered as a very wise man just as my cousin Malcolm is revered as a wise mortal. Of course, James has had a long time to perfect his wisdom; so Malcolm can hardly be compared to James. Elaine and James greeted us and we all sat down around Elaine's round table in her garden.

"Eric," Elaine began. "We look forward to your wedding next week as well. James says that he would like to perform the ceremony for you."

"Ah. Yes, mistress," Eric responded. He seemed to be somewhat taken back by this. "I will tell Lilia about this as soon as I see her. She will be so, . . . surprised. And blessed, I assure you." He smiled convincingly at James. James showed no reaction. We all sat in silence for a while.

"Now for your next and final assignment," Elaine said.

"Pardon, mistress," Eric interrupted. "May we know something about how we are doing so far?"

"You will both know at the end," Elaine said. "That is how it has to be."

'Certainly," Eric replied. He did not sound happy.

"This time we want you to make full use of your angel escorts," Elaine said. "We want you to explore any place, especially Imperial places, that they will take you to."

"As of now," James interjected. "You will have entry to the capital including the Temple area, as you wish it."

We both expressed surprise and thanked him.

"Fine. You are most welcome," James continued. "Furthermore, this permission is not temporary as such permission can not be given on a temporary basis. No matter what the final decision, no matter who becomes the Keeper, you will both always have access to the capital and the Temple area."

"Thank you again," we chimed in unison. This was a great honor to be bestowed on any mortal. In most cases we can only visit the capital when we are invited for each individual instance.

Elaine motioned for us to calm down.

"Furthermore," James continued. "Which ever one of you who does not become the Keeper will be designated as Vice Keeper in case the Keeper should have need of him. This will be a life long designation."

We both sat quietly. Finally Eric asked, "Sir, what exactly will the Vice Keeper do? Will he have an angel?"

"He will do whatever the Keeper needs him to do. When on official business he will be assigned an angel. Probably the one you have now. Of course, the one who becomes Keeper will have Lucius back instead."

We both nodded. I looked at Eric. He seemed to be examining all alternatives. I am content to proceed.

"To clarify," Elaine said. "We want you to learn as much as you can about the Immortal side of things. We feel that this will help you in your future duties. Use the angels. Explore. Ask questions. Go to many Dais' as well. Express yourselves to the judges there. Do you understand?"

"Yes, mistress," we answered in unison.

"Do we go together?" Eric asked.

"As you wish," Elaine answered.

Neither one of us knew exactly what to do first. Eric suggested that we go together to the capital first. That sounded good to me.

[N.D.] After Eric's wedding and wedding trip he and I went to the capital together. Our wives stayed behind this time at the residence. The first thing that we did in

Jerusalem was attend a General Audience so that we could get a glimpse of the Emperor. It was very impressive and inspirational although the Emperor did not do anything unusual. Afterwards our angels told us to stay. We waited and were glad to be welcomed by the Chancellor himself.

"You are Orin and you are Eric," the Chancellor said pointing to each of us.

"Yes, Sir."

"Exactly, Sir."

It is not too difficult to tell us apart. We are about the same height and weight but Eric has lots of curly hair and I am balding quite a bit already.

"Congratulations on your recent weddings," the Chancellor continued. "Your wives are thriving?"

"Yes, Sir," we answered.

King David patted us each on the back and told us to enjoy the capital. He did not make any recommendations. We had not brought our brides because we thought of this as an official duty and we were not clear if they should come. Eric seized on this opportunity.

"Lord Chancellor," Eric said just as the Chancellor had turned to leave.

He turned toward us and smiled.

"Sir," Eric began, "are our wives allowed at the capital as we are?"

"That was not made clear?" he asked.

"No, Sir."

"Yes. They may share your privilege," he answered.

We thanked him again. He waved back at us. This man was accustomed to command. Both as a mortal and an Immortal he has always commanded. I felt that his authority comes from his own relationship with the Emperor. I noticed in the Audience how almost casual the Emperor seems. He carries Himself as if He has all the time in the world, which He does. But it is more than that. He carries Himself as a man who has done everything that He has been required to do. Now he has only to enjoy everything. The Chancellor and the other Immortal governors, on the other hand, are still occupied with their duties as they serve the Emperor. They are comfortable in their duties, but they are still aware that they have duties to perform. That is the only way I can explain what I sense. Perhaps I will try to make it clearer in my final report. Yes, I will try to do that.

I went back to get Carin. Eric sent his angel for Lilia as he said that there were a few things he wanted to see right away. We all met again that evening at the guest residence at the Capital. All visitors at the Capital stay at the guest residence totally under Imperial hospitality. We ate supper together. Carin and Lilia talked to each other a lot. They seem to get along fine. They are both thrilled to be at the Capital. Eric and I planned our next step. I am pleased that we are working together.

[N.D.] I do not know where Eric went when I went back for Carin. When I asked him, he just smiled. I hope he is not up to something that could bring discredit on our office. I say 'our office' because now it seems that whichever one of us does not become the Keeper will still retain the title of Vice Keeper. It seems that it is the will of the Princes that Eric and I remain tied to each other indefinitely. Don't get me wrong, I like Eric. He is very smart and much more decisive than I am. I would not have had the nerve to call after the Chancellor like he did to get permission for our wives to be with us at the Capital. Perhaps he would make a better Keeper. I am better at considered decisions and research. Perhaps the Princes, and indeed the Emperor Himself, are convinced that whichever one of us is the Keeper that he will need the talents of the other to complete the office. I could certainly help Eric with the research and the detail work and he could help me with the public appearances and the bolder decisions. Oh well, we'll see. There is no use being overly concerned about this. They will do what is best.

[N.D.] We have left the Capital on a tour of most every Dais in the world. We are traveling with both angels and both wives. Our wives stay at the guest residence of whatever Prince we are visiting and the mortal hosts are most kind to them, taking them on tours of interesting places in that area. Eric and I stay at the Dais and try to learn from the judges there. When we come across a situation which we think might need further documentation, we ask permission to leave. It is always given as this is more of a courtesy than anything else, and we go to investigate the situation. This has been very interesting. Of course, the Princes always make the right decision; the guilty are always found out and punished. But we look into the details and get acquainted with all the people involved. Often, we find that someone else in addition to the person who was punished had some small part in the problem. For instance, the Metropolitan of Lisbon, Jorge Romero, judged a certain man guilty of cheating another fellow in a business transaction. He sold grain by weight and seemed to have a very heavy thumb on the scales. He had regularly overcharged most every customer by nearly twenty percent for the past several months. We wondered why he began this practice since he has been in business for almost twelve years. So we went to his place of business and met his wife of some two years. We talked to the friends and neighbors.

"He has not been the same since he married," one man said. "It's that new wife of his. She is greedy. She pushes him to make more and more from his sales. Now she has gotten him judged for this. Now he has to pay back double for each time he has overcharged and he is under supervision as well for who knows how long. He would have been better off not marrying."

We found that many of his old friends and customers were in agreement. And yet the Metropolitan had not judged the wife at all. We returned and reported to the Metropolitan.

"Well, men, what would you do?" he asked us. "After all she did not do anything illegal. Her husband is responsible for how he responds to her and how he conducts his business, is he not?"

"Yes, Excellency," Eric answered. "But it seems that she should be held accountable in some way."

"And you have an idea?" the Metropolitan asked.

We were prepared as we had discussed this between ourselves already. "She could be assigned to some sort of re-education," Eric said.

"You mean supervision?" the Metropolitan asked.

"Not exactly," I said. "There would not have to be an angel involved. Perhaps it could be handled on a mortal level." I looked at the Metropolitan. He waited for more.

"Actually, Excellency," Eric said. "We have in mind a sort of re-education center as a part of the Keeper's office. If we could get a governor to provide living facilities, we could assign people from our office to work with people like this woman to help her see how she has been a bad influence on her husband and hopefully change her ways."

"Since the Keeper's office is in Atlanta perhaps Henry Sawyer would provide the facilities," Jorge Romano said. "Have you consulted the prince Elaine on this matter?"

Uh, no Excellency, the idea is still in what you might call the seedling stage," Eric answered.

"Then I suggest that Elaine is your next step," he answered. "If it is approved and begun, I will give you Mrs. Valdez as your first student."

Reign II

[N.D.] Everything proceeded rather quickly. Since Elaine and Henry Sawyer approved of our project, we have opened our re-education center near the Dais in Atlanta. We have quickly grown to over three hundred students, as we like to call them, and there are more coming in each time we visit a Dais. We have employed over twenty teachers who have been recommended from as many Dais' around the world. The students are educated concerning the many benefits of the Reign. Once most of them see how well they can be cared for under the Emperor, they no longer see any reason to misuse their friends and neighbors. Of course, we do not accept blatant wrong doers. They are judged by the Immortal Princes and dealt with at the Dais.

11.09.361 C.R. Today Elaine announced that I am to be the next Keeper and Primate. She met with Eric and myself privately at her residence. She praised Eric for his foresight and boldness and added that overall I was her choice for the position. Eric tried to hide his disappointment and I quickly told him how much I need him as Vice Keeper. He asked me in Elaine's presence if he could be excused for a while to take his wife on a pleasurable trip to the Mediterranean. I, of course, agreed.

01.02.362 C.R. Eric has been gone for almost two months now. I have not sent for him, but I am concerned. The re-education center takes a good bit of my time and Carin's time. She seems to love the work. She has actually become the moving force behind that work. One of the best things about our lives now is the return of Lucius. I guess that I would have to honestly say that Lucius and Mario are very much the same in personality, if that can be said about an angel. But even if it is, in my own perception I still see Lucius as being the faithful one to me and my family. Since angels can be nothing except faithful, this must be in my own mind and emotions. I can see a definite facial difference between Lucius and Mario. But that is probably because I have had enough time with each of them to be aware of this. Most mortals say that they can not tell one angel from another. Since Eric is not at present on an official trip, the angel that he had assigned to him during our testing period, Andros, is not around. I presume that he is back at whatever place unemployed angels reside or that he has been reassigned by Elaine or another Immortal.

[N.D.] It has now been over three months since I have seen my cousin Eric. Carin says that I am within my rights as Keeper to send for him and give him something to do. Dear Eric seems to be good at beginning things and leaving them to me to finish. I don't mind the work we have done at the re-education center. It just seems that Eric and Lilia should be doing something useful with their lives and I suspect that they are merely enjoying themselves.

[N.D.] It is another week since I wrote in this journal about Eric. I have sent Lucius to get them.

"Cousin, it is so good to see you," Eric said when he arrived. We embraced. Carin and I also embraced Lilia. She seemed a little distant. I would hate to believe that she only married Eric in the belief that he would become Keeper. I hope for both their sakes that they were still very dedicated to each other. Elaine would not put up with any irregularities here; I imagine that they are also aware of this. I took Eric aside so we could talk.

"Cousin, I need you to do some field research for me," I began.

"Field research? What is that?" Eric asked.

We were sitting in the rose arbor at the rear of the residence. The weather was nice and the roses were beautiful. This particular arbor is covered with hundreds if not thousand of white roses which bloom almost constantly. The weather control at the Metropolitan's Dais seems to extend as far as the residence and this makes my gardens particularly nice. I leaned back and prepared an answer to Eric's question. He sat and sipped his tea as if waiting for an answer.

"Field research? Well, by that I mean that I need you to travel to various places where I have been told there is a potential rebellion brewing and study the situation. You know, get to know the locals and find out what the complaints are so that I, that is, we, can try to answer the questions. Usually when good people really understand all that is available to them in the Empire, they are happy to be contented and accept the generosity of the Emperor in all things."

"Do you mean that you want me to spy?" Eric asked.

"No, not at all, unless you see a reason and particularly want to. For the most part you can visit as the Vice Keeper and talk to those who are willing," I said.

"Orin, if they are really feeling rebellious, then they are not going to speak truthfully with the Vice Keeper. It may be necessary for me to conceal my identity," Eric said.

"In that case you know what to do," I answered. "You can disguise yourself and your angel can turn invisible while you discover what you need to know."

"I will have an angel then?" Eric seemed to become more interested.

"Yes, I have talked to Elaine about this. You can use Andros for your work as Vice Keeper. As a matter of fact, she says that you can keep him as long as you serve as Vice Keeper." I stopped and smiled. I thought Eric would be pleased. I did not quite understand the look on his face.

"That will be good," Eric responded. "Although, . . . I may not need him all the time."

"When you don't need him, just tell him to report back to his legion. When you need him again, you could either make a request at any Dais or contact me and I will send Lucius for him," I added.

"That should work," Eric said. He seemed cautious. I had thought that he would be very happy to be the second mortal in Imperial history to have his own angel. This concept of Vice Keeper was, after all, new to both of us.

"Well, where do I start?" Eric asked.

"I have knowledge of a lot of unrest in the Denver area. If you would go and check in with the Metropolitan there, then you can choose your own way to investigate. Just tell Andros to inform me through Lucius as you go along."

"Should I take Lilia?"

"That's up to you and her. If she does not go, she is welcome to stay here at the residence. I have designated the East wing for you permanent use as you desire."

"That is very kind of you, cousin, I am . . . well, I am grateful." Eric seemed to be out of words.

"It is my pleasure, cousin. Of course, you are not obligated. Whatever you think is best. You and Lilia are always welcome and you can have your privacy."

Finally, Eric seemed pleased. We all had supper together and they both departed with Andros for Denver the next day.

[N.D.] Eric has sent regular reports. He has uncovered the malcontents in the Denver area and sent the stronger ones to our school. I am pleased as he seems to have defused that situation very nicely. His students are doing well at the school and are contributing nicely.

[N.D.] Eric and Lilia are off for Germany to uncover potential rebellion there. He is working with the court of Prince Norval, the Metropolitan of Frankfurt.

Reign II

[N.D.] Eric has solved the problem in Frankfurt. He may prove to be very good at this. I am so pleased.

04.22.363 C.R. I have been told by Lucius that Eric does not keep Andros with him at all times. He often sends the angel back to his legion with a predetermined return date. I suppose this is necessary if he is not to frighten the mortals and loose their cooperation.

[N.D.] I dispatched Eric to Australia today. This time Lilia is remaining at the residence. He will work with the court of the Overlord of Australia.

[N.D.] Yet another problem solved by Eric in Australia. What next?

01.09.364 C.R. Eric and Lilia spent a wonderful week with Carin and I at the Residence. Then they left to work in Brazil with the Metropolitan of Rio De Janeiro.

[N.D.] I have not heard from Eric in over a month. Lucius says that Andros has not been with them for almost three weeks. No one at the court in Rio knows where they are. I will give him another week. They may be working under cover, but I am worried about their safety without an angel to look after them.

05.01.364 C.R. Another week and still no word from Eric and Lilia. I have sent Lucius for Andros.

"You sent for me, Keeper," the angel said as he appeared with Lucius in my dining room.

"Yes," I looked up from my dinner. Carin studied the two of them evidently trying to determine how much they look alike. "I want you to go and find the Vice Keeper Eric. Report to me as soon as you know something."

"Personally, Keeper?"

"Yes, personally, just come directly back here. If I am sleeping, Lucius will get me. Understood?"

"Clearly, Keeper."

I nodded and he departed. Lucius resumed his place next to the wall.

05.02.364 C.R. "Keeper, awaken please." I heard Lucius out of a deep sleep. Beside me Carin stirred.

"What is it, Lucius?"

"Andros is back. There is news," Lucius said. I thought I heard a hint of doom in his voice but since I was barely awake, I ignored the instinct.

"Show him in," I said.

Andros appeared and stood at the foot of the bed with Lucius behind him. I propped myself up on some pillows and Carin did the same. "What do you have to report?" I asked.

"Eric seems to have joined the group in Rio in their plans," he said.

"As an infiltrator, no doubt," I added groggily.

"Perhaps, Keeper, but he is using his own name and his wife is doing the same," Andros said.

"There may be nothing wrong with that," I added. "You did not show yourself?" I asked.

"No, Keeper. I remained concealed."

"On who's instructions?" I asked. I was fully awake now.

Andros turned towards Lucius.

"Your instructions, Lucius?" I asked.

"Yes, Keeper."

"It is unusual for you to take such an initiative," I said.

"I was instructed by those over me," Lucius said.

"Alright," I said.

"You're shouting, dear," Carin said.

"Am I? Sorry. Now, Lucius, please fill me in completely," I insisted softly but firmly.

"There has been suspicions for some time, Keeper," Lucius said.

"Suspicions? By whom?"

"Imperial security, Keeper. Eric has been too good at this. It now appears that he has asked for volunteers to come forth and go to your re-education centers while the bulk of them just go underground."

"You mean that he is actually involved with the rebels?" I asked.

"No, Keeper. He is their leader." Lucius said.

My heart sank. "Their leader? What does he hope to do. He knows that he can not overthrow the Emperor. What does he want?" Now I was shouting and Carin was not reminding me.

"He does not seek to overthrow the Emperor, Keeper."

"Then what. Does he want more 'mortal rights' or some other such thing. Why, he knows how things are, how things must be, he . . ."

"Dear, please calm yourself," Carin said. She grasped my arm. "Just listen to Lucius for a minute, dear."

I waited.

"He expects to overthrow you, Keeper. By showing your re-education centers useless he hopes to become Keeper. He has never resigned himself to not being the Keeper."

"Does Prince Elaine know?" I asked.

"She was informed as she emerged from the feast an hour ago," Lucius said.

"I must see her."

"Yes, Keeper."

I dressed immediately. The sun was rising and when I entered my meeting room, Elaine was there.

"You know." I said.

"Yes. I'm sorry, Orin. We had to give him enough rope to hang himself."

"I am having him brought to Prince Henry's Dais now," Elaine said softly. "I understand," I said. I could hardly fight back tears. Elaine embraced me for a few seconds. We did not speak.

"Do I have to come?" I asked.

"I'm afraid so. You should bring the charges."

"What will the punishment be?'

"The maximum, Orin."

I felt an emptiness in the pit of my stomach and then cold chills. Eric executed. I could not take it in.

"Yes," I finally said. "All crimes are against the Emperor Himself."

"Yes," Elaine said.

05.10.364 C.R. Eric tried to exclude Lilia but she insisted that she was as involved as he was. Metropolitan Henry Sawyer sentenced them to death for sedition. Eric appealed to the Chancellor and was taken to the Capital. The Chancellor judged them immediately and they were executed there. Eric did not appeal to the Emperor. Normally, no mortal would even think of appealing but as Vice Keeper Eric was a little bolder and they allowed it. I am desolate and it will take some time for me to recover. All the rebels that Eric was in with have been delivered by the angels and judged.

06.03.364 C.R. My Re-education centers have been a failure. I am closing them world wide.

02.02.365 C.R. I am opening my first center for Truth-Seekers. I will run it and speak there myself.

03.14.365 C.R. The Truth-Seekers have had some success.

11.18. 415 C.R.   The Truth-Seekers project is the crowning achievement of my career as Keeper. It has, however, exacted a toll on my life and my marriage. Carin and I are still close, but I have missed many important events in my life and the life of my family because of the demands of the Truth-Seekers. I was absent at the birth of my son James in 412 C.R. I have traveled extensively in this work. I have establish Centers for Seekers in many cities and I am usually the only mortal speaker at these centers.

[N.D.]   There are Immortals who are always ready to provide resources for the Truth-Seekers. We have been privileged to hear from Paul, Augustine, Martin, Jean and others.

[N.D.]   In order to stay inspired myself I have visited the Imperial Court and sought an audience with the Emperor as many times as possible. I find that being in the presence of His Majesty inspires me to be able to inspire others. In the rare instances where I have convinced some of my more promising disciples to seek an audience with the Emperor, they too have been an inspiration to others. However, most mortals are too afraid of the Emperor to want to get to know him. I can easily arrange for them to see Him. They do not understand.

09.12.428 C.R.   My son James is sixteen years old today. I have made arrangements so that I do not miss this occasion. I have succeeded in getting him recognized by the Chancellor as Keeper Heir. He is a very intelligent and conscientious young man and I have great expectations for the future.

Orin

08.09.429 C.R. My name is James. I am the new Keeper and Primate. My father Orin died in his sleep last night. The Immortal Elaine has taken his body to the Dais. What a dear man my father was.

Reign II

Patricia

503 - 568 C.R.

3.21.503 C.R. My name is Patricia the daughter of James the Keeper and Primate. My father died quietly in his sleep last night at the age of 91. I am the daughter of his second wife Jessie. Mother is my closest friend after the Governess Elaine. I am the new Keeper and Primate. I saw the Emperor at my investiture; I have looked into his eyes. I am not the same.

04.02.503 C.R.   Since Great Aunt May was so spiritual, she had several assistants to help her perform her duties as the Keeper. The first original was a male and he was in charge of the actual library and research. The second original was a female and was in charge of her ceremonial duties and actually appeared for her on many occasions. She resembled May and was on certain occasions mistaken for May herself. The third original was also a female and was in charge of implementing her spiritual innovations. These three were named Executives of the Keeper or E.K. for short: the E.K. for records and research, the E.K. for ceremonies, and the E.K. for spiritual growth. As the generations have continued, the offspring of these Executives have taken their parent's jobs.

The current E.K. for ceremonies is named Celeste and we have been fast friends since childhood. We grew up together at the residence. The other two Executives now are much older than Celeste, but they are nice and perform their duties very well. All of this structure is good for the Office of Keeper but the problem is that I seldom have enough to do. I have not mentioned this to anybody but I am starting to believe that I do not need these officers.

Actually, I plan to find a way to do away with these offices as soon as I can find a way to take care of the people in them. I don't want them to be hurt. When I became keeper, Celeste was only a little over a year into her office and just four months younger than myself. She is special to me. I have kept her close ever since. Most people think we look a lot alike. Celeste is often taken for me, but she quickly sets the record straight.

I do not want to be a nun like May who was the last female keeper. I love the Emperor. Praise His Name! But I do not feel the call that Aunt May felt. I have told Celeste that I will appear at more ceremonies and she was glad to hear that, but I still have too much idle time. I am not very good at research and at my age I do not feel much like a spiritual leader. You might say that I am still seeking my true calling. I feel that each Keeper has made their own contribution to society and to the Empire and I want to make mine.

06.12.503 C.R. I have decided to go among the people anonymously. Celeste has agreed to accompany me. She has assigned her necessary duties to others on my staff. Elaine has agreed and has supplied us with some common clothing. Lucius will come along but remain invisible.

06.14.503 C.R. "You two look like school girls," Elaine said when she saw us in the new clothes. "Why does each generation want to 'be among the people?' You remind me of Mark and his 'adventure' except that you two don't have an ounce of rebellion between you."

"Great Grandfather Mark was a guy, Elaine," I responded.

"So?"

"Well, guys are more adventuresome than girls. Most girls." Celeste and I looked at each other and grinned.

"O.K. Now you two, what exactly are your goals in this thing," Elaine asked.

"Elaine, I just want to be around some more people our age and . . ."

"And that is?" Elaine asked.

"You know perfectly well that it is twenty."

"And what are you going to learn from mortal twenty somethings?" Elaine asked.

"I don't know. How they think.. What they feel."

"Feel about what?"

"Anything, everything. Life, the world, the Emperor, families, Immortals."

"I can tell you these things. Lucius can tell you." She spoke with a frank serious look.

"But Elaine, that will not give me a feel for where they are. I have been raised here in the residence. I have been quite sheltered. I want to be a part of my generation and a good Keeper as well. I want . . ."

Elaine raised her hand for me to stop. "Very well, little one, your motives seem good enough. Lucius will keep you safe. Just promise me one thing."

"Of course, mistress, anything." I seldom called her 'mistress'. She took me by the chin and looked directly into my eyes. Her pale blue eyes always made me feel quite peaceful. My eyes are a darker blue. I don't know what she sees in them.

"Promise me, that if Lucius becomes visible and gives you advice, any advice, that you will heed him immediately."

"Yes, absolutely. I trust Lucius implicitly," I responded.

"Fine. When will you leave."

"In the morning, early," I said. She hugged us both and vanished.

06.15.503 C.R. We arose early. After we ate, we picked up our packs and strolled towards the gate of the residence with Lucius following behind. As we passed through the gate, Lucius vanished but I knew that he was still there. I had a purse full of gold coin. These were in twenty talent pieces, the newer kind with the Emperor's sign on one side and the Western Viceroy's sign on the other side. They are also good in the Eastern Viceroy's area as are the Eastern ones in the West. In this century the Emperor's sign is a faintly depressed fleur-de-lis with a bold raised cross of St. Andrew or "X". The Western Viceroy presently uses a faintly depressed simple castle design with a raised Viceroy's coronet, or small crown, outlined in the center. The Eastern coin has the same sign of the Emperor with a sacred heart, a human heart with a band of thorns around it. We intend to pay our way and not to stand out too much. We would tell everyone that we were two students from Metropolitan Sawyer's University and that we are touring as part of a research project on the opinions of those in our age group. This would enable us to ask lots of questions. Celeste and I should fit in as students quite well. And, with the Metropolitan's approval we are to report whatever findings we think appropriate to the student body when we return so we are not telling a lie.

[N.D.] We spent our first night at a youth hostel just a short distance on the North side of Atlanta. We had walked all the way. It is to the credit of the reign of our Glorious Emperor that two young women can walk openly without fear of danger. Angelic patrols are everywhere, seen or unseen. And, of course, my true identity is not known. I use my middle name, Marie, when asked to identify myself and I have not been the Keeper long enough yet to be recognized by sight. Indeed, Celeste could be recognized as easily or more easily as myself. We wore light head scarves to obscure ourselves a little more. We met a lot of people that first day, young and old, most of them friendly and certainly none who seemed too aggressive. At the end of the day we resolved to take the power train the next day to the North, perhaps staying the next night in the Carolinas.

[N.D.] We talked most of today with some students returning to the Metropolitan's university in Raleigh. Most universities these days are under the patronage of a Metropolitan although a few higher princes have also sponsored some. These students were all friendly and seemed to be impressed with my knowledge of mortal and Immortal history, but they did not seem to venture a guess about my true identity. Celeste has acted as if I were an advanced student, so they just took that at face value. I have, after all, been studying mortal and Immortal history from a child as my father had encouraged me to do so in order to be ready for my responsibilities as Keeper.

[N.D.] In Raleigh Celeste and I went out to eat at an outdoor restaurant. I noticed a group of people, about 15 in all, gathered together there and I became fascinated with them.

"I think I would like to get to know them better," I said gesturing in their direction to Celeste.

"Well, that is what we are doing out here, Ma'am," she said.

"Put away the Ma'am stuff. Remember who we are, or . . ., who we are supposed to be," I said.

"Yes, ... of course."

I don't know why these people fascinated me so. They were attractive although their clothes were very much like our own, loose fitting and colorful. They were certainly mortals, but they seemed to have something, something I could not put my finger on, of the immortal about them. Lucius did not appear in any form to warn me; he could have appeared as a server if he was so inclined so I pushed on. They were polite from the first, but only polite.

"We're from Atlanta, actually Buckhead, I volunteered."

Most nodded, some offered a hand.

"Do you mind?" Celeste nodded towards two empty chairs.

"No, no, go right ahead," one of the young men responded.

I noticed that he was particularly strong looking and graceful; all in all very nice indeed. For a while some of them made small talk with us but I got the definite impression that we weren't really welcome. I was about to decide to excuse us and move back to our old table which was still empty. Then something almost undetected passed between several of them and they became genuinely friendly indeed. Celeste gave me a hand sign, the first two fingers tapping the opposite wrist that we had agreed upon if she thought I had been recognized. I nodded back pensively; perhaps she was right. The conversation turned decidedly to history and I got very involved. They were very knowledgeable on the subject and I could barely hold my own. Before long nearly three hours had elapsed and Celeste was pointing towards her wristwatch. She was one of the few people who wore one these days. A very efficient girl. We all exchanged pleasantries and retired for the night to our rooms. I did not notice where these people were lodging.

[N.D.] The next night we met at the same place. After an hour or so of more conversation that agreed very well with me, the same young man that I had noticed at first spoke during a brief lull in the conversation.

"So, ... Miss Keeper, is that what we should call you?"

I was surprised that I was surprised. "Patricia will do," I answered calmly and managed to smile a little. Actually it was not that difficult to smile at this man although I was a little miffed at being found out. His name is Melcor, not a name I had heard before. They had mentioned a time or two that they were from the East.

"I guess I am not as smart as I thought," I mentioned after some more silence.

"Smart enough, Excellency," a woman named Melodi said softly. She was more respectful.

"No formalities," I said. "We are on a research trip. Help me keep my identity a secret."

They all nodded agreeably.

"There is supposed to be an angel, an escort," another fellow mentioned looking around.

I noticed Lucius over his shoulder in a server's apron and almost laughed out loud remembering my own thoughts of the day before. Sensing no warning from Lucius I went on. "He's there," I said nodding. He turned to look Lucius squarely in the eye and jumped.

"No problem," I said urgently but softly not wanting to draw any attention. I wondered briefly how he knew that what he saw was actually an angel or whether he had merely taken my word for it. No, he knew this was an angel. Few mortals do when Lucius intends a disguise. Who were these people?

The conversation did not go well from then on since everyone was obviously thinking of things much different that what we were actually talking about. The old emphasis on history, mortal or not, no longer held up. They drank a little but did not eat. I had not seen them eat at any time. I was not sure that I could actually see them breathing. Then there was that strangely ethereal look about them. Finally, I decided to assert my authority.

"Where are you staying," I asked.

"Not far," Melcor said. He turned his head to a building behind them.

"May I see it?" I asked.

There was a short silence. "Of course," several of them said at once.

We got up and made our way quietly out of the restaurant and went back to their rooms. They all seemed to be staying in one very large room on the top floor of the building. It seemed very clear that they had been there for some time. They were not mere tourists, neither were they natives. Knowing that they knew about Lucius and were somewhat afraid of him I pressed on.

"Where exactly are you people from?" I asked.

They looked around at each other. No one answered. Some looked towards the floor rather than meet my gaze.

"Lucius, appear!" I commanded.

He did.

"Who are they?" I asked.

"They will tell you, Keeper. But I do advise discretion on both sides." He said no more. He remained visible. I felt assured and somewhat bolder.

"We are not from here, Keeper," Melodi ventured.

"That is obvious," I said. "I know most all of the Over-Lords and Governor's. Who is yours?"

"Our Over-Lord is named Satay," Melcor said.

"I know of no such Over-Lord," I said.

Silence again. They looked at Lucius who now had a distinctly angelic bearing. He nodded.

"We are from off-world, Keeper," Melodi said.

"Off-world, are you immortal?" I asked. Perhaps I was in trouble.

"No, we are mortal, Keeper. But, ... different."

"Do you serve our Emperor?"

"Absolutely. He is Emperor in all places."

This was truly exciting. I could feel my heart pounding. I looked at Celeste, she looked as amazed as I was and a little confused.

"Another planet?" I asked.

"Yes."

"Named?"

"That is not necessary, Keeper."

"How long have you been here?"

"A long time."

"Do you die?"

"Eventually."

"Do you need, ... redeemed, like we do?"

"Yes, but we are not the children of Adam."

I felt a rush of excitement. I looked at Celeste. I was afraid she was going to faint. One of them offered her a glass of water. She drank some and looked a little better. Lucius was expressionless.

"Are you related to us?" I asked.

"Only by the same Creator," Melcor answered.

I had a million questions, but I decided to slow down and act more like the Keeper than an excited child. I realized that I had been participating in an exchange of information since yesterday and now it was my turn to receive some.

"What are you doing here?" I asked.

"The same as you, Excellency, learning."

"You, of course, have the Emperor's blessing to be among us," I said.

"Yes, we came first to the Viceroy John in the East. We are here now by the permission of the Viceroy Luis of the West." Lucius nodded in agreement so that I would be assured that they were telling the truth.

All seemed to be in order. Fine, now we could really talk. But Celeste interrupted. At first I was aggravated with her.

"Patricia, Keeper, could we get some rest?" she asked.

Rest? Now? I thought. But she really looked pale. I glanced at Lucius. He seemed sympathetic, although I knew he never needed rest. The off-worlders seemed relieved at the suggestion. So I agreed. They, in turn, agreed to meet the next day.

"You won't leave?" I asked.

They promised. We went to our rooms once again.

[N.D.]   We spent many days with these people. They are a lot like us. As near as I could tell their bodies are nearly identical to ours, male and female. But I was curious about a lot of other things.

"How old are you?" I asked.   "In your years," Melodi answered, "I am 152 years old."

"152?!"

"Yes, that is correct."

"Are you sure? You look so young. Is this in our years? Like in 365 twenty-four hour days?"

"That is correct."

"You appear to be so much like us," I said.

"We are. We eat. We sleep. We breathe. Our bodies look like yours. We have essentially the same internal organs. My heart beats like yours. Here, feel my pulse." She stretched out her hand. I grasped her wrist and felt her heart beat.

"If we live 70 or 80 years, it's a long time," I said. "How long do you live?"

"It varies, 400 years or so."

"How do you do that?"

"I do not know how, we just do."

"Do you reproduce like we do?"

"Yes, after conception, we breed like you do. The infants are born in 10 of your months."

"Ten?"

"Yes, a little longer. The child is considered to be an adult at 18 years, like yours."

"You said that you acknowledge the Emperor."

"Of course, he is our Emperor as well."

"He has been to your world?"

"Yes."

"What does he do there?"

"Holds court. Rules. Is greatly admired."

"Are there Immortals on your world?"

"Not yet."

"Not yet?"

"That is correct. Except those who come with the Emperor. We do hope to become immortal ourselves in time."

"In time?"

"Yes."

"Will it, ... er, do you expect it to happen suddenly, like the great cataclysm that happened when our Immortals were changed?"

"We do not know."

"Lately," Melchor continued. "We have desired to learn and have been given permission to come here."

"We are only talking to you, Patricia, Keeper," Melodi interrupted, "because of who you are. We trust that you and your assistant here, Celeste, will keep our confidence. We are not given leave by the Emperor to talk to everyone right now."

"How did you get here?" I asked. "I mean, how did you travel?"

"We studied and have achieved travel through what you sometimes call portals," Melchor said.

"You travel like our Immortals?"

"Sort of," Melchor answered. "But at a much lower and more limited level."

"This can be learned?" I asked.

"At a certain level," he answered. "Ours is limited whereas your Immortals' travel is not. At least as far as we can tell."

"You say that our Immortals come to your world?"

"Yes, as members of the court."

"Your Over-Lord is mortal or immortal?" I asked. I watched him closely.

"The Over-Lords that we can see are mortal as we are. But, we know that there are others."

"Do your mortal Over-Lords communicate with the Immortal ones?"

"Yes, in the Sacred Place."

"What is that like?"

"We, none of us here," Melchor looked around, "have ever seen it. We do not know."

"How have you communicated with our, . . .the Emperor?" I asked.

"Through a member of his court," Melchor answered.

"Can you tell me which member? I may know him, or her," I asked.

Once again Melchor and Melodi exchanged glances. I had another question now but I waited for them to answer the last one.

"Through one named Julia, she is a monitor for our world." Melchor answered.

"Just one more question," I said. They waited. "You two, Melchor and Melodi, you are the leaders? You have a special relationship here? What?"

"We are siblings, Keeper. We have the same parents, Father and Mother." I nodded. There seemed to be more to that than what they actually said, but I let it go for now.

"I know I said just one more question, but I want to say this," I said. They all looked directly at me. "Since I am on a trip of exploration near the beginning of my service as

Keeper, I believe that our meeting was no coincidence. There must be, therefore," I caught my breath, "some reason for this. There must be something that needs to be learned or done."

This time they looked at Lucius.

"Lucius," I said slightly exasperated. "Give!" I found myself sitting with my hands on my hips and looking very demanding. 'Had my own angel put something over on me?' I thought. Then it occurred to me that if he had, Elaine would most likely be at the bottom of it so I calmed down before he could answer.

"Prince Elaine," Lucius began.

"Yes, of course, please continue," I said acting somewhat amused. Any lesson set up by Elaine would have to be a good one. I half expected her to arrive.

"This one," Lucius pointed to one of the men who had been very quiet, "he holds a position similar to yours in his world."

'Ah ha,' I thought. 'Now the real secret is out.' Immediately the young, uh, who knows how old he is? Anyway, this young man stood and extended his hand to me with a big smile and said, "Alexor, Madam Keeper. My office is called something like 'Documentor' in your language."

I shook his hand and tried to act official. "You, you all speak our language well," I said.

"We have studied it for a long time," Alexor responded.

[N.D.] I spent a lot of time with Alexor over the next several weeks. I started leaving Celeste for long periods of time with Melchor and Melodi and the rest of them. Alexor and I would take long walks in the most beautiful places I could find. I still hesitated to try to travel by transport together as I was not quite sure how that would work out. I was not sure that Lucius would take Alexor with me or if I could go with them. I started calling him 'Alex' and I fell in love with him. He would hold me and kiss me and caress me but anytime we were tempted to go further Lucius would appear. He would just appear. He did not say anything or do anything. About the fourth or fifth time that this happened I got a little angry.

"Lucius! Why, why may I ask . . .?" I was beginning to splutter. Alex looked apprehensive.

"You should consult Elaine," he said.

"Very well. Alex, will you wait?" I asked.

"Yes, of course." We had slipped off to a private garden nearby.

"Please take me to her," I said to Lucius calmly.

"No dear, you can not. You can not even continue with this man" Elaine said.

I was shocked, shocked and hurt. I started to tear up. She sat down beside me and put her arm around me.

"I let you go this far to see if you would get your own bearings on this," Elaine said. "But I am afraid that you have strayed somewhat from the path, little one."

"How?"

"You can not have a, a relationship with this man or any man from their world. You, to put it simply, can not reproduce with them and that would be the natural result of the way in which you are heading," Elaine explained.

"Why not?"

"Because your children would inherit a lot of their traits and they are not the children of Adam. I am sorry, Patsy. That is just not allowed."

She was being very loving and kind. I could sense that she was sharing my pain and really feeling for me so I decided that any form of rebellious behavior was unacceptable although it did seem unfair. Why couldn't we have some more years? But I didn't say anything. Typical of Elaine I did not have to.

"I know it seems unfair. I am Immortal and your mortality is so short while theirs is so long. But it just doesn't, it just doesn't fit into, well, the overall scheme of things. I wish I could explain it to you better," she finished.

I sat there for a few minutes.

"I will find someone really nice for you to marry," Elaine promised. She kissed me on the forehead and I cried for a while. I had to go back to Alex and tell him what could not be. It was very hard for me to do. I was assigned a female named Mairi as my contact with our off-world friends. She was instructed to join my staff at the residence. She seemed a little sad about this.

[N.D.]   Back at the residence Mairi and I had a talk. My trip had been interrupted.

"Are you lonely," I asked.

"Yes, Keeper. I am to spend your lifetime here and there are no others of my kind here. Not that I do not appreciate your hospitality and the honor of being liaison here, I do."

She is really a nice girl, I wonder . . .

"How old are you, dear, in my years," I asked.

"92, I am one of the younger ones," she responded. She looked 22.

"Why don't we send for a companion for you?" I said.

She brightened considerably.

"That would be wonderful," she said.

"Do you know who you could ask?"

"Yes, I have a sister who would come."

"How old would she be?"

"92, Keeper."

"Please call me, Patsy, always," I said. "The same age. Are you twins?"

"Yes. Patsy, that is very kind of you." She now was considerably lighter.

"How do we, er, get her here, do you suppose?"

"I'm not sure," she answered.

"I'll speak to Elaine," I said.

I told Lucius that I needed to talk to Elaine.

[N.D.] "I'll arrange it right away," Elaine said. She left and returned with Mori in a few hours. The sisters hugged and acted quite excited. They were so excited I actually heard a few words in their own language.

"Remember, Patsy," Elaine told me in front of them, "Mairi is your liaison. Her people insist on this. Mori is her sister and companion."

I agreed. Mori did not seem to care.

"And be sure not to reveal who they are to any other mortals without my permission on a case by case basis. Understood?"

When Elaine asked 'understood', that was always serious.

"Yes, I understand," I said. A spoken response was required for this. Celeste had been sworn to secrecy.

[N.D.] I never saw Alex again. I even asked Lucius if I could visit his world. His immediate answer was, "No, Keeper."

Mairi even let it slip that Alex had been disciplined for his lack of discretion with me. I was always convinced that he had sincerely loved me. This report, although I hurt for Alex, was a confirmation of his love for me. Evidently the discipline involved only the loss of some privileges and nothing worse.

[N.D.] After Alex I gradually got back to my work. There is the usual researching and writing, the usual speaking and encouraging the people in the areas that they seem to need strengthening. But nothing really catches my attention.

[N.D.]   Mairi is very intuitive; she seems to be aware of things and knows many things before I am aware of them. She and Mori seem to be in almost constant communication. I don't think it is mind reading since that has been forbidden to mortals since before the glorious return of the Emperor. So if it is mind reading, then that rule does not apply to them although they are technically mortals no matter how long they live. I have a feeling that it is different. Sometimes it seems almost instinctual, like our animals.

[N.D.]   After my grief over Alex started to subside as Elaine said that it would, I started to get curious again about Mairi and Mori's world. I must admit that it did cross my mind once or twice as to why I should trust these aliens. Then I reminded myself that I did love and trust Alex and also that Elaine had placed these aliens in my household. This distrust of strangers must lie deep in my race.

A new relationship with the twins began as I accidentally overheard them one day as I went into my garden.

"Yes, it is quite bright," Mori was saying, "but then again it has to be since there is only one."

I asked myself, 'do they speak in our language all the time, even when they are alone with each other?' "Hi," I said, revealing myself. I did not want them to think I was spying on them.

"Good day, Keeper," Mori answered a little surprised.

"She wants us to call her Patsy, sister, you know that," Mairi said.

I had spent more time with Mairi before Mori joined her and therefore Mairi felt more familiar with me.

"Yes, that's fine," I said. "I was just coming into the garden and I did not want you to think that I was spying on you. You have every right to your privacy. After all, you are sort of exiled to our world." I turned and started to leave because I saw them glance at each other in that knowing way that they have when I said the word 'exiled.'

"No, please, . . . Patsy, stay," Mori said. I looked at them and they were both smiling so I decided to stay.

This was the beginning of endless questions from me about their world and culture. They did not seem to mind answering. As a matter of fact, they seemed to enjoy it.

"You always speak to each other in our language?" I asked. "Even when you are alone with each other?"

"Yes," they chimed in unison. I have noticed that they tend to do this when they are nervous.

"Yes," Mairi said. "If we do not, our ability to communicate with you and others here might be compromised and I am charged as Liaison to represent us well to you and any others that I am allowed to talk to. It is a great honor."

"I see. When I came upon you here, you were talking about there 'only being one of them'?"

"Yes, your sun. There are two that shine on our world."

"Fantastic!" I said. "Are they very bright?"

"Yes, much brighter than here," Mori answered.

"Doesn't that hurt your eyes?" I asked.

"No, we have . . ." Mori started to answer then looked at her sister and then continued. She had gotten some sort of permission. "We have another lid," she said. With this she came closer and transparent white lids closed over her eyes. It seemed to be under her normal eyelid.

"Oh, my," I exclaimed. "This is amazing."

"You, you don't think we are . . . freaks, do you?" Mairi asked.

"No, no indeed. You are just wonderfully adapted to your world. You are actually quite attractive." This fear of being thought a freak was probably why Alex never allowed me to see this second pair of eyelids. I thought of some of our animal creatures that have a second lid. I believe they are reptiles but I did not mention them to the girls as I was afraid of insulting them. Plus, I know they are not cold blooded after snuggling with Alex as much as I did. He was very warm.

"You think we are attractive?" Mori asked.

"Yes. Yes indeed," I answered truthfully. "You are quite attractive." The females are all quite thin but it is not unbecoming and they have nice figures. They are from medium to fair coloring and all have very large luminous pale blue eyes. The males are a little heavier with unusually broad shoulders and similar coloring with the same eyes. They have hair on their heads but no body hair. They are quite sleek and attractive. I imagine that if the girls travel much with me, we will have the problem of them attracting many male admirers.

"Most things come in pairs in our world," Mori said. "Even more so than here."

Mairi shot her a glance.

"Then guide me, sister," Mori returned. "Please excuse us," she then said to me apologetically.

"It is fine to be totally honest with the Keeper," Mairi said. "She knows what to share and what not to share."

I asked, "Are you two twins?"

"We are all twins," Mori answered.

"All?"

"Yes, we are all born twins on our world. Unless something goes wrong." This time Mairi answered.

"How interesting," I responded. "Are you what we call maternal twins, I mean from the same seed that splits, or are you fraternal twins from different seeds?" They did look a lot alike, but not completely identical in their facial features.

"We two are what you call maternal," Mairi answered. "All of our mothers bear twin young of some sort."

"All?" I asked again.

"Well, most all."

"But when I first met you and Alexor and the others, there did not seem to be any twins in the group," I explained.

"No, we did not travel as twins here. It draws too much attention. Although those of us who are unmatched, er, unmarried do terribly miss our twin."

"Drawing too much attention makes sense," I said. "Our people are often fascinated with twins. Then you are very close as twins?"

"Yes."

"And after you marry?" I asked.

"We usually try to marry twins," she answered.

I didn't say 'amazing' or 'interesting' this time. That had to stop since I had the feeling that I would be continually amazed by these two.

I continued my quiz, "Is the older twin, by whatever margin, a minute or whatever, always the one in charge? I mean Mairi seems to be dominant among you and Mori does not seem to mind at all."

"Not the older. Not every time. But the dominant one is established early and the other is happy to fall in behind. Is it not the same here with twins?" Mairi asked.

"I believe so," I said.

"Of course, it is not a perfect twin world," Mori added. "In some cases something goes wrong and twins are not born. In some cases twins do not marry twins. Then another set has to be broken up."

"Some of our best leaders have been singles," Mairi added.

"By singles you mean a non twin," I said. "Not an unmarried person."

"Yes."

"But your twin suns, . . " I began.

"They are perfect," Mairi said. "They share the sky perfectly and they are totally equal in their light."

"I guess that is what inspires your overall twinness," I said.

"I guess," Mairi said. "I had never quite thought of that before."

"Have you visited other worlds like you are visiting mine," I asked.

"Yes, a few," Mairi said.

She seemed hesitant. I pushed on.

"Tell me about some of them," I said.

Again, hesitation and then finally, "We, . . . we would have to ask permission of the Immortal Elaine," she finally said.

"Elaine won't mind if you tell me," I insisted.

"I would be afraid to without her permission," Mairi responded. "Please, Keeper, I must not."

So now we were back to formal names. I got the feeling that I was on the edge of setting back our new relationship if I pressed on so I quit. "I will talk to Elaine," I said and indeed I would. I was angry that information had been forbidden me but I could not blame Mairi. I was glad that I did not see Elaine right away as I might have shown my anger and then I would have had to apologize for that.

Lucius came for me for a meeting in Johannesburg so I had to excuse myself.

"We will talk some more after I return," I said smiling. I was hoping to continue our good relationship.

[N.D.] On the way back from my meeting I stopped off to see Elaine. Lucius said that she was at the capital and I also welcomed any excuse to visit Jerusalem. For some reason I was determined to speak to Elaine before something happened and I found myself around the

Emperor. He has a way of making me forget that I am upset or angry and I wanted satisfaction on this one although I have resolved to be sure to remain respectful.

I found Elaine at the house of her friend Martha. She welcomed me warmly. Martha had food and drinks brought and conveniently found something else to do. After a little small talk I came directly to the point.

"Elaine, why are the twins not permitted to tell me about other worlds?" I asked.

She looked up from pouring her tea. A slight smile crossed her lips. She sat back with her tea and looked at me.

"Well, you can know if you really want to," she said.

There. I said to myself. I was not cut off here. Mairi is just overly cautious.

"Will you tell the twins that it is O.K.?" I asked.

"Surely, if you want it," she answered.

"Why shouldn't I?" I answered. "After all I am the Keeper and knowledge is part of my job and I . . ."

She held up one hand and I stopped. "All that is true Patsy," she said. "But you might want to consider if you really want to know."

I did not answer.

"It is somewhat complicated how much you can tell others," she began.

"Yes, I did want to talk to you about that too," I said.

"We will. But let's finish this first."

I sat back with my cup and waited. When she saw that I was calm, she continued.

"In the first place, you can not visit any of these worlds. It is simply against policy. Also, even if we could get an exception for you, which I doubt, you would have to be very careful not to talk about them either in public or in your journals, even your private one. That puts considerable weight on you. Almost every member of the entire Annatic line has been compulsive tellers. For the most part that is good, it makes you good at your job. But until there is a change in policy, this tends to be sort of hush-hush stuff. Do you understand?"

We were down to important stuff now; she had asked if I understand.

"Yes, mistress."

"Don't start that 'mistress' stuff with me, young lady," she said still smiling.

"I'm sorry," I said. My bad attitude had already shown itself.

"Patsy, you know that I just don't want to cause you any more anxiety than necessary," she said. She had won my heart again. This smile was the one that said 'I love you and you can't stay mad at me.' What a friend my Elaine is.

I thought out loud. "O.K. So I can not go and I can not tell. That obviously comes straight from the top. I am an obedient subject and I will not question the policy. Can you help me to understand why, other than your concern for my personal comfort? I mean, since the Emperor is the Emperor on all world, why is the separation necessary? Why, most people aren't even aware that he is Emperor everywhere."

"True," Elaine responded. "And that is one place we need to have unity in our understanding." The Chancellor wants this world to know that the Emperor is loved and respected on all worlds. He made that pretty clear when he was a mortal King. His desires have not changed. However, and there always seems to be an 'however' in this world, this civilization, this world, is very near the middle of an extended trial. So it must remain relatively isolated until that trial is over. Too much contact with another race, one which is not in exactly the same predicament as this one, would mess up the trial. This is very important to the

Emperor, that this trial be completed properly and we all have to abide by that, Patsy."

There was more involved here than I had expected. I did not want the responsibility.

"O.K., fine, I don't want to go. I would like to know just a little about Mairi and Mori's world since I do know them and maybe some things about other ones. But I'll keep that to a minimum. Now, how much can we tell about Mairi and Mori? After all, they do live with me, obviously for some reason." Elaine said that she would get back to me in a few days.

[N.D.] True to her word Elaine returned in four days. We were both more relaxed now. "The Chancellor now wants the mortal public to know enough about Mairi and Mori so that they will realize that the Emperor is supreme on their world as well. Soon you will start introducing them as off-worlders."

"That will be excellent," I said. I liked that.

11.21.513 C.R. The public has welcomed the off-worlders with enthusiasm. They have presumed that they were brought to our world by the Immortals. This is actually true as they would not have been granted access without the Emperor's approval and the cooperation of the Princes. The fact that they have developed inter-dimensional travel was not announced. I have not yet learned how their travel is inferior to that of the Immortals. I have just taken Mairi's word for that. However, in the process I have learned that their name for their planet is unpronounceable in our language so they have begun referring to it as Astride. It is pronounced as-tree-dee. No one is willing to reveal what our name for it is and I am beginning to presume that it does not appear on any mortal star charts. Since they have described their world with two suns, there has been much speculation among our researchers as to where it is. I consider these arguments useless. The kind of people they are seems to be more important to me.

[N.D.] There are now almost fifty individuals from Astride on earth that I know about. About twenty of them are twins, ten pairs. This tendency for twins is now known to our people so they are now free to appear in public. There have been several occasions when our visitors have been in danger but this has not been allowed to go beyond mere threat. They seem to be under a strong invisible angelic guard. Obviously the Princes do not intend them to come to any harm. I have come to the conclusion that our off-world friends are somewhat naïve; they have a certain innocence. They tend to always believe that anyone that they are talking to is telling the truth. They have no sense of when someone is trying to cheat them. The women do not sense any danger of sexual assault.

[N.D.] At any one time I have from two to thirty off-worlders at my residence. I have had to ask Henry Sawyer for supplies to help host them. They eat well and like everything. If you set it before them, they will eat it but they do not overeat. None of them is overweight. The married couples sleep together and seek privacy every few days. The unmarried ones all prefer to stay together in one large room. They are very supportive of each other. I have been learning some of their ancient stories.

They believe that they had one set of ancient parents. They are very aware of their genealogy. They believe that everyone should have something productive to do. They have a mortal government on their home world, but it is always subject to the Emperor. Their leaders, or elders, meet with the Emperor and some angels regularly and about 500 of our years ago Immortals started appearing at Court. I am convinced that these are our Immortals although I do not recognize any of the names that they have mentioned. It was, after all, just over 500 years ago that our Immortals began their resurrection and reign with the Emperor. We usually think that any Immortals that we do not see are on the other side with the Emperor. Now we are beginning to realize that there are any number of places that they can be. However, apparently the Immortals do not hold court on their planet. The government is left to them as mortals under the overall supervision of the Emperor. Their Emperor is our Emperor and they have never heard of another.

Mairi and Mori are my principal 'aliens.' They coordinate all the activity at my residence. They surprised me today. I had just asked them how the supplies were holding out.

"We still have plenty of food, Keeper," Mori said. "But we do need certain items of clothing."

"Fine," I answered. "Can you check with the Metropolitan's supply master on that?"

"Yes, Keeper," she answered. "Then, Keeper, what if there were to be more of us in your world? How would that work?"

"I don't know. Right now those of your people who are not here are spread around at various Dais' studying our world and people. How many more are likely to want to come?"

Mairi and Mori exchanged glances. "Many, Keeper," Mairi answered.

"Sounds like a lot," I said. "Is that like hundreds?" Again they looked at each other. I had been polishing an article while I talked to them, but now I put the writing down. I was getting the impression that this was a big issue.

"Thousands?"

"Many thousands," Mairi said.

"I see. Has permission been granted?" I asked.

"The Lord Chancellor has approved it," she said.

"Then, it's done," I answered.

"Yes, but he has also said that there must be some effort from your mortals in hosting them," Mairi said.

I got the feeling that I had been set up. "And the Keeper and Primate should lead in this I suppose?"

"You are the Keeper of the Ancient Books, the primary Interpreter of the books of Anna, the Chronicler of Imperial Truth and the Spiritual Primate of the mortals on the earth," she recited.

I smiled. " And now, Hostess," I said.

We all laughed together. "I have learned well?" she asked.

"Indeed you have learned well," I answered.

I asked to see the Chancellor.

01.11.514 C.R. I am now apparently the mortal go-between. I saw the Lord Chancellor just a few hours ago. He was as gracious and decisive as ever. He told me that it was his will and the will of the Emperor that these foreigners be allowed to live among us, but for their own protection they should be established in enclaves in several places. I could start with one enclave in the Over-Lord Janice's area. As this is a large area to consider, I decided to visit Janice next. I kissed the Chancellor's ring and departed. I was somewhat relieved to learn that the primary condition to their living among us was that they swear loyalty to all the Princes and agree to abide by the Imperial Code and our mortal laws. They seemed to have no problem with this.

[N.D.] "Patricia, welcome to my Dais," Janice welcomed me. "And where should we put our visitors?" She was already ahead of me. We decided to establish the first enclave in the Appalachian mountains. Since they liked to be together, several large dormitories would be built along with a series of cabins for the married couples.

This first enclave would support about three thousand off-worlders. There was certainly no one easier to host than these people. I wondered what they hoped to learn from us.

09.12.522 C.R.   It was a grand day when Elaine brought me my Robert. I had resigned myself to an arranged wedding. But I was not dreading it because I knew from the journals that Elaine was such a good match maker that I would love him dearly all my life. Robert is a good man, quiet and deliberate. He is tall and dark and usually attracts considerable female attention when he enters a room. He is absolutely loyal to me and helps me a lot. Officially he is a law clerk, but he spends most of his time helping me. He has no problem with a low self image. He says that my job is an important one in the Empire and that the best thing he can do is help me as much as he can. He is a steady and attentive lover and I can honestly say that I lack for nothing. Our wedding was held at the Metropolitan's Dais and it was quite an affair, the Chancellor, our Viceroy, and Janice were there. The Viceroy performed the ceremony. I was relieved when all the ceremonies were over and Robert and I could depart on our wedding trip to the French Alps. We returned to the residence and settled down to as normal a married life as one can have in my position.

03.12.550 C.R.   We have been married many years now and I am finally with child. Elaine says it will be a boy so we plan to name him Andrew. I feel like quite an old married woman to be a mother.

03.11.553 C.R.   The morning before Andrew's third birthday Lucius wakened us at the residence. I sat bolt upright in bed.
"Yes."

"Keeper, your presence is needed at the off-worlders enclaves," he said.

"Which one?" I asked. There were now nine of them scattered throughout the world.

"Actually all of them, but you can start with the Appalachian enclave," he answered.

"I will need some briefing," I said as I prepared to leave.

"I can brief you, Keeper," he said. "Elaine is occupied on the other side right now."

"Then, brief me," I said.

"Yes, Keeper," Lucius began. "It seems that their Elders of all the enclaves have just revealed to them the reason for their living in this world."

"Good, finally. And it is?"

"The suns of their home world are moving closer to each other and before too long their entire population will be relocated to another world. This in itself is quite an uprooting and the Emperor does not choose to do anything about these suns."

"I can see how they would be shocked," I said as I picked out some knee socks. The Appalachians are chilly to me.

"But that is not all, Keeper."

"And . . . "

"The conditions on their new world although not particularly hard will not lend themselves to such a long lifespan. They will not live as long there and their offspring born on the new world will live just about as long as our mortals." With that Lucius was quiet.

I stopped in the middle of pulling on a knee sock. I looked at Robert plaintively.

"Will you go with me?" I asked.

"Of course, my dear," he answered. He had already begun to get dressed.

"I imagine that their visit here has had some effect on their lifespan," Robert said.

"Good thinking, my love," I said.

"Lucius, how are they feeling now?" I asked.

"They will, I suppose, be paying more attention to how you mortals handle your mortality from now on."

"Yes, I expect they will, and be wondering about an afterlife as well. Well, my off-world friends, welcome to true mortality," I said. "Lucius, are you quite sure that Elaine can not be interrupted this time?" I asked.

"Quite, Keeper. No angel has ever interrupted a feast on the other side," he answered.

I still could not understand all about their feasts, but I certainly knew better than to go against over 500 years of precedence. Robert and I stood close for the short trip with Lucius to the enclave.

When we arrived, they were all in a state of shock. Mairi and Mori and all my residence off-worlders were at the enclave. They had all gone there the week before for what we might call a family reunion. Apparently their Elders had known about this for some time in their meetings with the Emperor, but they had, for some reason, chosen not to announce it until now. They broke the word early in the morning at this enclave but the entire announcement had been coordinated so that all the enclaves heard it at once. Soon shock turned to sadness. I embraced Mairi and Mori for quite some time. Finally we sat down with some more of their family and it was quiet for a long time.

"I guess it is hard for you to have much sympathy with us, Keeper, as we are about to go into something that you have always known," Mairi finally said.

"Oh no, I can sympathize," I said. "This will be a big change for you."

"And just what does your family's accumulated wisdom have to say about an afterlife?" Mori asked.

"Well," I began. "For our Immortals there certainly is one. We hope to attain to the same thing."

"But there is no promise," one of them asked.

"Have you had a promise?" I asked. "You have always been mortal even though you have lived much longer than we do."

"Our sacred writings say that the Emperor is capable of giving us Immortality. But we have never seen one of our own in an Immortal state." Mairi said.

"And the implication is?" I asked.

They were all quiet for a while. "The implication is," our old friend Melchor began. "The implication is that if we are obedient and love the Emperor that it will come to us, immortality that is."

"We have no more promise than that," I said. "We rely much on the sacred writings that our Immortals had when they were mortal. They were promised Immortality through their relationship with the Emperor. He is the same Emperor. One thing we have learned by living under his glorious rule is that he is always true to Himself. He is not whimsical or cruel in any way. We ended up mortal at the glorious return because our parents had no relationship with him prior to the glorious return. If we choose to have a relationship now, we expect Him to run true to Himself." When I finished that, I was quite happy with myself. Robert gave me a big smile of approval. I had never thought it through exactly like that. This crisis for my off-worlder friends had helped me to crystallize my thinking. I made a mental note to write it down. Robert has an excellent memory and will help me do that.

"Of course, your ancestor May was the one with the most real relationship with the Emperor," Mairi said.

"She was my great, great aunt, I believe," I said. "And yes, she specialized in a relationship with the Emperor."

"I guess that is the key," Mori said quietly.

They all nodded and it was quiet for some time again.

[N.D.] I have not seen my off-world friends for some time as I needed to go on an extended trip in my duties as Keeper. When we returned last evening, Mairi was still here at my residence. We were glad to see each other and she hugged me and Robert robustly. I asked her about her twin and she said that Mori was temporarily visiting the nearby enclave and would return soon. I invited her to join us for breakfast in the garden.

"You look rather sad. Are things not going well? How are things at the enclaves?" I flooded her with questions as I poured her tea.

"No, I don't think things are going well at all," she answered. Robert and I waited expectantly.

"Most of our people have been cycled out at the enclaves," she said. "After the announcement about the big move for us the enclaves here were opened to volunteers so that they could come here and learn about how you live with such a short lifespan. We, your original group here, expected that many would want to come. There has not been a great response. We had hoped for a more enthusiastic response. Something more, how can I say ...?"

"Spiritual?" I offered.

"Yes, I suppose that is it," she answered. "You see, Patsy, many have taken a different attitude at home. They say that since our lives are to be shortened, they might as well live for all it's worth. I fear that they may offend the Emperor. They don't seem interested in investigating immortality. We don't know what to do."

Robert and I exchanged glances. We had been concerned that this would be the response.

"Who can we get to help?" I asked.

"I'm not sure," Robert replied. Mairi managed to eat some of the food that had been brought to us.

"We mortals don't seem to have enough answers," Robert continued. "But our Immortals seem so much above it all. I don't think that Elaine or Henry Sawyer or even Janice could help much. I don't think Mairi's people could identify much with them."

I thought for a minute. "Maybe an Immortal who lived earlier in time. The ones you just mentioned lived during the Second Testament. Their way to immortality was pretty clear to them. What about those who lived before the Emperor first came?" I asked.

"You may have something there, dear," Robert said.

Then I remembered something that I had read in May's journal. I had been reading May a good bit on the trip because I felt that if my off-world friends needed help she would be the most likely to offer it.

"Robert!"

"Yes, dear."

"I've got it. I think I know who to call on."

"Please tell," Mairi said.

"May says that the Chancellor's second wife Abigail was sure of her immortality because David himself was sure. She gained her confidence from him. And they were from the First Testament period," I said.

"Was immortality known to them?" Mairi asked.

"Yes, it was known but it was not as clear as during the Second Testament period when Elaine lived," I answered.

"The Chancellor was the most spiritual man of his time," Robert added. "But, will he do it? Can he take the time to instruct the off-worlders?"

"Maybe, maybe not," I said. "But I'll bet you that the lady Abigail can and will."

[N.D.] I have met the Chancellor, but I have not met Abigail. I decided that I should put my case to the Chancellor with the request that Abigail be asked to help. I ran the whole thing by Elaine and she was very supportive. She said that she would arrange another audience with the Chancellor for me.

[N.D.] In a few days Mori came back to the residence. She said that things were still pretty gloomy in the enclaves. The ones that are here are at least the ones that are interested in studying the possibility of immortality, but they are not doing very well at this. The morning after Mori returned Lucius told me that Elaine wanted me to collect all the off-worlders from my original group to stay for a while at the residence. I managed to get all of them except my old flame Alexor. That was probably for the best.

Two days later there was quite a flurry on my front lawn. Even Lucius seemed flustered as he sped into my presence.

"Keeper, in front, the Chancellor comes," he said.

I nearly collided with Mairi and Mori at the front door. "Is it, . . .is it the Emperor?" they asked.

Despite Lucius' warning I looked quickly for the angel Gabriel and did not see him. Then I reminded myself of what Lucius had said. Lucius has never been known to make a mistake. The Chancellor's full escort is quite large, but it is not the Emperor's. After most of the escort had arrived and positioned themselves just above and in front of the residence, there were about twenty levels of them as far as I could see, one large angel appeared on the ground just in front of the Chancellor who appeared with several other Immortals. I rushed forward to greet them and gave my best curtsy. David took my hand and then pulled me to his side and gave me a big hug.

"This is Abigail," he said motioning to a striking looking Immortal with a female appearance. I curtsied to her as well. She smiled a big smile and nodded to me. "And this is my son in mortality, Nathan," the Chancellor continued. Nathan smiled also and he seemed a genuinely caring person. I was ashamed to admit that I was not aware of who his mother had been or anything else about him. "He is my son by the Lady Bathsheba," the Chancellor said. I recognized that name. "He is also of the Imperial line," David added. "yet another generation closer to the Emperor than I." All of this information was as if David was aware of my lack of knowledge. Obviously, Nathan was also a direct ancestor of the Emperor's.

"And this is our son Chileab, Abigail's and mine," the Chancellor concluded. He did not introduce any of the other Immortals at that time. I recognized our Over-Lord Janice and, of course, Elaine and gave them a quick hug.

"Elaine has advised me of your concerns," David continued as we stood there. He nodded towards Elaine. He spied my front garden and started walking in that direction and the entire entourage moved with him including the lines of angels just above us. Abigail and I and Nathan and Chileab are willing to do anything that we can to help." We neared some seats in the garden and he sat in one of them. I waited to see what the Immortals wanted to do. Abigail sat down and motioned for me to sit next to her.

"So, you remember what I said to dear May 200 years ago?' she said.

"Yes, mistress. It was hard to forget," I said. Then, just in case she thought too much of me, I added, "Of course, I have been reviewing her journals of late."

"Good," she responded. "It is true that we did not have the specific promises that they had in the Second Testament." I was honored that she used mother Anna's title for that particular record. "And it was David's conviction that sustained me," she said.

"Yes, mistress," I said weakly, "I know that this is the most important of subjects."

"Since there will be no Imperial decree on this subject," David added, "we shall proceed to help people to understand our ancient belief in immortality as we understood it as mortals."

"That will be wonderful," I said. Mairi and Mori were sitting on the grass nearby and they were beaming with joy. I had never thought of an Imperial decree on the subject, but apparently the Chancellor had and already had his answer.

"We have a plan," Elaine said. Dear Elaine, she had really taken my request to heart and was managing a large part of the answer herself. I loved her all the more.

"Yes," I said expectantly.

"We shall, with your help and the help of your Astridian core group here, organize rallies in the enclaves. His Excellency, the Chancellor, will share his thoughts and then questions will be entertained by the Lady Abigail and the Lord Nathan. They and others from the Chancellor's ancient court will be on hand to answer questions and lead discussions of smaller groups within the enclaves until your off-world friends have a better understanding of the issue. Then they will be sent back to their world both before the move and after the move to share with their people. Other groups will then be brought here to learn the same truths for themselves." She stopped to see my reaction.

"That is wonderful, Elaine, to all of your excellencies, it is wonderful." Everyone voiced their agreement.

"And there will be one other," the Chancellor added looking at Abigail.

"I know that my Redeemer lives," Abigail said.

"Yes, that one," the Chancellor said.

"Job, himself," Abigail said.

"He will share occasionally," David said.

[N.D.] The rallies are turning out to be a great success. The Chancellor has pointed out that in the very oldest book in the First Testament a man named Job affirms his own belief in immortality when he says that he expects to see the Emperor yet many years after his death with his own eyes. He believed in immortality. Since this book was already ancient during the Chancellor's time, these words had been a great comfort to him personally. The man, Job, has even shared once or twice. The Chancellor himself had said, "The Lord has said unto my Lord, I will make your enemies your footstool." The Chancellor actually worshipped the Emperor in his own heart before anyone really knew about the Emperor. What a wonderful example for us all.

Abigail's talks have also been very helpful. She is less formal than the Chancellor and often meets with smaller groups in which she will sit and entertain questions. She is gracious and beautiful and both men and women enjoy listening to her. She explains that her sureness regarding immortality grew as she lived with David as his wife, and that it was his sureness that helped her to believe.

"Of course, he was not equally sure all of the time," she said once. "As mortals we were never that constant in our beliefs, especially in the First Testament period. Those in the Second Testament period were surer because they had the Presence living inside of them. But we did see God move on our behalf and our sureness, if nurtured, would grow."

"Well," one off-world mortal asked her, "since our conditions are more like the First Testament period than the Second Testament period, we should try to nurture our faith like you did. Do you agree with that?"

"Yes, I do," Abigail answered.

"How do we do that? How did you do that?" he asked.

The room fell quiet until Abigail formed her answer. "There are a few things that I would suggest," she said thoughtfully. "Our people in those days formed some habits over the centuries that are helpful in nurturing a person's faith. The Second Testament people also used them, so that should be good for all mortal times. First of all, we would recount the faithfulness of the, er... Emperor at all times. Since immortality depends on him alone, his faithfulness is absolutely central to believing it."

Several of the people started taking notes. I knew that she was getting through.

"We also read the sacred writings. You can do this as well. Read the First and Second Testaments and the writings of Anna and the other Keepers. Rely on the Keeper Patricia here to put you in mind of the Emperor's faithfulness."

They all looked at me. I nodded enthusiastically. This put a lot of responsibility on me and it came directly from the mouth of the Lady Abigail, a wife of the ancient King of Israel and the Chancellor of the present Empire. I know that I would have to work long and hard to meet this challenge. However, later, as Robert and I talked, he reminded me that this was no more than what had always been expected of my office and that by holding the very meetings that we were holding I was, in fact, doing this.

"Is there anything else," the same off-world man asked. I noticed that there were as many of our mortals taking notes as off-worlders. I was seeing an interest in Immortal things grow among our own people because of the concern of the off-worlders for their shortened mortality. This is wonderful. The wisdom of the Emperor and the Chancellor is also wonderful.

Abigail answered. "Yes, you need to gather together and share what you learn and what you feel," she said. "Our people did. They had the Temple and later they formed local schools called synagogues. We also shared around the family table a lot."

"We called it 'church'," Elaine chimed in. I had almost forgotten that Elaine was there because Abigail's presence seemed to fill the room.

We had many meetings in many places both in and outside the enclaves for several years running. Gradually the off-worlders became more and more sure that immortality for them was possible and many of them believed that they personally would achieve immortality one day. Much of this spread to our own people and Robert and I were deeply effected and rejoiced in this.

"There is something else," Abigail said. This time she was showing a big smile. "This may take some, shall we say, arranging. But I am sure that the Chancellor can help us on this."

Everyone waited expectantly for her next words.

"The Emperor himself is the vital key. Any true seeker would be immeasurably strengthened by attending an audience with him."

Many showed a visible fear at this suggestion. Most have never been in the presence of the Emperor.

"There is nothing to be afraid of," I said. "If you are not a wrongdoer, you have nothing to fear."

"How do we know if we are not a wrongdoer?" one of our own young mortal men asked.

"If you are a sincere seeker, you will not be a wrong doer, " I answered. "You may not be perfect in thought or deed but you can not be a seeker and a true wrongdoer at the same time."

There, I had said it. Based on Abigail's comment I had coined the term 'seeker' and given an official opinion about seekers. This term caught on immediately and spread the world over. I was finally beginning to live up to my office. It felt good.

[N.D.] Before long there were groups of Seekers everywhere. There were great increases for permission to attend Imperial audiences. The Chancellor arranged for Seeker Audiences on a regular basis with the Emperor. No Seeker ever left his presence unchanged.

[N.D.] This morning Elaine arrived unexpectedly.

"Good morning, Patsy."

I got up from my work immediately and went to her side. I motioned that we move from the musty library to the kitchen garden and she went in that direction. We sat and I waited for her to talk.

"You suspect that something is up, don't you?" she said with an impish smile.

"Yes, why shouldn't I?"

"Well, there has been a change," she said acting very pleased with herself.

"Tell, please," I said. She obviously wanted me to act a little excited.

"You have been given permission to go to Astride with Mairi and Mori and the lady Abigail to speak on the subject of the afterlife," Elaine announced proudly.

"That is wonderful! I am so excited. Why the change? That is, if it is all right for me to know."

"Just that the Chancellor is so pleased with the grasp that you have obtained on the subject as a mortal and the Keeper. You have, after all, started a world wide Seeker movement. Due to the Astridian seekers who have returned to their world, this movement is also growing there. Their leaders are actually considering petitioning the Emperor for Seeker Audiences so that their people can get the encouragement and strengthening that earth mortals can get. But He wants you to go and help."

"He? The Emperor himself?" I asked.

"Yes, the Emperor and the Chancellor," Elaine answered.

"When can I go?" I asked.

"Soon, Patsy. I will get back to you soon."

"Will you go with me?"

"I am not sure about that just yet."

As usual, we had tea together and she departed.

[N.D.] Today I had a surprise visitor. Since he was unknown to me, Lucius rushed to tell me.

"An Immortal at the front to see you, Keeper," he said.

I went to the front to meet this person. I found a smallish blond man who had the slight appearance of having died at an older age. I do not know how to explain this appearance, but you can tell if you look closely. None of the Immortals actually look old in the sense of being wrinkled or injured or deformed in any way. But in their ageless faces you can detect a certain level of natural maturity if they lived a long time as a mortal. At the same time those who died young seem slightly less wise in their present state. It takes a while to learn to see these things.

"Hello," this Immortal greeted me cheerfully as I held the door opened for him to enter. "My name is Jack," he said.

"Hello Jack," I answered. He seemed so informal that I did not resort to the usual formality when first meeting an Immortal such as calling him 'sir' or 'Excellency.'

"It is good to meet you, Keeper Patricia," he said. "Let's talk."

I showed him into my reception room and he picked a chair with a certain amount of care. This is obviously an old habit as no Immortal would have any aches or pains that would require such a careful selection. He must have had such pains as a mortal.

"I do not want to shock or upset you," he said, "but Elaine has been called to the other side for an extended period of time and I have been chosen to help you with the Astridian project. There is nothing to be concerned about and you will find me to be quite helpful," he said.

I wondered about so long an absence on Elaine's part but I was not upset. There is no accounting for

Imperial matters and I have learned not to tax my mortal mind over their affairs. If I did, I would be stressed often. This Jack seemed like a very likable person.

"May I call you Jack?" I asked in order to fulfill all protocol.

"Certainly," he responded. "And I will call you Patsy in private and Patricia or Keeper in public."

"Fine, great," I said and I offered him a big smile which he returned readily. I am quite excited about going off-world and I know that Jack and I will get along fabulously.

"We need to do a little planning," Jack said, "and then we can be off for Astride."

I was more than ready. Since the first trip would involve the Chancellor and the lady Abigail we had to coordinate our plans with them. Jack said that after that we could go on our own as much as I wanted to. I learned that since the initial appearance about 500 earth years ago of Immortals on Astride that the Chancellor was know there as the Chancellor. Before that the angel Gabriel had served in that function. He was not called the Chancellor, but he had done the job of the Chancellor. The Astridians are aware that something monumental happened 500 earth years ago.

[N.D.] The Chancellor informed Jack of the dates for our first visit to Astride and he was at my door before I was out of bed. I told Lucius to beg his pardon for me and hurried to see him. He had breakfast with me in the kitchen garden. Jack is one Immortal who really likes to eat whether he needs to or not. We had already made our plans flexible so we just altered them to match the Chancellor's schedule. I was nervous as we prepared to depart but Lucius took it in his stride. Jack and I and Mori left from my residence with Lucius and we arrived ahead of the Chancellor and his party and escort. Mairi was waiting for us there in an open field with a large stone Dais. At first I had to look around, my first time on another world.

The sky was more purple than on earth and the two suns together did not seem to shed as much light as our one. I could understand the coming problem. Mairi and Mori were anxious to show me around. There were many Astridians loosely lined up around the field. Actually it was more like a meadow. Most of these Astridians were dressed in a sort of robe. I presumed that it was some sort of formal attire. I walked on their grass towards the Dais. The grass was more dark blue than green; the blades were very fine and spongy. Some of these officials greeted me in front of the Dais. They addressed me as Keeper and were very polite. They spoke to me first in my language. I found that they also spoke the Emperor's native language as some then greeted me in that language. That is how they learn if you can speak it as well. I returned their greetings in that language as well as I am quite fluent in that language. Lucius was visible with me, but he moved across the ground with me as if he were walking. All of the Astridians noticed Lucius and when they were forced to pass by him they nodded respectfully. Evidently no one here had a personal angel. Some of those who had greeted me moved onto the Dais with some others. They stayed to the side and awaited the arrival of the Chancellor. Mori then told me that this was the sacred meeting ground and that only the leaders, or elders, came to this place to meet with the Chancellor and the Emperor. This was about to change.

[N.D.] I have now been on Astride for over a week. It is a very interesting place. It is too bad that everyone must now leave. The first special Imperial audience was held yesterday and it took most of the day. I stayed from beginning to end. About 500 Astridians were there plus a number of the elders. Most of these people had never seen the Emperor before. They had all been to Seekers classes and this group consisted of some of their builders and record keepers. They are the first to go to Astride Two, as they are now calling their new home. These people leave today under the supervision of some of our Immortals. At the audience they listened to the Emperor speak for a few minutes and then any who wished could approach him for a blessing. The Emperor can speak in more than one voice. His normal conversational voice is quite calm and pleasant. He can also speak in what I call his 'waterfall voice.' He usually speaks in this voice when he is speaking to a crowd. The only way that I can describe it is that it sounds like a lot of little waterfalls. He is easy to understand in this voice and he can speak many languages although the court language is the ancient language of His natural people. Yesterday he spoke in Astridian. Their people seemed a little shy to approach him at first. I knew that they did not want to miss this opportunity to approach him. Since there were so few going up, I decided that I would go for a blessing to show them the way. As I approached, he looked my way and spoke my name. I can not express how I feel when he speaks my name. He spoke quietly and in his normal human voice.

"Patricia." That was all he said. I felt that my name and my person had just been affirmed throughout all of time and into eternity. He knows me. He KNOWS me. HE knows me. He knows ME. I already had my blessing, but I knelt before him just the same. I felt his hand touch the top of my head. I was flooded with peace and warmth. I did not feel any tendency to pass out. I wondered how many different kinds of blessings he could give. I felt greedy. I wanted them all. After a short time he touched both of my shoulders and indicated that I should stand. I stood and accidentally looked into his eyes. Just as at my investiture I then lost all track of time. All I knew was that there was not a particle of doubt or fear in me while I was locked in his gaze. When I came out of it, I was surrounded by

Astridians. Evidently I had accomplished my purpose because no one left that day who did not get their blessing. I thought later that their mental questions would still have to be answered at the Seeker groups, but their inner affirmations were supplied by seeing the Emperor. Jack has been a big help all along. Apparentl, he had been a missionary after being a sea sailor in his mortal life so he fit well into this role in his Immortality.

[N.D.]   I have had to return to my residence on earth to take care of a few matters. I have missed Robert as he was not asked to go with me. I intend to ask Elaine quite clearly if he can go when I go again.

"Yes, he may go," Elaine said. "What's the matter, dear? You look absolutely green?"

"I don't know. My breakfast has not agreed with me for several weeks," I answered.

"Are you sure that Andrew is not about to have a little sister?" Elaine asked.

"I never felt like this with him," I said.

She came and touch my stomach. "Yes, and it is a girl," she said.

"That's wonderful," I said.

"You don't sound pleased," Elaine answered.

"I am, really. But I have been away from Astride for longer than I expected now. I do hope that this child is not going to hold me back. I want to get back there for a while very soon."

"Here, let me help," Elaine said. She touched me again. My nausea vanished. "There, Patsy, you will hardly know that you are pregnant," she said. "You and Rob can leave today if you wish." That sounded good to me. We prepared to leave.

[N.D.]   When we arrived back on Astride, things were changing fast. The Emperor was still holding audiences and the word had spread about the blessing, so everyone wanted a touch from him. He would appear from who knows where just on time and depart just as quickly. He might have come from the capital on earth or from the other side. Some people were saying that there were more than one of him; that he had somehow duplicated himself so he could do more things at one time. I asked Elaine about this. She had come with Robert and Lucius and I, and she said, "absolutely not!" There is only one Emperor and he goes where he will. If a presence is needed in many places at once, then The Presence takes care of that, but that usually requires some explanation from some Immortals since he can not be seen."

I found that almost one half of the Astridians had already moved to Astride Two. Elaine said that we could go there. At first the Astridians had been determined to move their people through their own mechanical movers. But they soon found out that they did not have the capacity for that. It was then that the Chancellor insisted that his people provide the transportation. A small group of angels would take the Astridians several thousand at a time. At first when they arrived, there was housing for them all. But now that they were arriving so fast they had to camp out until they finished their homes. All the archives from the old planet have been moved and a new sacred place has been dedicated. The Emperor is now meeting with them on both the old and the new planets. This new world also has two suns and it is quite beautiful. The bluish grass is just as beautiful as their old world and the green seas are also quite nice. The night is different but breath taking. There are two moons here but they are eclipsed by a breathtaking nebula of purple and blue and green which takes up almost a fourth of the night sky. It really doesn't get very dark here. The children love it. They seem to be less afraid of the night. The adults are quite fond of it as well. If it were not for the shorted life spans, I am sure that they would like their new world better than the old one.

There are some small animals here. They are small and furry and quite friendly. They come in many colors and sizes. They seem to be mammals. But there aren't any insects or reptiles here. There are fish in the seas and they all look different than any we have on earth or on old Astride. All in all it is quite a beautiful world. Mairi and Mori greeted us warmly and showed us their new home. The native trees are quite good for building and we are told that the buildings will not deteriorate much over time. They should all be quite thankful.

06.14.555 C.R.   We came back to our residence today and I promptly went into labor. Little Marissa was born at suppertime. I ate a few grapes while I nursed her. I shall have to leave the Astridians on their own for a while. After I recuperate from this baby, I have much to do on my own world.

03.12.566 C.R.   It has now been many years since I first met Alexor, Melchor, Melodi, Mairi and Mori and the other Astridians. They are all gone now. Their enclaves, and indeed they themselves, are now but a faint memory among our people. I remember now how their presence among us was first a secret and then the enclaves came and they became public knowledge. Then, surprisingly, I was allowed to visit both their old and new worlds. Then Robert was allowed to go with me. I am sure that our contact with them and the changes in the rules as we went along was all the work of the Chancellor. As far as I know, we were the only mortals that ever went there. Elaine has put no restrictions on what I can write about them in my journals. I am honored to have been helpful to them during their time of great change. Meanwhile our own people's problems do not seem to change much.

04.17.567 C.R.   My dear Celeste died yesterday. Although she left my service to start her own family many years ago, we still kept in touch and this world will be a poorer place without her.

01.11.568 C.R.   Today Andrew became a man. We had an eighteenth birthday party for him at the Dais of Metropolitan Henry Sawyer of Atlanta. The Over-Lord Janice declared him to be the Keeper Heir. He is a fine man, if I do say so myself, and he will make a wonderful Keeper.

11.12.568 CR.   My name is Andrew. Mother died last night in her sleep. Father is doing well under the circumstance. I am the new Keeper and Primate. May the Emperor help me.

ANDREW

568 - 639 C.R.

3.18.568 C.R. My name is Andrew. The year is 568 Christus Regnus, the 568th year of the Glorious Reign. I succeed my mother Patricia today as the Keeper and Primate. My father Robert still lives and is my closest advisor. My sister, Marissa, and I are close. She will have a place beside me. I plan to be unique as a Keeper just as my mother and most of the Keepers have been. I was well trained for my office and I intend to keep it in the dignity and respect that the office deserves. In order to do this right I have already chosen a wife. Her name is Zoë. She is the daughter of a prominent builder and an upright man here in Atlanta. We will be married the day before my investiture. Our Governor, the Immortal Elaine, has approved everything. Our wedding will be here at my residence and the investiture will be at the Dais of the Metropolitan Henry Sawyer. The Imperial Chancellor will perform the wedding. My mother was one of the Chancellor's favorites.

9.20.568 C.R. Today is my wedding day. Zoë is beautiful and the ceremony was just right. The Chancellor brought many Immortals with him and his escort was most impressive.

9.21.568 C.R. Morning. This is the day of my investiture. We had a wonderful wedding night. I believe that it is going to be a great blessing having Zoë for my wife.

9.21.568 C.R. Evening. I am invested as Keeper and Primate. I hold all the titles of my predecessors. The responsibility of it all is almost overwhelming. I will combine my first tour as Keeper with my wedding trip and visit the Dais' of all the Over-Lords of the Empire. Zoë is agreeable. At each Dais after I finish my official duties we shall take a day or two to rest and see the sights together. I think I have invented the working wedding trip.

11.02.568 C.R. We are near the end of our wedding trip. We have been to many places and met many people. All the mortals we have met have been very respectful of my offices and the Immortals have been most kind and supportive. Zoë has particularly enjoyed the many festivities.

11.23.568 C.R. Evening. It is late at night. We are in Amsterdam. I have returned to our suite because I am exhausted. Zoë decided to stay out for a while with some friends that we have made here. Today I met with the Metropolitan here and we planned for me to speak to the people tomorrow so I must get a good nights' sleep.

11.24.568 C.R. Evening. My address went well today. I spoke on the history of my family as it reflects the goodness and generosity of the Emperor. I spoke for almost an hour. Zoë insisted on coming with me even though she was tired from her night of celebration. She is a wonderful person.

12.31.568 C.R. Today there is a big New Years' celebration at the Dais of the Metropolitan Henry Sawyer. Even though they are no longer subject to the tyranny of time, the Immortals do like celebrations. The Over-Lord Janice should visit shortly after the turn of the day and the New Year.

01.01.569 C.R. Private Journal. What a wonderful celebration. There were thousands of people at the Dais. I lost track of Zoë somewhere in the crowd. I returned home at about 2 A.M. and she was not here yet. I awoke at 8 A.M. and she was beside me asleep. She must have been very careful not to wake me.

03.12.569 C.R. Private Journal. I am beginning to become concerned. Zoë has made many friends here and she goes to many celebrations. Her friends seem to have a celebration for almost anything and she does not like to miss even one.

04.19.569 C.R. Evening. Private Journal. It is almost midnight and Zoë is not home yet, again. I shall have to talk to her about this.

04.23.569 C.R. Private Journal. Today I tried to talk to Zoë about her many social engagements. She asked if I needed her somewhere and she had not been available. I told her, of course not. She does not seem to understand that I need her to stay close to home so that we can grow closer as a couple. Well, she is young. I shall have to be more patient with her.

5.30.569 C.R. Private Journal. Evening. I am close to despair. I have not seen my wife in nearly three days. I am going to send Lucius to find out where she is.

"Do not bring her back," I said to the angel. "In fact, don't even let her know that you are there. Just find out if she is all right and come back and tell me. Understand?"

"Yes, Keeper."

"Then, be off. I will wait right here," I said.

Lucius was back in about five minutes. I was still in my chair in the library. He stood directly in front of me at floor level.

"What did you learn?" I asked.

"Your wife is fine. She is in good health and she is, … resting as we speak."

"Resting? Where?" I asked.

"In a bed. The bed of a friend," he answered.

"What kind of a friend? I mean, is this friend a man or a woman?" I asked.

"A man," Lucius answered.

"Is the man there in the bed as well?" I asked.

"Yes, Keeper."

The angel never lies and he never expresses an emotion. He is simply faithful and true, evidently unlike my wife. I now have to make a decision. I can not allow this to continue. My office is at stake. This is a terrible example to all. I decided to ask Lucius to take me to the public entrance of the house where Zoë was resting.

"I could take you directly to her," Lucius suggested.

"No, the public entrance will do," I said.

In a few minutes I was standing in front of a door to a townhouse in Decatur. I knocked firmly. No one came. I knocked again. Still no answer. I am afraid that I lost my temper because I knocked loudly and shouted Zoë's name until someone answered the door. It was a young man and he had hastily dressed. Lucius was visible behind me. When the young man saw Lucius, he looked startled.

"Keeper, Excellency," he began.

"Never mind the formalities," I interrupted. "My wife. Tell her to come down here." I demanded. At that moment Zoë appeared just behind him and pushed her way through to me.

"Husband, dear," she began. "I did not mean to upset you. You see, the celebration ran late last night and

Brett here was kind enough to put me up because I was so tired. Come, you and Lucius take me home."

I nodded and Lucius did just that.

After we were back at the residence, I confronted her with what Lucius had told me.

"You had that angel spying on me?" she exclaimed.

"Yes, yes I did. That is my privilege," I said.

She glared at Lucius for a few seconds. He started to grow larger and she immediately became afraid.

"You must respect him, dear," I said. "He has no ego as such, but he will not tolerate disrespect." She was now considerably calmer. Finally I said, "I want you to talk to Elaine."

"Elaine, what for?" she shouted. Then she looked back at the angel and toned down. "What for, my dear. I know that I did wrong, but I will never do it again, I promise. You do believe me, don't you?"

"Lucius, has she done this before. Had intimate relations with other men since she has been my wife?" I asked.

Lucius was still almost twice his normal size. "Yes, Keeper," he answered.

I was deeply wounded. "Do you want me to ask how many times?" I asked Zoë.

"No, I mean, if you want. I guess . . . oh," she could not speak.

"Lucius?" I asked.

"Keeper," he responded.

"How many, . . ." I could not continue.

I insisted that Zoë talk to Elaine. She agreed. She went to clean up and I sent Lucius to ask Elaine if she would see us. Lucius returned to say that Elaine would see us at her residence. So we went there.

06.20.569 C.R. Private Journal. After our meeting with Elaine things went well for about two weeks. Zoë seemed genuinely repentant and we had a good time at home. Then she started going to celebrations again.

"Honestly, dear, I just have to get out. I am not the scholarly person that you are. I promise that I will be a good girl. I promise."

She looked so sweet and sincere that I gave in. Perhaps everything would go well this time. I had made it a point to give her more intimate attention and she seemed to like it fine.

08.02.569 C.R. Private Journal. Evening. After I returned from a nine day trip to Lisbon, I worked late in my library writing up my account of the trip. Zoë is not home yet and I had allowed her to skip going on the trip with me since she said that she did not feel good.

"Lucius," I called. He came directly to me.

"Please go wherever and collect my wife. Bring her directly to me here and be prepared to tell me what she has been doing," I said. He departed without a word and was back in less that a minute. Zoë was only partially dressed.

"Uh, what! Andrew what is the meaning of this?" she demanded.

"The meaning is that you have been dishonoring me and my office again," I said. She started toward me in anger and Lucius restrained her. This calmed her considerably.

"You know that he will not allow me to be attacked by anyone," I said.

She did not answer.

"What am I to do?" I thought out loud. Zoë just looked at the floor. Lucius loosened his grasp, but he did not leave her.

"Go to bed. In the Rose guestroom," I said.

"Lucius, she is not to leave the residence without my permission," I said.

She shuffled off looking quite pitiful and small. I felt sorry for her through my rage.

08.03.569 C.R. Private Journal. I have asked Elaine for an appointment just for myself. She sent word to have luncheon with her in her kitchen garden at Noon. I arrived exactly on time.

"We can not force her will," Elaine said. "She has to want to change."

"I know, mistress," I said. "But I do not know how to get through to her. I am trying to be a thoughtful and considerate husband."

"You are spending time with her? You are attentive to her needs? You can be rather official in your private life, Andrew. You are aware of that?" she asked me.

"Yes. I am aware of that, especially lately," I admitted. "Perhaps if I change, she will want to change also."

"Perhaps," Elaine said. "Would you like to confer with anyone else? Anyone? My feelings won't be hurt if you do."

"No. No one; not just now."

"There are many Immortals who had this same kind of problem in their mortality," she offered. "It would probably be helpful. There is a man named Hosea, he . . ."

"No. Please. Not just now," I interrupted. "I will get back to you. Really, I will get back to you soon," I promised.

10.11.569 C.R. Private Journal. It has been two months since my talk with Elaine and things are no better at home. Zoë is obedient but not friendly. She resents the fact that Lucius will not let her leave the residence. She has tried to walk off several times and he blocks her way.

"It's no better than being under supervision," she told me. "It is being under supervision. Only this is at the command of my mortal husband."

"Dear, I can not be sure what you will do if I let you travel freely," I said softly.

"I promise, Andrew. If you love me you will trust me. This time it will be different. Pleeeeeeease."

"Very well. Lucius, my wife may go where she pleases."

01.22.570 C.R. Private Journal. It is now over three months since I gave Zoë her freedom. She has gone out for a few hours a day or evening but she always comes back and she seems to be in good condition when she returns. I have gone out with her on a few occasions. I don't particularly enjoy the celebrations she attends, and I suspect that she takes me to the milder ones. The music is too loud and most everyone drinks too much. I have made a few friends, both male and female, with some others who accompany their partner like I do. We talk quietly in a corner and console each other. They are very respectful of me and ask a lot of questions that I enjoy answering.

02.12.570 C.R. Private Journal. Zoë is sick this morning again. I have asked Elaine if she will come and check on her.

02.12.570 C.R. Private Journal. Elaine has been. I did not tell Zoë that she was coming as she usually refuses any attempt to make her well. Zoë was obviously upset when Elaine arrived. Elaine spent about 20 minutes with her and then joined me in the library.

"Andrew, the news is not good," Elaine began.

"What? Mistress, is it something that you can not fix?" I asked startled.

"Not this, my dear Andrew. This is not something that I can fix."

I waited anxiously.

"She is with child and you are not the father," Elaine said clearly.

"Perhaps she is not telling the truth," I countered. "She will lie to hurt me and I called you in without telling her," I said.

"She did lie," Elaine answered. "She said it was yours, but I know better. The child in her is not related to you, dear Andrew. I am so sorry."

"I see." I should have known that Elaine would use her Immortal powers in this regard. She is never wrong and she never lied.

"There is more, Andrew," Elaine said.

"Yes."

"This child can not be here. He can not be involved in your office. As soon as he is born, he must be placed with foster parents."

"Of course. I understand. I fully agree. Did you tell her that?" I asked.

"No. That task falls to you," Elaine answered.

As Elaine departed, she said, "Send or come to me for anything."

02.13.570 C.R. Private Journal. Zoë did not receive the news well. She said that she would leave when the child was born or even sooner. I implored her to stay.

08.27.570 C.R. Private Journal. Zoë's child was born this morning. He is a fine looking boy. I have arranged for a place for them. I have hired a woman there who is a competent nurse and cook to help. I will be lonely here, but also somewhat relieved.

03.02.571 C.R. I have just returned from a tour of the Western Viceroy's area. I spoke almost daily on the advantages of living as a mortal in this reign as compared to before the Glorious Return. It was a great trip and I feel like I am really back into my work.

05.11.571 C.R. Private Journal. Zoë is dead. She was killed by someone who followed her home early one morning. Because of my position, we have never been legally separated, Imperial Security is working on this. I am sure that the guilty person will be caught and executed soon. The child is fine with his nurse. I shall make arrangements for his continued security.

05.13.571 C.R. Private Journal. This morning a very intimidating angel arrived in my reception room unannounced. Lucius came to the garden for me; he almost seemed excited for Lucius. I hurried to the reception room. When I entered, this angel nodded respectfully.

"Those who have killed your wife have been apprehended, Keeper," he said flatly.

"Good. Where are they?" I asked.

"At the Dais of the Over-Lord of the Mediterranean," the angel answered.

"Fine. Thank you for your report," I said. "I will go there."

"I can take you, Keeper," the angel said.

"No, thank you," I said. "Lucius will take me."

This angel looked at Lucius for a second as if Lucius might not be capable. Then he nodded and flashed away.

"Who was that?" I asked Lucius.

"His name is Bright," Lucius answered. "He is a Vicar. He is from Imperial Security."

"He makes me shiver," I said.

Lucius did not respond.

The offenders, two men and a woman, were found guilty and executed on the spot. I returned to the residence a sad and lonely person.

07.21.571 C.R. Private Journal. Elaine paid me a surprise visit this morning.

"Are you ready to see the Emperor yet?" she asked.

"If you think I need to," I answered.

"You have needed to for some time," she said. "Just being with him for a short time will take away your sadness and heal your broken heart."

I nodded and began to tear up. I did not like to tear up.

"I will make an appointment for you," she said.

I nodded again. She kissed me on the forehead and departed.

08.03.571 C.R. Private Journal. Today I had my private audience with the Emperor. I had seen him only once when I was a child at the Dais of Janice Holland. I did not get very close at that time. This audience was as private as one gets, I suppose. There were several massive angels in the corner of the room at the palace and a couple of Immortals talking softly at a table some distance away. I soon lost notice of anyone but the Emperor. He entered after I was shown to my seat by an Immortal named Martha, evidently a member of the inner circle of the Imperial court. I knelt immediately and lowered my eyes. He sat down and spoke.

"Andrew. Rise. Take your seat," he said quietly. I was instantly reassured. I took my seat and his eyes caught mine. I don't know why I waited so long. We talked for a while. I will never record this conversation. It was too special to me. His answers anticipated my questions. His wisdom is unfathomable. But it is not his wisdom that heals. It is his very presence. I left the audience a new man. Back at my residence I floated in joy for weeks.

02.04.572 C.R. Today Elaine came with another surprise for me, a mortal woman.

"Andrew, this is Mary," she said.

I extended my hand. "Mary, it is always good to meet a friend of Elaine's," I said.

She took my hand gently and I shook it. She smiled as if she had a secret.

"Andrew, I want you to court this woman," Elaine said.

I knew that I was blushing and there was nothing that I could do about it. Mary smiled. It is a very sweet smile. "Mistress?" I asked.

"Andrew, you really must start calling me Elaine," she said. "And yes, you heard right. I have chosen Mary as a prospective wife for you. She is from Richmond and Janice is very fond of her. She will be staying at my residence here and you may, and will, call on her there. For today I leave her with you for luncheon in your garden. Your staff have been instructed." Then she departed.

At first I was nervous and self conscious with Mary. We talked haltingly there in the reception room for a while. She was very pleasant at conversation. I learned that she was the older daughter of a court clerk for the Over-Lord Janice Holland. Her two younger sisters were already married. She has helped her father a lot with his work and has actually been his assistant for the past two years. She was very curious and interested in my library and research. We are a lot alike. Apparently her father had asked the Over-Lord to help find her a husband. Her mother had died some years ago and the father did not want her to end up unmarried. Janice and Elaine had talked and the plot was hatched. I would have been angry over this but who could be angry at Elaine and I have not been angry at anyone for six months now. Besides, she is the Imperial Legate over my office. I must obey her. But I have the feeling that this obedience was not going to be difficult. As we left the room to go to the garden for luncheon, I found myself gently taking Mary's hand. She did not mind and came along obediently. She is easily led, at least by me. She is as far from Zoë as a mortal woman can get. I pulled out a seat for her at the garden table. Then my cook, an older woman named Giselle, mentioned that she might want to "freshen up." Mary nodded and Giselle took her to the bath. When she returned, we talked calmly over lunch. She held nothing back about herself and I tended to do the same. Before I knew it over two hours had passed. I had an appointment so I had Lucius take her back to Elaine's.

04.10.572 C.R.   The last two months have been wonderful. I have seen Mary almost every day. I want to be with her always. I have proposed and she has accepted. I have requested this time that we be married by the Emperor himself and he has agreed. Furthermore, the wedding will take place at the Capital. The Immortals love weddings, men and women alike. It is because the Immortals as a group are considered to be the Bride of the Emperor. At mortal weddings every Immortal present wears white in some form. Many of the female Immortals wear white dresses and even some of the men wear white suits. At the least each person wears a white scarf or armband. They seem to celebrate their group oneness with the Emperor at their feasts on the 'other side.' They tell us that they do not practice sex as mortals know it. Instead it is some kind of spiritual group unity with the Emperor Himself.

05.02.572 C.R.   Our wedding day. It has been a wonderful day. The whole capital turned out for our wedding. We stood before the Emperor himself and somehow managed to say our wedding vows. In every wedding that I have ever witnessed or seen recorded the official says something like "In the name of the Emperor I pronounce you husband and wife." Today he said, "I now pronounce you to be husband and wife." There is no higher authority. Surely our marriage will last our lifetimes.

The city was beautiful today. The angelic canopy was enormous, at least 21 levels high, the sounds coming from the canopy were beautiful. Everyone at the ceremony also wore garlands of flowers; they must have come from all over the world. The ceremony was held on the steps to the temple because the plaza in front could hold thousands. I did not think of how grand an affair this would be when I asked the Emperor to marry us. Mary is swept off her feet but she is a humble person and I am sure that it will not go to her head. Our wedding night is to be spent on the Imperial island of Capri in the classic Inn there.

05.04.572 C.R.   Capri is magnificent. It has sweeping overlooks of the ocean. There is a small permanent canopy here. The Inn is not far from the Palace and it is sumptuous. We are truly well cared for. This island was the Imperial residence of some of the ancient Roman Emperors. Our Emperor, The Emperor of all time and space, was executed under the authority of this ancient empire. So, when he returned and subdued everything unto himself, he chose to make Capri one of his royal residences.

09.12.589 C.R.   Word today from Spain. It seems that Zoë's son has been quite active. The boy was named James after my grandfather, a fact that I was several years learning about but did not take much note of it. James is, after all, a fairly common name. He is now past nineteen years of age and has been letting it known that he is the son of Zoë, the first wife of the Keeper. I can not deny this. He has made no direct statement that he is actually my son and there is enough public record of the entire matter that I am content to let the mortal press respond to this for now. I have asked my current events clerk, Heidi, to watch the matter and report anything that she thinks I need to know directly to me.

01.05.590 C.R. I was told today that James Hardwick, he uses the surname Hardwick now, that was Zoë's mother's name, has been speaking at various literary and historical circles in and around Spain on the worthiness of mankind and the benefits of the present empire. He seems sincere enough. He is evidently a very good speaker. The report says that he is quite interesting and weaves a good deal of humor into these presentations. Several humanitarian groups have begun to sponsor him. He is fluent in several languages and can speak in any of them at the drop of a hat. I am told that there are no direct references to me in the publicity although some of his critics have accused him of taking advantage of his "relationship" or lack thereof with me. My people will continue to watch.

04.11.590 C.R. Another report regarding James Hardwick. He spoke at a large student rally in Berlin two days ago and was very well received. The content of his message was still on the extraordinary nature of the human race and the wonderful opportunities that all mortals have under the Emperor's present reign. Although some of the students got a little too spirited, the mortal authorities kept things under control and the incident ended well.

06.02.590 C.R. Another report of James' speaking. This time in Amsterdam. The crowd was heard to shout for more freedom of expression in the Empire but this was not clearly defined.

08.12.590 C.R. I am informed that James Hardwick was arrested by mortal authorities in London today and that he refuses his freedom until he can talk to me. I have asked to speak to Elaine.

"He wants to see you," Elaine said flatly.

"Yes, that's what I'm told," I said.

"Then why don't you go to see him. Size him up. Size the entire situation up. And then get back with me," she said.

"O.K., if that's your advice," I said. I had Lucius make the arrangements.

08.14.590 C.R. When Lucius and I arrived at the London police station where James was being held, it set off a torrent of activity.

"Keeper, what an honor," the station captain said. I was taken to an interview room and James was brought out. I must admit that I was not prepared for what I saw.

James Hardwick is a striking young man. I suppose that a lot of the impression that he makes is because of his personality as well as his looks. He is tall, almost six and a half feet, with lots of blond hair and piercing steel blue eyes which also twinkle with a bit of seemingly harmless mischief and still manage to contain a generous amount of warmth and sincerity. He took my hand immediately and did not act at all like a man who was being held against his will.

"Keeper, Sir," he said earnestly. "It is such an honor, sir, to finally meet you."

"I saw you as an infant," I added.

"Yes, sir, I know that, but, of course, I don't have much of a memory of that," he said. Then he flashed a broad smile and I instinctively smiled in return. So much for my determination to be "all business" with this man. He had disarmed me entirely as I suppose he does most people. I arranged for his release – that only required a word from me - and had Lucius take us to my hotel rooms. I noticed that James hardly acted like he acknowledged the presence of the angel. This is most unusual for a mortal as most mortals either revere or fear Lucius or both. Those who are guilty of something always fear him. We talked for some time in my suite. By now most major hotels around the world keep rooms available for me. He thanked me sincerely for coming and having him removed from his confinement.

"You see, sir, I am afraid that I am somewhat misunderstood by the mortal authorities," he began. "I mean absolutely no disrespect for the Emperor or the Empire. I sort of think of myself as a reminder. I want to remind all mortals of our real worth. We are, after all, all creatures of God. I believe that if we look for the best in ourselves and in each other, we can be better subjects of the Emperor and lead more productive lives. I am so glad to be in your presence and to hopefully look forward to your advice in all things. After all, even though I am not related to you, you were my mother's husband for a time and I feel that we have some things in common except that, of course, I do not have the stature or standing that the Keeper has." He stopped talking and looked me straight in the eyes and that enticing smile gradually worked its way across his features.

I waited a few seconds before responding. I felt like my response was very important. I searched for the right words. Finally I said, "Well, James, may I call you James?"

He nodded. Still smiling.

"I think, rather I believe," I was stumbling. "I believe . . ." I cleared my throat and determined to speak clearly. "I believe that I can offer you some advice. I would like to establish, shall we call it a dialogue with you." I tried to sound firm and fatherly.

"Good," he replied and he extended his hand. I shook his hand. It took him a few seconds to release me.

We talked for some time about many things. I was particularly struck with his humor. He acted like a man without a care in the world. I even thought at one point that he somehow reminded me of the Emperor but I quickly put that from my mind. I ended by instructing him to be careful and to maintain a low profile for a while and agreed to a meeting with him again at his request in about four weeks.

My secretary, Edward, was with me but he had not been in the interview. "I have some background information on him," Edward said. Edward was big on thoroughness and research.

"Good. What have you got?"

The summary of Edward's report was that the boy was generally well liked. He had no record of any violations of either the mortal or Imperial law. He spoke frequently for a group known as "The Committee For A Better Humanity Today and Tomorrow." And, last but not least, his living seemed to be from donations from some of the most responsible and successful mortals on the planet. I decided to reserve judgment for at least a few more meetings.

09.17.590 C.R. I had another meeting with James Hardwick today. A prestigious local civic leader in Atlanta relayed a message to me that James would like to visit me, if possible, at my residence and I sent Lucius for him.

He arrived smiling as usual and apparently still unimpressed with Lucius and his first journey with Lucius. Lucius had fetched him from London where he had been speaking on "More Responsible Service to the Emperor and Mankind."

I enjoy the company of this young man. I had Lucius return him to his activities in England.

10.06.590 C.R. Today Edward brought me some more "background information" on James Hardwick. There were some "dishonorable" press articles which claimed that James was actually my son and pointed out some physical similarities that he and I seem to have in common. I discounted the articles as they are obviously prejudiced against James. I also thought that although there are some facial features that I share with the boy, they could be entirely coincidental.

01.12.591 C.R.   Another meeting with James Hardwick today. He was in the area and requested a meeting. I had us served luncheon in the garden and enjoyed the meeting very much.

02.03.591 C.R.   I have put off talking to Elaine about James as long as I can. Today I brought him up at our regular meeting. Elaine had not pressed me to talk about it.

"I am still not sure about him," I said. "He does not appear to do anything seditious, although it is a little difficult to understand exactly what he does. What do you think of it?" I asked.

"I don't know if it's all good, Andrew."

"What harm is he doing?" I asked.

"None to speak of yet. But he seems to be playing off of his relationship to you and although his message is still rather vague, I am sure that he has some sort of a goal in mind."

"Only his opposition in the mortal press has mentioned his relationship to me," I answered.

"But don't you think that is just a bit too handy?" Elaine responded.

"How do you mean?" I asked.

"Andrew," Elaine leaned forward and caught my eyes with hers. Her eyes are so beautiful and peaceful. "Andrew, listen," she said. I regained control and acted attentive. I suppose that she knows that every male Keeper from Mark on has been a little bit in love with her.

"That is a common trick with subversives; they have their 'opposition' make the 'wrong' accusations. They are often not really the opposition, except, of course, to the Emperor."

"Then what do they want?" I asked.

"It is very important that you find that out," Elaine said.

"I will put some more time on it," I said.

"Be careful, Andrew," she said.

"I will, Elaine."

On the way back to the residence I thought a lot about Elaine's warning. Be careful, she had said. Careful of what?

03.10.591 C.R. I am going to take some time to travel incognito with James. It will take a few weeks to arrange it.

04.06.591 C.R. Lucius deposited me in London this morning where James is conducting a rally in Hyde Park. There is a large sign which reads, "Welcome To The Second London Rally For Human Significance." There is a large and expressive crowd and James is an exceptional speaker. I am well disguised.

04.27.591 C.R. I wish that James' staff did not know who I was, but it is too late now. James told them when I arrived. I am convinced that they are not telling anyone outside the staff, but I can feel their tenseness when I am around. I guess that having the Keeper so close makes them nervous. And then again I make frequent notes in my journals. This, of course, is my job but it makes them nervous none the less.

Reign II

06.15.591 C.R. I am very impressed with James' abilities. He always seems to lift the mortals into a new level of confidence. He is much loved.

[N.D.] Private Journal. I overheard two of James' assistants talking today. I am somewhat disturbed about it and I intend to talk to James about it.

[N.D.] "I really do not think they meant exactly that," James said to me.

"Then what?" I asked.

"Probably just that we should not bother the Immortals with anything that we can improve," he said.

"But their exact words were 'not the Emperor's business,'" I objected.

"That was their exact words?" James asked.

"Yes, exactly," I insisted.

"I will talk to them," he said. He went immediately to do just that.

James got back with me to say that his two disciples were properly corrected and that even though mortals can do much to improve themselves and their lot in the Empire that nothing is outside the realm of the Emperor.

[N.D.] I have missed Lucius so I have instructed him to be visible when we are alone. It is not that he says much, but I feel more content when I can see him. He takes me home every few weeks for a visit with Mary.

03.09.592 C.R. "My dearest, must you leave again so soon," Mary pleaded with me. Her eyes filled up with tears but not quite enough to spill out.

"I guess I could stay another day," I answered as I moved to hold her very tightly. She does not understand why I must spend so much time with James. I will tell her tonight.

03.10.592 C.R.   I do not think Mary understands why I want to adopt James. After all they are about the same age. Maybe she is just a little jealous of him. It is wonderful to have a pretty young wife, but sometimes she acts just a little childish.

"You what?' Elaine said. This is the first time I have ever caught her by surprise and she even seems a little shocked.

"Adopt him, yes, Elaine. He is like a son to me. You might say the son I never had. I am not sure that we should have turned him out when he was a baby. Especially after Zoë died. I could have shown more interest in him then." I waited. Elaine sat down in her favorite thinking chair and was quiet for a few minutes.

"Andrew, I will never consent," she finally said.

The words went through me like a knife. "But El . . Mistress, why?" I asked.

Again silence.

"It is time for you to see the Emperor," she responded.

"I would love to see the Emperor, but I would rather solve this first," I added.

"It is solved, Andrew," Elaine said calmly. "Lucius," she called. Lucius appeared at once. "Take your charge to the Chancellor's waiting room immediately," she said. I have moved quickly with Lucius before, but this move was instantaneous. There were several other mortals waiting to see the Chancellor. They all stood when I arrived.

"Please resume your seats," I said. As I took a seat alone near a corner, it occurred to me that I had been recognized. I moved quickly to a mirror just up the wall to discover that not only had Lucius changed my clothes but my face was back to normal as well. It was unsettling. In about an hour I was shown into the Chancellor's main council chamber. I was the first from the waiting room to be called in. His Highness was not there so I waited another few minutes. King David arrived smiling as usual. He walked directly towards me and embraced me. This also was a first for me.

"Sir," I bowed as he stepped back.

"Andrew, you are disturbed," he said.

"Yes, Sir. What?" I stuttered. "What have I done wrong?" I asked.

"You have evidently failed to discern," he answered.

"Discern what?" I asked.

"It is an old device, Andrew," the Chancellor responded. "But let me show you some things that are happening now." He motioned to a nearby sofa and sat next to me. "Just relax and watch this," he said.

There appeared before me a "Betterment Of Mankind" rally that James was speaking at.

"And the final truth, my friends," James was saying, "before too long we will improve our condition to where we do not need the rule of the Emperor and He will depart this world and leave us on our own. We have learned our lessons and he has much to do elsewhere. The time is near my friends."

"He has only held these meetings when you are at home with your wife," the Chancellor told me. "As a matter of fact you have slowed down his timetable of late by staying with him so much."

"But this is wrong," I said amazed.

"Yes, indeed."

"But he seems so fond of me," I said.

"He is, he truly is," the Chancellor answered. "But he also wants to be your adopted son. He thinks it would help his cause."

"But I suggested it," I confessed.

"Look at this," the Chancellor said. I saw a surgery. James was having his features altered to look more like me.

"You mentioned it first with words," the Chancellor said. "But he had this done before you first met him. "He wants you with him. He actually believes that this will happen."

I sat stunned for a while. The Chancellor sat quietly beside me. Suddenly I heard a sound in the room and turned. It was the Emperor Himself. I fell to my knees. The Chancellor stood.

"Majesty," the Chancellor said. He took the Emperor's hand and kissed it.

"Grandfather," the Emperor answered smiling.

They embraced.

"Andrew, sit," the Emperor commanded.

I resumed my seat and the Emperor took the seat beside me while the Chancellor scurried to pull up a chair in front of us. The Emperor touched my temple with one finger.

"Look," he said. In a minute I understood it all.

"You see, Andrew," the Chancellor said. "It is the subtlest lie of all. Mankind can not stand on its own."

"We are but mortals," I admitted.

"You don't quite understand," David said to me. "We can not stand without Him either." He pointed to his own chest with one hand and to the Emperor with the other. "Mortal or Immortal, He alone gives direction and life."

The scales were now removed from my eyes. "What will you do with him, Sire? " I asked the Emperor.

" I leave that to my Viceroy," the Emperor said. He touched my forehead and said, "I bless you, Andrew." I fainted.

When I awoke, I was in Montevideo at the Dais of Viceroy Luis Cepata. James Hardwick stood before him. I was seated at the side of the Dais being supported by two mortal members of his court until I regained my composure.

"What made you believe that you could do this," the Viceroy was asking James.

"Excellency, what did I do wrong?" James asked with his usual composure. Then he saw me over at the side and acted a little shaken.

The Viceroy continued, "No one, no one, young man incites sedition and gets away with it. Dependence on His Imperial Majesty is the destiny of the human race, mortal and Immortal, and you will not be allowed to continue."

James looked very small and very afraid.

"Keeper Andrew," the Viceroy said.

I jumped to my feet and hurried to his side.

"My Lord," I said.

"I am exiling him to your farm in Georgia for an indefinite sentence until he learns better," the Viceroy said.

"Very good, Sir," I answered.

"Do you need another angel to watch him?" Cepata asked.

"Yes, sir," I answered. "I need Lucius for other duties as well."

The Viceroy motioned and an angel from his canopy moved down next to James and the invisible cord was attached. A portal opened and they both disappeared. My mother Patricia had turned an old off-worlders camp near our residence into a farm for mortal probationers. I have not continued its use. Some graduates from her program live there now but it still belongs to the Keeper.

[N.D.] I have taken Mary and we are vacationing in Jerusalem for a few weeks. We attend the Emperor's public audiences regularly and spend a lot of time at the little Inn in Bethany. It is like a second honeymoon. I have a wonderful wife.

[N.D.] Gradually I have mulled over the entire James Hardwick episode. I believe now that he was not executed because he actually believed that the Emperor would leave voluntarily. He now knows better. At first he was not very humbled, but as his probation continues, he seems to be learning. I have spent some time with him but our relationship can never be the same again.

02.19.621 C.R. Finally, we have a daughter. Joan was born early this morning and she seems to be a fine healthy child.

03.14.623 C.R My beloved Mary gave birth today to our second daughter Marie. She is as beautiful as her sister.

01.21.624 C.R. All my life I have been concerned, as have others of my family over the generations, about what lay in store for us mortals who have lived during the Glorious Reign after this life is over. As the Keepers we understand what was involved for the mortals of the past who have been our Immortals during this Glorious Reign. They lived and died as mortals through their generations over the centuries just as we have been doing during the Reign. Although the Emperor was absent while they lived as mortals, they had the Sacred Writings and the Presence with them during their mortality. And, this is the most important part, they were virtually guaranteed a resurrection and life forever in the Sacred Writings. If they believed in Him and accepted His covenant, then they were included in this magnificent future and they had the actual indwelling Presence as their guarantee of their inheritance.

We have had no such promise during the Empire. The Emperor has been visible and his rule has been absolute due to the government of the Immortals, the assistance of the Angelic legions, and the power of the Presence among us if not within us. As mortals we have just hoped that the Emperor would do the most generous thing and that we would have some kind of a future even if it was not as glorious as what Elaine and her fellows have. At least we hoped that by obedience and love to the Emperor we would not be consigned to everlasting punishment. The Keeper May encouraged us to believe this and each Keeper since her time has offered this assurance as best he or she has been able.

I have studied my mother Patricia's work with her off-worlders and their quest regarding the after life complete with the help of the Chancellor and his family. This has been a great help to us all.

I have also been fortunate to have formed a relationship with the Lord Chancellor over the matter with James. I must have a better idea of what awaits us in this life and beyond.

Rather than push Elaine on this at this time I have asked Lucius to get me an interview with the Chancellor as soon as possible. It is not that I do not trust our beloved Elaine, but she has been away so much beyond the veil lately and I feel that she would only refer me to some other Immortal on a subject as important as this. It is well known that as Chancellor David spends most of his time on this side unlike the Master of the Feast, Peter, who is hardly ever here. Also, Elaine was the one who got me my opening with the Chancellor. She said that she believed that I would remind the Chancellor of some of his own sons in mortality. The Chancellor was a very loving father in his mortality and, as you probably know, he was the Emperor's own distant grandfather.

[N.D.] Lucius was back to me in exactly 4 hours. "Your audience with the Chancellor is immediate," he said.

I found myself in the Chancellor's reception room at the Capital. Lucius and I were alone in the room. In a few minutes I tired of pacing and sat down. Hours went by. I got up and looked out the window several times. I sat in the seat by the window. The Imperial Parks are magnificent and I enjoyed watching as mortals and Immortals moved freely around the parks. The canopy of angels over the Capital seemed somewhat subdued but it was still magnificent. All the colors and lights and haunting music that came from it were very comforting. I finally fell asleep at my seat by the window after many hours of waiting. Once a mortal girl entered and offered me food and drink. I took a slight repast and freshened myself at an adjoining bath. I was warm and comfortable after the bath which is probably why I fell asleep.

I was awakened by a touch on my shoulder. It was Elaine. "Mistress," I managed to mumble. The thought crossed my mind that she might be displeased because I went directly to the Chancellor but her smile put me at ease. I sat up to see the Chancellor himself directly behind Elaine. I stood so fast that my head felt a little light. Both Elaine and the Chancellor took an arm and steadied me.

"I am sorry for the wait, Andrew," the Chancellor said. "I was otherwise involved, but I trust that you have been comfortable." His kindness always puts me at ease.

"Yes, Chancellor," I said. "Quite comfortable. It is, …it is very good to see you again, Sir."

He motioned and we all sat down.

I started slowly and got faster and faster as I expressed my sincere desire to know the final end for us mortals. After I had passed several good stopping places, I finally decided to be quiet and listen. They had both been listening quite patiently. The Chancellor spoke to Elaine in a language that I do not understand. This is most unusual and I knew that it was not the Emperor's native language which is usually spoken at the Capital. I had never heard this language before but I suppose that they can speak scores of languages that I do not know. The Chancellor nodded in the positive and told me that he would see me in a short time and left me with Elaine.

"Andrew," she said quietly. I listened intently.

"You will have to be, shall we say, prepared for where we are going to take you."

"Fine, Elaine, anything," I answered.

She stood and motioned for me to follow her.

We walked deep into the Palace structure past places that I did not know mortals could go. We passed Immortals and mortals along the way. The mortals who were obviously working there looked very happy and contented and I wondered briefly why, as the Keeper, I had never been in these halls before. Finally we entered a room where the Chancellor went along with several other Immortals and some angels. The angels were obviously very high ranking as some of them had characteristics that I do not remember seeing before. Elaine had me sit down in a chair in the center of the room and the lights seemed to change to a golden glow. My awareness of the Presence was very strong. I felt intoxicated. I was surrounded by Immortals and angels and Elaine never let go of my hand. I heard snatches of conversations around me. Some in the common language and some in another language.

"Careful, not too fast . . ."

"He's doing fine...."

I felt a little dizzy but I was not frightened.

"Almost ready..."

"That is enough..."

"Andrew, Andrew, open your eyes," Elaine commanded softly.

I did as she said. I felt wonderful. I felt very light.

"You will have to have a reversal after we return," Elaine was saying. That was fine with me. Anything was fine. After a few minutes she got me to my feet and we moved across the room to another door, not the one that I had entered by. It opened and there was a very thick mist on the other side. Elaine took my hand very firmly and walked into it. I was still too much under the influence of what had just happened to me to feel any fear and Elaine's hold on me was very tight. We walked through the mist for a short time and then the light seemed to become stronger and the floor under me seemed to become firmer. It had been very soft at the beginning.

"There you go," Elaine said. A sort of a sky was appearing in front of me. I began to realize that it was me that was changing and not my surroundings. Elaine had been seeing all along what I was now beginning to see. We walked on some more and we were now surrounded by the most beautiful scene, a fantastic countryside. Immortals were now all around and I could see a great distance in every direction as we seemed to be on a hill. Suddenly I recognized a friend from my youth. It was Jeffery Lind. I had grown up with Jeffery. He died about 12 years ago. I attended his funeral. He saw me and waved. What? I was perplexed but not frightened.

"All those you see here," Elaine began. "Lived as mortals since the Glorious Return and sincerely loved the Emperor. They have a place. And there is more."

I saw the skies lower and an opening appeared. These new Immortals were going in and out of another realm. Before I could ask, Elaine answered.

"Yes, they have some access there."

Then inside the giant opening the mist cleared and I saw another higher layer in the other realm. I saw thousands of Immortals walking the streets of a great city. I briefly recalled some of the accounts in the journals of the Keeper Joan where her young friend had described his dreams of the other side.

"There only we can go" Elaine said. That was fine with me. It seemed only fair to me that Elaine and her

Immortal brothers and sisters should be allowed a greater access than we who have loved the Emperor in my era. I was just so happy that there was so much wonderful life ahead for me and my people. We sat down on the hillside while Elaine explained more to me.

"You see, Andrew," she said. "We lived our mortality during the age of faith and grace. We believed in and were joined to an absent Emperor except for his short sojourn with Peter and the others. Our reward is everlasting in these worlds and the other side, even to the Eternal City. Your people have seen the Emperor in his Magnificence in your mortality. Those who loved Him will have a reward."

I nodded. Now I knew. I was beside myself with joy. "What about those who have not loved the Emperor?" I asked. "In your day and mine?" I added.

Elaine sighed and stood. She took my hand again. "I will show you," she said. We walked to one side for a while and it grew dark. I could not see anything. Elaine held my hand very tightly. I trusted her implicitly. After a while I saw an orange glow ahead. It got brighter as we approached. Suddenly Elaine stopped and jerked me back firmly. I did not know she was so strong. She looked down and my eyes followed hers. I was startled. We were on the edge of a great cliff. Below I could hear screams. Somehow my vision grew sharper and I saw thousands and thousands of people burning in a great pit. Thousands of evil angels beat them with whips of steel. I choked and threw up into the pit. My vomit vaporized as it proceeded downwards.

"How, …how do they survive?" I asked.

"That, my dear Andrew," Elaine said, "is truly the Hell of it. They are also Immortal. They can not die. They can not escape."

In a few minutes she mercifully led me back to that beautiful meadow and we sat there for hours while I recovered and started to appreciate the beauty of the place. As we waited, she stroked my back. I felt strength coming from her. Without her help I do not think I could have recovered. After a while she took me back to the room that I had been prepared in and the process was reversed. I felt well but heavy again. She took me from that room and to a bedroom within the Chancellor's apartments. I slept for days.

07.13.636 C.R. In looking over my life's work the past year. I must admit that I am truly disappointed. My beloved Mary has been gone almost seven years now. My daughters are a great comfort to me. Elaine has never criticized my work. I suppose that I have been competent. I have spoken many times for the good of the Empire and the Emperor and I have endeavored to keep good records. But I do not think that I have done anything noteworthy in my office. Of course, no one can attain to the spirituality of May, or the originality of our mother, Anna, or the unique work of my mother, Patricia, with the off-worlders, but I had hoped to do more.

03.11.974 C.R. *IMPORTANT NOTE: There follows here a gap in the journaling of the Keeper and Primate Andrew. There is an oral tradition in our family that he himself either hid or destroyed many years of journals before his death. His beloved Mary died almost ten years before his death. His private journal was hidden away and discovered by his granddaughter the Keeper Mandie in 704 C.R.*

Tim, K. and P.

Reign II

Mandie

699 – 749 C.R.

The Keeper Joan said in her journal, "My sister Marie's daughter, Mandie, is a good girl. She has attained womanhood now and she is very interested in the work. She is a tall girl with fair skin and hair and very graceful. I am short and dark and have always struggled with my weight. She will probably deal with the ceremonial portions of the office much more gracefully than I. She is also a capable researcher and scholar. She says that she will remain unmarried just as I have, but that will remain to be seen. If too many of us remain unmarried, the succession will get complicated although I am sure that the ageless Elaine who watches over our work will be able to deal with it all quite well."

10.03.699 C.R.   My name is Mandie, actually Amanda, but I've never been called that. I am the new Keeper and Primate. My beloved aunt Joan died last night in her sleep. She labored until the last spreading the news of love. There was not a single day that she did not feel the Presence since she started this work. I long to be her faithful successor. I have had some experience in my unique position as "Keeper Heiress" and I hope to please my mistress, the Immortal Elaine, in all that I do and to please the Emperor himself as well.

01.22.700 C.R.   At present I have three suitors and my mother Marie, my most trusted advisor, is in quite a state over this abundance of suitors. Mother is so upset about this that when Elaine was here at the residence yesterday, Mother asked her, "Elaine, can't you just assign one of these men to be her husband. You have done so for the Keeper in the past."

"I would rather she made her own choice, Marie."

Mother did not take it well. I smiled at her.

Elaine continued, "Marie, this is actually a part of Mandie's training, the first thing that she needs to do as Keeper."

"Choose a husband?" Mother asked.

"Precisely, and she must do this on her own. We can advise if she asks, but only if she asks."

"Just one more question, Mistress," Mother asked politely.

"Yes."

"Why do you allow Mandie this freedom when you picked mates for others? I have read the journals."

"Mostly because some of them would have never found a partner without my intervention. Mandie attracts many men, right now there are three 'front runners.' I want to see what she will do."

"You see, that's quite a responsibility young lady," Mother scolded. Before I could answer, she added, "I hope you will ask Elaine's advice even if you are not interested in mine."

"I will, Mother. I will ask you and Elaine." There was a slight pause. Then I continued, "So Mother, which one should I choose? Jason? Andrew? Josh?"

"Oh, I don't know. I just wish there weren't so many."

I looked at Elaine and shrugged. Mother left the room to 'freshen up.' She did that a lot.

"Elaine, what should I do?" I asked.

"You know perfectly well, Mandie, that when I say that I will advise you, you have to have specific questions," Elaine said firmly.

The Immortals have a lot of interest in mortal marriages for a people who do not marry among themselves. I sometimes think that they are hopeless romantics, but then again there is the belief among them that they are all, as a group, married to the Emperor. I know that this is not a physical union for them. I guess we mortals just can not understand why courtship and marriage interests them as much as it does.

"O.K., sorry. Help me judge which of them is more suitable for me. Jason is, well, I guess you could call him 'stormy'. That excites me. Andy is so very sensitive. When we look at the sunset, he will often say exactly what I am thinking. Now Josh is, I guess you might call it, 'steady.' That's nice but I don't know if I want to spend the rest of my life with him. So what do you think?"

"I think you are starting to think. Keep up the good work. I have to go now to the Capital. I will be back in a few days. If you really need anything, send Lucius." With that she was gone.

I was going to continue this thinking process when it occurred to me that some help from the Presence would be good, but Elaine was already gone. Still I shouted after her even though I knew perfectly well that she was already in Jerusalem in the few seconds that I had let elapse.

"Elaine, uh, the Presence . . . "

Lucius answered, "She says that He is here. Go ahead and ask."

That was unusual but I have learned one thing as Keeper Apprentice, don't ask how they do it, just enjoy it. I have asked Lucius to greet everyone who comes to the residence since my major domo died last year. Old Cecil had been the head servant at the residence from the beginning of Aunt Joan's term. When he died, we had a grand funeral for him and I needed a new greeter. There were several who thought they should have it. Since they all seemed to have less than the purest of motives, I just assigned it to Lucius. Lucius is, of course, always willing to help and his total absence of emotion or self seeking makes it easy. However, some say that I have overdone it and I want to be too impressive. They say that I take advantage of my privilege as the only mortal with a personal angel. Those that call are quite impressed, of course. But I believe that some of the less well intentioned ones just stay away since they know they can not fool Lucius and are actually a little bit afraid of him. Fine. That works. No more salespersons and people collecting for unregistered charities. Apparently my using Lucius in this way, at least temporarily, is no problem with Elaine or she would have mentioned it. I will, however, try to do something about this later.

05.12.700 C.R. Well, the 'boys' as I call them are not the least bit put off by Lucius. Mother calls this 'the power of hormones.' They each check in with Lucius upon arrival if I am not in the front part of the residence. They know that he will announce them when the time comes in the order that they arrived if I have left instructions not to be disturbed due to some research project I am conducting deep in the library. Lucius is eminently fair. They just wait in the parlor unless Elaine arrives. In which case they greet her very politely and find a reason to go away and come again later.

"Keeper, Mr. Andy awaits," Lucius informed me. I was just taking some tea with Mother in the garden.

"Do you mind, Mother?"

She began to get up to leave.

"No, Mother. Please don't leave. Can he come back and have tea with us?"

"If you want." She sat down and tried a weak smile.

"Please tell him, Lucius."

"The sensitive one," Mother mumbled before he arrived.

"Good day, Keeper Mother," Andy greeted her with a smile.

"I have never been the Keeper, young man. My sister Joan was the Keeper. You may call me Mrs., ah, er, . how about just Marie?"

"Wonderful, Marie. Of course, I am just Andy.

"Your proper name is Andrew, is it not?"

"Yes, Ma'am." He thought that she missed the 'just' part.

"Good, I will call you Andrew. Andrew is a good name. My father's name was Andrew."

"Great," Andy responded. Then he turned his attention to me. I looked into his eyes for a long time until Mother started rattling the tea set. I am not sure just what I was hunting for. Then he turned back towards Mother and said, "I would like to take Mandie to the Metropolitan's gardens today. The gardeners have outdone themselves with a new display of annuals. They . . . "

She did not let him finish. "Our Keeper is capable of her own decisions on courting, Andrew. I am just an observer." With that she filled her mouth with cake. I glared at her to no avail.

"Sounds great, Andy. I will be ready in a few minutes."

On the way out we ran into Jason at the door. Both Andy and I asked him to go with us but he responded that he would not but that he would be back. He seemed a little angry, but maybe it was just his normal storminess.

05.13.700 C.R. Jason did come back the next day. I was in the library but when I came out, I invited him to join me in the garden for some refreshments. He was brooding.

After a while I said, "You know that I am seeing Andy and Josh, Jason. You and I have come to no 'agreement'."

"I know. I just wish we could come to an 'agreement'."

"But you agreed that we would not rush. Not only for myself but for my office."

"I know, I know. It's just that I want you so much."

"And you may well have me, and live to regret it," I added.

"I could never regret it, my lovely," he responded. He has a tendency towards mushiness when he feels romantic. He took my hand and smiled. I returned the smile. He started to move in for a kiss so I picked up my drink. He pulled back and looked into the distance. In a few seconds he said, "Let's go skiing."

"Skiing? Where? It's May here in Atlanta right now."

"In the Alps, Switzerland, Austria, whatever, your angel can take us."

"Well, he certainly could." I thought for a while and urgently tried to contact the Presence. I sensed nothing. So, it was not a 'no'.

"O.K. Lucius!"

We spent most of a day skiing in the Alps and when evening came, I said that I must return to my residence. He wanted to spend the night in a romantic little cabin there but I reminded him of who I am and he reluctantly agreed to return home. I offered to leave him there but he was aware that he would have to get back by mortal transportation so he came along. I told him I was very tired when we returned and he excused himself. For Jason it is never enough. I wonder how that would be if we were married. I began to miss Josh.

[N.D.] Several days later Lucius appeared in the library where I was studying.

"And . . .?" I asked.

"Mr. Josh is in the parlor." he answered.

I started to say, 'and you interrupted me for that?' But I did not. As a matter of fact I apologized for my tone. I had been deeply involved in my research about my ancestor Mark's travels. Dear Lucius simply nodded in agreement.

When I saw Josh, I squealed and jumped to put my arms around his neck. He picked me up and twirled me around in the parlor. He felt very good. He is tall and strong. He is a woods manager for the mortal department of parks.

09.02.700 C.R.   After a few months of spending time with all three of my suitors and much thought and communing with the Presence, (I am so thankful that He is near,) I have finally decided on Josh. I wish all of the mortals had the access to the Presence that I have enjoyed. Even though it is not as intimate as it was for Elaine when she was mortal, it is as intimate as it was for leaders in the First Testament and I am so very thankful for that.

Andy took the news quietly and told me that if I ever needed anything to call him no matter what. He is such a dear and I appreciate his offer.

I called Jason to the residence the day after I told Andy. Andy had just dropped by. Jason looked like he would explode. He said that he would love me forever and angrily bolted for the door. I have no regrets there.

Josh was the last to know. I did it this way in case he turned me down so I could not offer myself to a second choice. I resolved that if he turned me down, I would just have to start all over again. Elaine said that this was very wise. I had to send for Josh too. I was a little nervous. I decided to trust his instincts. I left the entire luncheon and afternoon free. I ordered his favorite foods and waited. He was, as usual, on time. We ate and talked for quite some time. Finally he asked if I had appointments.

"Nope, nothing all day," I said. I moved to a small bench to watch the fish in my pond. He sat beside me. My heart was racing and I felt like I was blushing. In a few minutes he put his arm around me. I snuggled in. He kissed me very softly and tenderly.

"You've decided," he said softly. It was not a question.

I nodded and looked into his eyes.

"And it's me," he said just as softly and just as surely.

I nodded again. All I could seem to do was nod.

"Darling, that is wonderful," he said looking deep into my eyes. Then he gave me the longest, sweetest kiss I have ever known. I knew that I had chosen the right man.

Mother was her usual self.

"Yes, of course my dear, I am glad that you have finally made up your mind. It's just that he is so descent that I hope he can do his duty to provide you an heir."

"Oh, Mother. He's not too descent. Just don't you worry."

"My dear, I . . . "

"That's all right, Mother."

Just then Elaine arrived. I remembered again how much the Immortals love weddings because they see each one of them as symbolic of their relationship between themselves and the Emperor.

"Good choice, Mandie," Elaine said putting her hand on my back. "Now let's plan the wedding."

Somehow I had the good sense and peace of mind to let Elaine run with it. She is, after all the Imperial Legate for the Keeper and she will make a grand affair out of it anyway. I figured that I might just as well go along quietly.

04.10.701 C.R. Our wedding was in the spring and Atlanta was at its flowery best. It was held at the Metropolitan's Dais and Elaine had full charge of how everything was arranged. Since my father died some time ago, the Metropolitan brought me down the aisle that Elaine created with thousands of blooming plants. Viceroy

Cepata and the Over-Lord Janice performed the ceremony.

I was calmer on my wedding day than I had expected to be. As I waited in the little garden building, I took a deep breath and felt quite calm. It would have helped if I could have seen Josh that morning but we still kept the ancient mortal custom of not seeing each other on the wedding day. Our trip was planned to the Bahamas and the Prince of the Bahamas had personally supervised our accommodations. She was also to attend the ceremony. Finally at 3 P.M. the mortal orchestra began to play and my escort arrived. There were many escort angels in the sky because of the presence of the Viceroy but it also made a nice addition to my wedding. I came down the aisle quickly and as soon as I locked eyes with Josh everything was fine. The Viceroy stepped forward to begin. He acknowledged some sort of signal from an angel somewhere above my head and smiled and paused.

I felt a flurry above and behind me and then a heavy feeling like warm honey being poured out on us and the Dais. Viceroy Cepata spoke clearly. "The bride and groom and wedding party need only to bow low." Then it struck me. Our beautiful wedding clothes including my gigantic white gown were to be spared the grass stains. The Emperor was coming. He was actually coming to my wedding. I had been calm, now I was speechless. Josh handled it well.

In a second the great angel Gabriel was facing me on the Dais.

"His Imperial Majesty !" was all that Gabriel said.

The next thing I knew the Emperor walked around me on the right side and stood facing us between the Viceroy and the Over-Lord. He nodded to the Viceroy who asked us each if we would have each other in marriage. We answered. Then Janice charged us to be loving and faithful to each other. Then the Emperor pronounced, "You are one." He then nodded to Josh who kissed me. Josh then looked quizzically at the Emperor who gestured with his finger that we were to turn around and recess. This we did. We got to the little building that I had started from and I nearly passed out.

"Look," my husband pointed out the door to the sky. With the Emperor's escort the sun was practically blotted out. But it was so light. The light was coming from the Dais. The Emperor was still here.

The Emperor soon blessed the people and left. There was dining and dancing for hours. The Immortals do love a good wedding.

[N.D.] Now that our wedding trip is over I must get down to the business of my office. We haven't managed to get pregnant yet, but it is not for lack of trying. Mother's concerns about Josh were totally unnecessary. I'm sure we will succeed before too long.

[N.D.] One winter morning I was studying in my library. Josh was off on a two day trip concerning his work. Lucius appeared and announced, "An angel prince to see the Keeper."

Really? I was very curious. "Well Lucius," I was thinking as I talked.

"You may summon him in here or come to the front garden to meet him," Lucius said helping me out.

I started for the garden and Lucius came along. I was startled when I saw this angel. We do not see many like this.

"I am Vicar Bright," he said bowing slightly.

"Yes."

"I am from Imperial Security." I remembered his name and description from the journals and yet for some reason I still felt a flash of fear, although I did not believe that I had done anything wrong.

"Wait here," I commanded and I went into my parlor. Lucius followed.

"Get Elaine," I blurted. I calmed myself. "Please ask Elaine if she could help me." I said more softly.

"There is no need for alarm, Keeper," Lucius assured me.

"I still need Elaine, Lucius, please!"

He nodded. I visited the bathroom and returned and looked out the window. The large angel was standing patiently waiting. Why are they always so patient? It seemed that Elaine would never come although it was only a matter of minutes.

"Sweetheart, don't be alarmed," Elaine said as soon as she appeared. She came over and sat next to me. That was what I needed, any arm of flesh around me in Josh's absence even if it was a different kind of flesh.

"He will do you no harm, little one," Elaine said.

"What does he want?" I asked.

"You will have to ask him. Obviously, he wants your help with something."

"Is Josh all right? Is he O.K. Elaine? Please tell me."

"Josh is fine, Mandie."

I took a deep breath. I don't know why this large angel unnerved me so.

"He is constructed to unnerve mortals," Elaine said as if she was reading my thoughts. "But he is no concern to you personally or to Josh. Now get ready to go out there and find out what he wants."

I nodded and asked, "Will you go with me?"

"Yes, since you want me to," Elaine answered.

We went back to the front garden. When Vicar Bright saw Elaine, he bowed deeply. I felt much better.

"What is your business with me," I asked somewhat curtly. I took another deep breath.

"Keeper, you know a certain Andrew Carrolton I am told."

"Andy? Yes, of course I know Andy. We are old friends."

The angel spoke slowly. "Keeper, he and his wife have been charged with high treason."

I felt Elaine's arm around my waist steadying me.

The angel continued, "The Imperial Chancellor requests your involvement on this matter."

"Yes, yes, I can come right away."

"Will the Prince Elaine accompany us?" the angel asked.

"To the Capital?" I looked at Elaine pleadingly.

"She will," Elaine answered. We waited a second for Elaine's escort to arrive; she ordered her full escort as the Legate, I was reassured.

[N.D.] I had visited the Capital with Aunt Joan once as the Keeper Heiress. I don't know how I could have forgotten the glory of it all. The angelic canopy is breathtaking. Neither Viceroy would even attempt to approach such sheer extravagance over his capital. We were shown to guest quarters near the Temple mound. I sent Lucius to get Josh. Elaine told us to relax and she disappeared for a few hours.

I asked Lucius, "Who decides about the canopy? I mean the size and the formations and the choral sounds?" The sounds did not follow any particular melody. They were more like complicated chords, but they were beautiful and mystifying.

"The leaders of the choirs, Mistress."

"Choirs?"

"Yes, some angels are in choirs."

"I see."

Josh and I just sat by a window and enjoyed the beauty of the Imperial Capital although I was worried about

Andy and Maxine. He had married Maxine not long after I married Josh. I was sure that this business was all a terrible mistake and that Elaine would probably have it all sorted out by the time she returned.

[N.D.] "I am afraid that it is quite serious, little one," Elaine said when she returned.

My heart sank. "What? How?" I asked.

"They have been members of a seditious cell ever since they were married." Elaine continued, "She actually was a member before they married and got him involved but he has been very committed and active."

"His wife got him involved?"

"Yes, it appears that she recruited him from the first."

"Poor Andy. She deceived him and now he's involved," I muttered.

"Make no mistake about it, Mandie," Elaine added quickly. "He is totally involved himself."

"How could he do this? He is so sensitive and sincere?" I asked.

"That's the thing," Elaine said. "It is that kind who are so easily led into things like this and who commit so strongly."

"I would have expected something like that from Jason," I said.

"He's not likely to be so involved with other people," Elaine said. "He's doing quite well as a businessman."

"I had heard that. But what can we do for Andy? Never mind Maxine. She got him into it in the first place."

Elaine came over to me and grasped me by the shoulders. "You have to hear me, little one. Andy is personally and totally involved."

I hesitated before I asked my next question, my heart was heavy. I took a deep breath and asked, "What could be the end result, Elaine?"

"They could be executed," she answered. "I am so sorry, Mandie."

My knees got weak and Elaine reached out to support me. Josh dashed to my side and helped me back to a chair.

"Executed," I said softly. I couldn't take it in. "Executed." I kept saying it softly over and over.

"You have been invited to luncheon with the Chancellor," Elaine finally said.

"I don't feel like luncheon with the Chancellor," I said rebelliously.

"You have to Mandie," Elaine insisted. "You must remember your office. You must show no sign of rebellion in sympathy with Andy or his wife and friends."

"Do you know any more details?" I asked.

"Yes. Some," Elaine responded.

"Tell me all that you know, please?" I asked.

"You won't like it. It is not easy to hear," Elaine warned me.

"Please go ahead. I must know," I insisted.

"O.K. Here goes," Elaine said. "This is an old cell of rebels. They are a seed cell for starting other ones. Imperial Security allowed it to continue for their usual reason, to see just how far those involved would go. Those who were successfully recruited had been warned through someone, a family member or close friend, to get out. Some did, but Andy and Maxine were not at all interested in getting out."

"What was their plan? What did they hope to do?" I asked.

"Evidently, they realized that open rebellion was hopeless, but they thought that they could remain secret and resort to harassment and guerilla actions."

"Like what?"

"Like stopping supply vehicles to various Imperial courts and either ruining the supplies or stealing them."

"Did they hurt anyone?"

"Sometimes, in the course of their actions. Of course, the ones that did injury were punished immediately. But the others were left to see how far they would continue to go," Elaine continued.

"What else, " I continued.

"They would print and distribute leaflets calling for the replacement of certain Immortal judges. They would warn and rescue other criminals, thieves, extortionists and the like before they were caught."

"What fools," I said. "They are always caught. What was Andy's involvement?"

"He was a strategist. He planned much of their activities. His wife was a recruiter and a spy. She got them information." Elaine seemed to be finished.

"What time does the Chancellor expect us?" I asked.

"In half an hour," Elaine said.

08.11.709 C.R. We arrived at the mortal side in the Temple right on time. Elaine brought only one angel and Lucius was with us. There was a lot of activity in the waiting rooms. Elaine took us right into the Chancellor's meeting rooms.

"David, my brother, it is so good to be with you again," Elaine said.

"And with you, my sister, Elaine," the Chancellor responded. "And our new Keeper."

When he took my hand, I felt a great strength and peace. His red hair and beard are striking. It was good to see him again. "Your Excellency," I did my best curtsy.

"And your husband . . ." he reached for Josh's hand and shook it warmly.

"Come sit with me," he said. We moved to a sitting area where there were several chairs.

"You know this Andrew, I believe," he said to me.

"Yes, Excellency, he was one, ah . . ., of my suitors."

"Well, you chose well. Josh's reputation as well as your own precedes you both."

I wondered what he had heard and from whom but I let that pass. I suspected that angel Bright, but he did not appear to be present. I was still a little intimidated in the Chancellor's presence. The resurrected King of Israel and Chancellor of the present Empire has a very high office. I kept seeing the position instead of the person probably because I knew that Andy's life was in his hands.

"I am afraid that the evidence against both the mortal Andrew and his wife Maxine is flawless. They were given every chance to change. Now there is nothing left to do."

We all fell very silent.

The Chancellor broke the silence. The sentencing will be held at the Dais of the Over Lord Janice Holland in the morning."

"And that will be?" I asked flatly.

"Death," was the only word the Chancellor spoke.

"And there is nothing that I can do to help?" I asked. "Put him in my custody. I will accept full responsibility." I was willing to try anything by now. I wondered why he had called me here.

"No. He has gone to far. I know how difficult this is for you. As a mortal I had to pronounce judgments that stuck in my throat. But there was nothing else to do. I will ask a special portion of the Presence for you to help you through this time. I asked you here because I wanted you to hear this from me. I knew that he was a friend of yours." He put his hand on my wrist and I felt a certain peace. But even that was not enough.

Elaine got us out of there gracefully. I thanked the Chancellor for his time. We went to New York to wait.

Janice pronounced the sentence because Andy and Maxine were under her jurisdiction. They died instantly and without a word. Their bodies were delivered to their families. Josh and I went to the services. They were full of regret and shame, all very sad. No voice of rebellion was heard.

"You have got to remember that these things are dealt with every day, Mandie," Elaine told me when we got back to the residence. "It is just that this one was personal for you. Take a while to grieve and then pull yourself together. I love you." She embraced me. "I leave you in Josh's capable hands. Love her, Josh."

"I will, Elaine. Thanks for your help and strength."

"You are, of course, most welcome," Elaine said. "Call me for tea?" she asked.

I nodded.

"Soon, little one. Soon!"

I nodded again.

[N.D.] After two weeks I felt no better. In my mind I even questioned the rightness of the Emperor. Wasn't he supposed to represent mercy to everyone? I chided myself for mental infidelity but things still seemed so dark. The angel Vicar Bright called again to ask if I was going to handle the public report on the matter. I flew into a rage and ordered him from my residence. In my grief and anger I no longer felt any fear. Afterwards I wondered if I would be corrected, so I finally invited Elaine for tea. She arrived on time and Josh and I were all set up for her in the garden. After a little small talk Elaine asked, "You're still pretty low aren't you, dear?"

"Yes. I just can't seem to throw it off."

Elaine looked at Josh.

"Josh has been wonderful," I added. I took his hand and managed a weak smile.

Again quiet. I looked at the floor, Josh looked at me and Elaine looked at both of us.

"Elaine?" I asked.

"Yes."

I looked directly at her. "Can I resign? As Keeper?"

"Yes. If you want to. But you can not come back."

I stared at her blankly. "I ordered that angel from my house."

"No matter. They don't have feelings," Elaine answered. She continued, "You could live quietly in the country on Josh's work. We would still be friends, I hope."

"Oh, Elaine, I will always love you. I just don't know if I can continue. I . . ." I was at a loss for words. I guess I had loved the gentle Andy more than I thought although I certainly did not regret being married to Josh. I just could not get over what I perceived as the severity of the Imperial reign.

"Take a few more weeks before you decide anything, dear," Elaine said as she stood and came to hug me goodbye.

I nodded. She left me alone with Josh. Josh did not say much. He is not a man for idle words. I know that he understands and supports me completely. For days I called upon the Presence for comfort and it seemed to help. After a few days I asked Josh, "Who do you suppose would succeed me?"

"I'm not sure," he answered. "Perhaps your cousin Charles."

"Um, maybe. Perhaps a man would be better. O well . . ." Josh gave me that 'you really know better' look.

[N.D.] Elaine arrived one afternoon a few weeks later. "I have one suggestion before we consider your resignation or wait through any more of this gloom," she said.

"What," I asked.

"I can arrange a private audience with the Emperor."

"The . . . the Emperor? For what? I mean what will that accomplish?"

"It might just change you, Mandie. The Emperor is more than a ruler. You have lost sight of that. Andy's treason, like all crimes in the Imperial Code, was against the Emperor himself personally. Some time with Him might just change your perspective a bit. It is a great honor, you know and other Keepers have had the privilege."

"I know. But I will need time to prepare. I don't want to insult Him," I said.

"Fine. I will be back," Elaine said. She left immediately.

In a few days Elaine was back. "One week, little one. Do all the preparation you can. I will come for you."

[N.D.] Josh and I filled our days with things to do and I meditated most of the nights. After all, I have seen the Emperor before; he married us. I was a little sleep deprived when Elaine came for me. She had a small escort. I expected that we would all transport to the Temple area where I would wait for my appointment as we had when we saw the Chancellor. I was surprised. Josh and I and Elaine and her escort and Lucius all left together but I landed in a private meeting room with the Emperor by myself.

He motioned for me to sit beside Him on a large soft settee. I obeyed. He took my hands in His and looked into my eyes and I looked into His. He explained some things which I can barely remember and I got lost in his eyes. Afterwards he actually hugged me and I passed out. I came too on the settee by myself and somehow everything made sense. I was overflowing with joy. I was not tired anymore. There was only light in my life. I remembered Anna's account of her encounter with the Emperor and May's as well. I now understood. How wonderful and merciful he is. How just and righteous are his judgments. Josh and Elaine came into the room and got me and we returned to our residence. I took up my duties, both public and private, with strength and joy. I can not explain any further. The Emperor is not only a ruler.

11.22.714 C.R. I have persuaded Josh to quit his work and to travel full time with me and Lucius. I told him that I believe that it is my calling to travel a lot and that I can not stand to be without him while I do this. He agreed after only a day of meditation and was free from his duties in two weeks. With Josh and Lucius I feel like I can do anything. Lucius is always nearby, all I need do is call out, but he is never in the same room with us in private. In public he is very present just above and behind me.

01.05.715 C.R. The Viceroy John's father, a man named Zebedee, is one Immortal who has been experimenting with undersea colonies in the South Pacific. He is very interested in under sea life. He is himself Over-Lord of a chain of islands there and he conducts his projects from his Dais on the Island of Tonga and he has underwater colonies in the Tonga Trench and at other places in the area. For some reason the marine life there has not been enriched as some other animal life has been. This is probably because Zebedee is a fisherman and he intends the fish more for food than for friends, except the Dolphins.

We found it to be an amazing place. I greeted the people and scheduled a series of talks on the benefits of the present Reign compared to past mortal life on earth. These were well attended. We had allowed plenty of time to visit some of these underwater colonies and I actually scheduled some speeches in them as well. Zebedee is an amusing man. He is quite glad to have his own island principality as his son has his own island at Patmos. At first I bowed and greeted him as the Over-Lord.

"Oh, my, child, we don't stand on ceremony here. Just call me Zeb and we will get on fine," he said. He shook Josh's hand long and hard and they hit it off wonderfully.

It was a little difficult calling him 'Zeb.' I could not imagine calling Janice 'Jan' or even Elaine 'Lane,' but I got used to it. Zeb is short and well tanned. It seems that Immortals do tan when exposed to the Sun. He has a full head of black hair which is always tousled. He could wear it shorter just by willing it, but he chooses to wear it longer and messy. He dresses very casually and always keeps half a dozen angels nearby to help.

[N.D.]   The underwater colonies exist under enormous air bubbles which are apparently constructed and maintained by angels and are not a part of any mortal technology. Mortals do well in the colonies. Most of them are shallow enough to benefit from the sunlight above, but the deeper ones seem to benefit from some sort of light also provided by the angels. I am not sure if the Immortals actually require air to breathe.

Everybody, both mortal and Immortal, willingly and cheerfully follow Zebedee and do whatever he suggests or orders. Marine life swims over the bubbles which are all situated on the ocean floor. Inside various floorings have to be installed to cover the sand once it dries. Angels can be seen scattered around the top of the dome in any colony. Their backs are to the sea and they face the colony below them. They do not seem to be under any strain. Josh and I honestly believe that they are supporting the air dome in some way. They never seem to get tired.

I asked Zeb if these angels ever change places.

"Oh, once in a while I notice that some of them seem to be replaced with others," he said looking up at the dome. "That is all up to their Legion commanders. I just tell my guys here what I want done." He motioned to the six angels who regularly accompany him.

Josh and I have decided that these six are of a higher rank than Lucius, but we do not know exactly what they are.

"The thing is," Zeb continued, "there are soooo many of them and many have little to do. I believe that they should be kept employed, so I do everything I can to occupy them." He continued examining a small yellow fish which had been brought to him on the floor of the colony in a bubble filled with water. One of his assistant angels was holding the bubble. It doesn't seem to matter if it is an air bubble in the water or a water bubble in the air. It works either way. Zeb is interested in every conceivable kind of aquatic life and every new discovery is brought directly to him and he surely does take full advantage of his opportunities.

"I used to wonder when I was a fisherman in Galilee about all the creatures that lived in the water. When we were returned to life on this earth, I asked my son John if there was any chance of doing this kind of thing," Zeb said as we explored inside a city bubble one afternoon.

"I see," I replied.

With that little bit of encouragement he continued. "You know this is our fifth city under the water and we plan even more."

Josh and I nodded.

"There seems to be no end to the wonders of aquatic life," Zeb continued. "And we can go anywhere, anywhere at all. Do you want to leave this bubble and explore more of the ocean floor?" he asked.

"Oh yes, we would love to do that," I answered. "How?"

"Watch this," he said motioning to some of his angels. An angel positioned himself over each of us, Zeb and Josh and myself. They lifted us and we moved toward the bubble wall. As we approached the wall, I felt a surge of panic but I looked at my husband and he had nothing but joy and wonder on his face so I calmed down. When we got to the wall, we penetrated it without causing a leak of any kind and found ourselves surrounded by individual bubbles created by our angel escorts.

I looked around for Lucius as I am accustomed to having things done for me by him. He was just behind us. I thought to myself that next time I would ask if Lucius could do this for me. About that time Lucius came close and joined with the other angel and me in the bubble and then the other angel departed. Lucius had learned to do what was necessary and the other angel willingly departed. I still tend to forget that they do not have any jealousy or envy among them. I smiled and nodded at Lucius.

We explored the ocean floor for hours. The air remained always fresh inside our bubbles. Zeb flitted from one thing to another and picked up several samples and brought them into the bubble with him. We learned that if we extended our hand we could reach outside and pick up things and draw them back inside with us. Our hand was wet when we drew it back but there were no leaks anywhere. If the sample was living, a small water bubble would appear around it when we pulled it into our air filled environment. The wonder of the Emperor's creation amazed me again. I thought that this was a unique and wonderful environment that Zeb had brought about at the bottom of the sea.

[N.D.]   I was speaking one evening on the generosity of the Emperor in this present reign to a group of about 300 of Zeb's mortals. Each settlement is composed of about the same amount of Immortals and mortals. They all seem to get along well and being here is considered to be a great privilege for mortals. All the mortals here are volunteers and all have an interest in exploring the seas and the life that is in them. As I was nearing the end of my talk, I was referring to the privilege of us mortals being here and recounting the wonders of the angelic help without which this would not be possible when I noticed a disturbance in the back of the crowd just over to my right. I continued but the noise from that area just seemed to get louder. I stopped and demanded to know what was going on.

"You there, in the back, what is all the fuss about?" I shouted.

"Nothing, Keeper," one man shouted.

"It is not nothing," another shouted after him.

I left the platform which is for all intents and purposes the Dais of the Over–Lord Zebedee of this island chain. His permanent Dais is on the surface. It took me a few seconds to arrive at the rear of the assembly and by that time most of the mortals there had cleared away to leave five men in a group awaiting me. At once I noticed a rather young looking Immortal man already on the scene so I stopped and deferred to him.

"Go right ahead, Keeper," this young Immortal said. "You have got to hear this."

"Thank you, sir. Now, you men, what is the problem?"

"I told them to be quiet," one of the men said. He looked a little more cooperative than the others who all just stood cross armed glaring at me. I turned towards them. Lucius loomed up large behind me. I heard Zeb's voice as he arrived at the platform.

"Out with it," I demanded. "What is so important, so egregious, that you interrupt my talk?"

They seemed to be looking at Lucius.

"Don't be afraid of her angel," one man said. "That's what they want you to be. It's all for effect."

"Never mind my angel, answer me," I demanded.

"You have no idea," another man said. "You live under constant privilege from a family of constant privilege."

"If you don't come to the point, I will just turn you over to Immortal investigation," I finally said clearly.

"You have her attention, possibly the most powerful mortal in the world," I heard Zeb say as he approached from behind me. "You might as well make the best of it now."

The men made faces that revealed their distain for Zeb himself. Granted, Zeb was more of an explorer than a ruler and he was probably very lenient on all those under his power. But I was beginning to dislike these men very much.

"We come here and we work hard," the first man began again. "But when we want to take something back and do a little business with it, we are slapped down."

"Not that again," Zeb said. "I do not want a business made of these creatures or my work. How much do these people want?"

"Apparently more than their due, your Excellency" I answered.

"You men have no gratitude. The Over-Lord, indeed the Emperor, does not owe you a thing. You said it yourself, you should be slapped down. You have not heard a word of what I have been saying, have you?"

"You are not in our shoes. You don't understand," the second man answered again.

"Do all of you agree with these two?" I asked.

"Not me. Oh, no," the man who had tried to warn them said. Then he moved away from them as if to say he wanted nothing to do with them.

"Excellency, I leave them to your judgment," I said stepping back.

"What is your recommendation, Keeper?" he asked.

I looked quickly at Josh who had come to my side. He looked back as if to say, 'go on.'

"Well first, Excellency," I considered very hard for a moment, "these five and any who agree with them should be sent back to dry land permanently. Secondly, they should be watched by whatever power at your disposal as if they are on probation. They all have a terrible attitude." I took a deep breath as this was the first time my opinion had been asked on a disciplinary matter as the Keeper.

"Fine," Zeb said. He looked at the other Immortal who had been on the scene when I arrived. This Immortal moved towards the five and in a flash all of them were gone. There arose an applause from the crowd and we went back to Zeb's camp for supper.

So I have had my first influential experience as Keeper. I asked Josh when we got by ourselves, what he thought of my decision and he said that it was perfect. He is a wonderful husband.

01.30.730 C.R.   We were married a long time before I started having children, but once I started they all came very fast.

Ken is our first born and we have always planned for him to be Keeper after me. After Ken is Chloe, then Jason, Anne, the girl twins Jan and Jean, then Preston, David, Pamela, Roger, Marie (named after my mother,) then Donald, Candace, Denise, and finally the baby Margaret. Instead of asking Elaine to help me conceive, as she has others of the women Keepers, I was ready to ask her to cause me to stop conceiving. We love all of our children dearly, but fifteen is quite enough. Mercifully, I have now passed beyond my childbearing years. Having children was also easy for me. They all came quite quickly when they were due and there was not much pain. We have quite a family life here at the residence and rooms have been added so that each child can have their own room, except for the twins who prefer to share a room. Josh is a wonderful father and takes good care of the children.

[N.D.] Josh has expressed a concern that so many children of the Keeper complicate the succession and even pose some other problems as by this time in the Empire the family of the Keeper is now considered to be very special and there are always plenty of people who are willing to do practically anything to be in our favor. My large family will need much wisdom and strength to sail these waters.

03.11.974 C.R. *Mandie apparently did not do a lot of writing in her journals after the birth of her sixth child. She died before they were all grown. Ken speaks much in his journals about his brothers and sisters. Tim, K. & P.*

Ken

749 – 810 C.R.

05.12.749 C.R. My name is Ken. I began my duties as Keeper and Primate after the parting of my mother Mandie who was the niece of the great Keeper Joan. Joan was my great aunt and her influence as Keeper was the greatest since May, although for entirely different reasons. May was, as everyone knows, the most spiritual of the Keepers to date. She actually was recognized as a wife of the Emperor although the Immortals including the Emperor do not practice any sexual behavior like we mortals do. The obvious reason for this is that they have no need to bear children through the generations since they are Immortal. They say that they do not miss the sexual pleasure because what they have as members of the corporate resurrected bride of the emperor is so much more satisfying, both spiritually and emotionally, that they could not wish for more. Since we do not get to attend their "love feasts," we have no way of affirming this. We take them at their word.

After May, Joan has been considered the greatest of the keepers in the now over 700 years since the line was started by the Immortal Elaine with our ancestress Anna. Joan, like May, did not marry in order to dedicate her life entirely to her work. Joan was great because she had three especially strong abilities. She was exceptional in her appearance before the public; she always made a strong, almost royal, impression. She had considerable administrative ability. She also had the ability to pick outstanding staff members. These staff members not only made the Keeper's office run smoothly but they made the Keeper look even better at her job. I doubt that anyone will ever equal Joan in any one of these abilities, not to mention all three at the same time.

I truthfully do not understand why Elaine appoints some of the Keepers that she does. Speaking only for myself I do not know what particular contribution that I can make to the office. I am not as spiritual as May. Even without the sex it would seem to me to be inappropriate for me to "marry" the Emperor. Make no mistake, I do love Him. I love Him as my Emperor and as the head of a whole new race of Immortal people. I once thought that I might petition to be "adopted" by the Emperor and in that way have a special relationship to His Majesty. Elaine said that the majority of the Immortals are adopted by the Emperor and His Father. I asked her who are the people that are not adopted. She said that these are his blood relatives but they also came to their inheritance in Him by faith just as the adopted ones did. Not completely understanding this, I did not ask any more questions of Elaine on the subject. I abandoned the adoption idea.

I have looked inside myself for some of Joan's strengths. I am not that good with crowds. They frighten me. I often feel that there is someone in the crowd who wants to assassinate me even though I know that Lucius is an effective protector. By the way I am extremely fond of Lucius. He is so gentle and quiet. I do not feel that I am much of an administrator either, and as for picking a staff I haven't a clue. I talked to Elaine about this and she told me that she was confident that I would find my place among the Keepers. I do like the research; the library is quiet. But there has been so much of that done since Anna. She did a lot herself. Mother was strong in research and pretty good with the staff. She dreaded public appearances and giving orders to the staff. At Elaine's insistence Mother finally appointed a Chief of Staff who ran everything for her. We know from her dairies where Mother excelled and I can not do much in that area either.

02.12.750 C.R.   If you have read my mother's journals, you are aware that I have fourteen siblings, all the offspring of my mother, Mandie, and my father, Josh. Mother excelled at having babies fairly late in her life. My father, Josh, was also a very nurturing father and spent a lot of time with us kids while we were growing up while mother was about her duties as Keeper. I have wondered why Elaine has not picked one of my brothers or even one of my sisters as Keeper. They are a varied lot and have many talents between them. I asked Elaine about this just after Mother passed beyond the veil.

"You have been the Keeper Heir since you were born, Ken," she answered me.

"But you can put anyone in the office," I protested.

"I want you as Keeper," she answered.

"May I ask why?"

"Certainly. I believe that you are the man for the job. You will do well. Just follow your heart and don't be concerned," she said.

Elaine is hard to argue with.

"Could I get some of my brothers and sisters to help?" I asked.

"So long as they understand that you are the Keeper," she said.

"I thought I would appoint some of my siblings to do certain things."

"Fine. That is your choice. But not Vice Keeper, that did not work out very well. They can be Assistant to the Keeper if you like, just as long as it is clear that you alone are the Keeper," Elaine repeated.

I told Lucius to refuse all visitors except for emergencies and took a few days to consider my siblings. Being the oldest Chloe and Jason and I have always been particularly close. There is only a year between us. It was two years before Anne and then the twins. Anne always stayed pretty much to herself, she is quite a scholar and a researcher. She helped mother a lot with research and writing. I will definitely make her an Assistant to the Keeper and head librarian. She will love that.

Chloe and Jason can help with public functions as they are both much more out going that I am. That's two more assistants. The twins, Jan and Jean, are rudderless. Right now they wouldn't be good for anything. Perhaps when they are older, if they stay out of trouble. They are both very attractive young women and have a lot of suitors like mother did. But they lack discretion. They were rather spoiled until Preston came along and then they resented not being the babies any longer. Little did they know that there would be eight more after Preston.

Going from the other end, Margaret, Denise and Candace are all too young. Margaret is the baby and she misses mother terribly. Denise and Candace are still in their early studies. There are five tutors here at the residence. All of us brothers and sisters pitch in to comfort Margaret and the other young ones, but Preston spends almost all of his time with them. He is a lot like father. I believe I will leave that alone as long as it works well.

That leaves, going from the top down again, David, Pamela, Roger, Marie and Donald. They are all young adults and fairly close together in age. Marie is like her namesake, our grandmother. She is a great helper. She will be a great helper to me as Keeper. I shall make her Assistant for administration. David and Donald want to pursue their studies in Europe; David in philosophy and Donald in history. I shall help them to do that. That leaves, finally, Pamela and Roger. Roger likes the women too much. He is friendly to everyone, but not particularly ambitious. I will continue to consider him.

Pamela loves children, but she does not attract many men. She is attractive enough but somewhat standoffish around adults. May's childrens' centers are still with us and doing a great work. I will send Pam to work with them as my liaison Assistant; she will love that.

05.22.750 C.R. After I had been Keeper for about a year I had relaxed some about my calling. Elaine appeared early one afternoon.

"Ken, we're going on a trip," she proclaimed as she entered the residence. She always appeared just outside and walked through the door without knocking or being announced. This was her way of respecting my privacy without standing on ceremony. She is, after all, an Immortal Prince and the Imperial Legate in charge of the Keeper's office.

"A trip, mistress?"

"Yes, to the court of the overlord of the Mediterranean."

"Wonderful, wonderful," I replied while trying to think of who that is.

"That's Marco the Centurion," she said as if to read my thoughts. I do not believe that she actually can read my thoughts. It is just that she has been around for such a long time and is a student of human nature.

"Yes, Marco," I replied. "From the Second Testament."

"You know your Scriptures, Ken."

I was flattered. I read these writings over and over again. "Thank you, mistress. Wasn't Marco the one who believed the Emperor when the Emperor's blood relatives would not?"

"You know he is, Ken. Such a show off."

"I do not intend to 'show off', Mistress. It's just that there are so few things that I am good at."

"I thought you were working through that," she answered. See, she can not read minds.

"I am. I am, really."

She smiled. I shut up.

"Actually, Marco is an excellent choice for a ruler as he so readily recognized the importance of authority," Elaine continued after a short while.

I nodded again.

"His faith was actually based on his recognition of authority. He obeyed his superiors and expected his soldiers to obey him. So when he told the Emperor that he did not have to come and heal his servant but to merely say the word, it was because he understood authority. Now he has been given as lot of authority over the very part of the world where he served as a captain of a hundred."

I nodded again.

"If you are ready, Ken, we will go. There is someone else there I want you to meet. He is a Prince in Marco's court."

We went outside where Elaine's escort appeared and we were there in Constantinople or Istanbul as it was once called. The Over-Lord's Dais is just a few miles from the Metropolitan's Dais there.

"My Brother, Marco," Elaine exclaimed. "I haven't seen you since the last Great Feast." She hugged him long and hard.

I was a little surprised. I knew that they had not been mortal at the same time, but they seemed to be very close. Marco hugged her in return with some zest. But I soon discovered that Marco did everything with some zest. Something to do with his lineage.

"Marco, this is our new Keeper, who has been in office about a year now. I brought him to meet Francis," Elaine chimed.

I approached the Over-Lord who was still standing from Elaine's arrival. His considerable court was standing as well. The sky was full of angelic presence and escorts.

"And so you come to us as Legate," Marco said to Elaine as he extended his hand to me.

"And as a sister and a friend," Elaine said smiling her biggest smile.

"I am so glad to meet the new Keeper," Marco said as he shook my hand so hard my shoulder actually hurt.

"Marco, your strength ..." Elaine said.

"Oh, so sorry, young man," the Over-Lord said. "Didn't mean to injure you. Are you O.K.?"

"Yes, my lord, just fine," I said rubbing my shoulder.

He put one hand on that shoulder and it was immediately fine. "So you came to meet the Prince Francis?" he asked.

"Evidently, my lord."

"Evidently! Ha! So she only tells you so much, my young Keeper. No worry, she is the same with us." Then lowering his voice slightly, "always some great secret, you know. But she is delightful."

He nodded expecting agreement so I nodded as well. Elaine just smiled. Do Immortals actually fall in love with each other? No, I know better than that. But this was new to me. I had never seen Elaine so 'delightful.' She must really like Marco. So they do have favorites.

Clasping me on the back Marco led me back to his seat and motioned for me to sit on a nearby stool. This was a high honor for a mortal and I was glad for it.

"Now, let's see," Marco continued as he scanned the area. His court seated themselves. "Where is our brother, Francis?"

"I believe he went to his reserve in Australia," a female prince offered.

"Oh yes, Australia, such interesting animals there," Marco nodded.

"Trieste!" Marco called to a particularly impressive angel just above and in front of the Dais.

The angel swooped down and bowed to the Over-Lord.

"Please go and beg my brother Francis to meet with us here," Marco said.

I thought 'please beg'; this Over-Lord was extremely polite. Again probably his bloodline. In a few minutes Trieste and another escort appeared and Francis stepped onto the Dais. He had a beautiful parrot on one shoulder and a small shaggy black and white monkey in his arms.

"What animals do you bring us today?" Marco asked. Francis gave the particular names of the animals both technical and common. I was fascinated.

"No, my brother," Marco continued. "I mean what do you call them, what do they answer to?"

"Oh, of course, this in Arthur," he pointed to the multicolored bird on his shoulder. "And this baby has not been named yet. His mother was injured and I have adopted him." He caressed the infant monkey who was very still.

"Say hello to the Over-Lord, Arthur," Francis said.

"Hello, your Excellency," the parrot said. "It is a great pleasure to be at your Dais today. I trust that the Over-Lord is quite pleased with all that is around him this beautiful day," the parrot continued.

I was amazed. My jaw dropped open. Elaine clapped and said,

"Marvelous, Francis. Arthur is absolutely marvelous."

Then she said to me. "Francis has expanded the talking abilities of many animals. He is quite fond of them all."

"Mistress," I said softly. She leaned in my direction. "Is this Immortal Francis from the Italian town of Assisi?"

"Smart, Ken. You have guessed it. He is the great champion of animals."

Now I knew who she had brought me to meet. Francis sat down on the other side of me and handed me the little monkey without speaking a word to me. I caressed it and loved it. The tiny creature almost appeared to purr like a cat.

"You like the monkey?" the parrot asked me.

I nodded before I could catch my own surprise. What had Elaine said? "Expanded the talking abilities?" I should think so. This parrot seems capable of a conversation. I decided to explore this right there in front of the Over-Lord and his entire court.

"Yes. How about you?" I asked the parrot. "Do you like monkeys?"

"Yes, they are fine," he answered and continued, "we are all God's creatures, children of the Emperor, but I generally prefer birds."

The entire court chuckled. I was dumfounded once again.

Francis leaned forward and said to me, "Yes, he can actually carry on a conversation. And I see that you like animals."

"Yes, my lord, I do. Very much. They are so innocent and pure. Don't you think?"

"Indeed I do."

Then every prince on the Dais had to speak to the parrot who was passed from arm to arm. He readily accepted each new arm and chatted to everyone who talked to him. This went on for quite some time. I just held the little monkey while he took a short nap.

Later Francis held out his hands to retrieve his monkey. Reluctantly I gave it back. He saw my hesitation and said, "After the meal we should talk, Keeper."

I nodded as I remembered how hungry I was. I learned that the Over-Lord Marco of the Mediterranean had many chefs and outstanding meals. I also learned that Francis was a vegetarian.

"These are just domestic cows and birds," Marco said in an attempt to get Frances to try a meat dish. At the word 'birds' Arthur the parrot squawked loudly. I felt strange so I looked around and noticed that the entire court did not know just how to respond. Some smiled but did not laugh. Others acted as if they had not heard Marco's remark or the squawk.

I waited for what seemed to be a very long time after the meal until Francis was ready to talk. By the time I saw him walking across Marco's beautiful garden, I was sleepy so I stood and tried to be very much awake.

"I am so sorry," Francis said as he approached me. Let us get you a cold drink. He motioned to one of the mortal waiters who brought me some wonderful lemonade. It was cold and it revived me.

"I remember when I was mortal how a big luncheon would make me so sleepy afterwards, especially on a warm spring afternoon like this one. There now, are you ready for a little talk?"

"Absolutely, my lord."

"You are just going to have to call me Francis. May I call you Ken, Keeper?"

"Yes, of course. And thank you Francis."

We got along great from the start. Later when talking to a friend about my first meeting with Francis, my friend asked how I felt when he handed me the little monkey and did not speak a word. I said that this did not even occur to me at the time. Actually any one that Francis hands a defenseless infant animal to should be honored with the trust extended. I guess that somewhere inside I actually felt like that.

"You see, Ken, I would like to take you to see my animal friends. I feel like you would enjoy it tremendously. I loved animals as a mortal, but here in the reign it is so much better. They no longer have their natural fear and ferocity that they had before. And I am able to do so much with them."

"Yes, the parrot, Arthur," I began.

"Yes, he is one. The Emperor has allowed me the power to actually improve some of them. If you come with me, you will see."

I was ready to start right then.

"So, Ken, I will come to your house in about a week and we will plan our travels. Is that good with you?"

"Of course," I said. I wondered how I would wait that long.

[N.D.] Almost exactly a week after I met Francis, I was reading in my parlor. I find the library too dark to stay in. When Lucius suddenly appeared and announced, "A large party is approaching, Keeper, a Prince from Italy."

I bounded out onto the lawn. I knew it was Francis. His escort was not particularly large and it arrived and stood on my lawn. There was a short delay before Francis stepped through the portal. He, of course, had animals with him and they were mortal. There was Arthur the parrot, a baby giraffe named Twigga who was at least 8 feet tall and a beautiful red Irish setter dog named Ralph.

"Ken, my friend," Francis began. We embraced and Arthur moved to my shoulder.

"Hi!" Arthur said softly as he was standing next to my ear.

"Hi, yourself," I answered. I expected more but all the bird said was, "Um Huum," followed by a slight rattling sound in his throat. Francis smiled.

"He likes you, really," Francis said.

I nodded.

Arthur rode gently on my shoulder. He did not dig his claws in too deeply.

Francis introduced me to the giraffe and the dog. The giraffe nodded repeatedly and the dog extended a paw to shake. When I took his paw and shook it, he chuckled out loud, "Heh, heh, heh, heh." It seemed to be a friendly laugh.

"May they run?" Francis asked.

"Yes, yes of course. Tell them to feel free," I answered.

"You just have," Francis answered.

The giraffe took off and the dog scampered to catch up with the long legged juvenile. Arthur left my shoulder with a flap of his wings and caught them and landed on the giraffe's back. And they were off running in large circles around my garden while skillfully missing the flower beds and shrubbery. I thought them to be very considerate animals.

"Arthur will ride on Ralph's back when Twigga is not around," Francis said. "But he always chooses the fastest ride."

I learned that Twigga was Swahili for giraffe. But Francis had made it this giraffe's proper name. I wondered who had named Ralph.

Francis asked for a table and I had one brought out. He unfolded maps from a large pouch carried by an angel who was always at his right hand. He called him Genile.

I had no idea of the number and sizes of Francis' animal preserves. I remember one report by one of my ancestors but I had no idea about the size of Francis' 'reserves' as he called them. We planned an initial trip that would take just over six weeks. I hurriedly considered how to rearrange my schedule with as few 'pop backs' as necessary and enlisted the aid of my best administrator sibling. Finally, we rested and I had some drinks brought for us. I was expecting Elaine to drop by at any time. Arthur landed on Francis' shoulder and whispered something in his ear.

"Some drinks for my friends?" Francis asked gesturing towards the animals.

"Oh, yes, I am so sorry," I said. "I thought they would help themselves with the ponds."

"He says they don't taste very good."

"No doubt." I ordered three containers full of fresh water for them. They all drank heartedly. The bird and the giraffe drank very politely. Ralph drank long and loud. When he finished, he approached me.

"Than Kweu," I heard the dog say.

Still taken by surprise I answered, "You are most welcome." I could see that I had a lot to learn.

"Each type of animal has different strengths," Francis said. "The parrot, of course, is a good talker." He thought for a few seconds. "And wait until you see some others," Francis said patting my knee. "Just wait until you see them. Wait until you meet the dolphins, oh yes, the dolphins."

"Very smart, the dolphins," said Arthur. "Very smart."

That night I thought of the words from the sacred scriptures, "The wolf and the lamb shall feed together, and the lion shall eat straw like the bullock . . . They shall not hurt nor destroy in all my holy mountain," and I promptly looked these words up.

[N.D.] In contrast to the enormous animal parks that Francis oversees in the world are the thousands of smaller ones in the midst of human neighborhoods throughout the world. When I say human neighborhoods, I mean places where people live both Immortals and mortals. In most areas the Immortals have their own enclave which spreads out from the local prince's Dais and blends with the homes of the mortals in the area. However, there is a place in almost every area where this blending meets that is what you could call a mixed neighborhood or blending area. Such neighborhoods can be in the city, the small town or even in the country areas; mortals and Immortals living sometimes next to each other. Although there is never any doubt who is the mortal and who is the Immortal, the fact remains that most of the Immortals are not rulers. They evidently did not do anything during their mortality to warrant being a ruler of any kind during the present great Reign. Some of them even keep up the homes they had as mortals. These Immortals are not required to do this. They can live in the Palace beyond the veil or even off world. But those who want to can live among us. There is even the strange case in some instances where a mortal family continues to occupy the house that their ancestors have always lived in next door to an Immortal that their ancestors knew in mortal life.

In many places, but especially near these blending areas Francis has established animal reserves where people can bring their animal friends to play and frolic. Sometimes these parks are quite large. These animal friends were once called "pets." The only thing about the animal friends is that there are no Immortal animals; they are all mortal and die like the mortal humans in a matter of years.

Regarding this I have found Francis' animal friend Ralph somewhat unusual. One day Francis told me that Ralph was nearly 40 years old.

"Do all the animals live such long lives under the Reign?" I asked.

"Not really," Francis answered. "I have extended Ralph's life, but he will die one day as well. There is only so much that I can do. I keep some of his puppies around so he can live on in them."

"I see." Or at least I think I did.

03.11.756 C.R. The residence has changed. Some say that I have made it a menagerie; there are a lot of animals here. It has gone from many children to many animals. All of the animals are well trained; they train very quickly and easily. They never leave droppings in the wrong places and they are not destructive to people or property. Francis says that this is because their natural instinct of fear of humans has been removed and they no longer have to worry about food or survival. The animals no longer eat each other, they eat fruits and vegetables instead. Animals raised for human consumption are raised on farms for that purpose and do not seem to be aware of their end; this is an obvious mercy. There are not many species of these.

I was surprised at the number of Immortals who have animal friends now during the reign. Most of them are near replicas of the beloved "pets" they had as mortals. They simply pick parents and allow them to breed. Then these Immortals touch the mother and bless the offspring with certain characteristics which cause them to be born an almost exact replica of their beloved departed pet. The mortals are less picky; they usually just chose the young animal they want and take it home to raise it as a companion. I have heard of cases, however, where a mortal will ask an Immortal friend who lives nearby to bless a mother animal for them in order to get a near replica of one of their own departed pets. The Immortal animal lover is more than willing to do this for a mortal neighbor. I asked Francis why there are no immortal animals and he said that this is not granted to them. However, most everyone seems quite happy with their blessed animal offspring.

Francis even has some angels who help care for the animals. They all seem to be from the lowest rank of angels like Lucius. Some of them are smaller than Lucius. I assume that they take this form intentionally in order not to scare the animals or that may be their created form.

I asked Francis why he thinks he is more remembered for his love of animals than for the religious order that bore his name. He says it is because Immortals during this reign are more interested in their animals than in an ancient religious order. There are many Immortal brothers from the order who help Francis with his animal work.

[N.D.] Francis was correct; I was very impressed with the dolphins. They live at the aquatic reserves. They speak human languages fluently. They are obviously the smartest of the animals. But my fascination is not reserved to dolphins.

All serpents now have legs; there are none who crawl on their bellies now. That was the result of an ancient curse that the Emperor has lifted during the reign.

I love lions. They are so gentle now. I have moved several to the residence where I have had to construct appropriate dwellings and exercise lawns for them and the other animals. There is plenty of room at the reserves for all of them, it is just that I want to have many of them around me at the residence. If the next keeper does not want them, they will not be forsaken. Francis and his brothers and angels will take care of everything.

[N.D.] My favorite lion pair, they seem to pair for life with one mate now, is Casper and Grace. They live with me here; I mean they really live with me. They have the run not only of the property but of the house as well. Casper is a medium size male with a great golden mane and Grace is a perfect match. They eat lots of soy beans and other grains. They are gentle and intelligent. They can speak a few words and understand almost anything in the universal language. They aim to please. Nearby children come to see them and they ride them all around on their backs. If they attempt to enter the house when mortals are here who might fear them, Lucius blocks the way and forbids them. They obey angels absolutely as do all the animals. Sometimes I think they see angels that we do not. I have always thought that it was a matter of which angels appeared, not a matter of our ability to see them, but that may not be the case.

[N.D.] Angels and animals would seem to be at the opposite end of the wonderful creation spectrum. In other words, we are most likely to think of angels as very intelligent and eternal super beings and animals as stupid and very short lived. Some of this is, of course, true and actually we mortals are closer to the animals than we are to the angels. But I have found some similarities between the angels and the animals. In the first place, neither of them is as confused as we mortals tend to be. They both know who they are and accept it absolutely. We mortals are frequently trying to be what we are not; we are either trying to be more than we are or we are acting as less than we are. We are either grandiose or we are debasing ourselves. Not true with angels or animals. Because they do not try to be anything that they are not, this gives them both, angels and animals, a sort of built-in dignity that we often miss as mortals. This is strange since we mortals are actually made in the image of the Emperor. But somewhere along the line we have lost something. When our original parents lost their favor with the Emperor and His Father, we all fell out of favor with them. Of course, the Immortals have regained this favor. Until we discover our chances of regaining favor, I often prefer the company of angels and animals. I have never seen Lucius angry, embarrassed, sad or ecstatic. He may miss out on some of the joy, but he is certainly spared the sorrow that we often experience. The animals from time to time get to share our sorrows. Sometimes they are abused in spite of the present laws.

But even then they bear it with dignity. Now they are free to be our friends. Francis and I find them to be fine friends indeed. When I want to move some of my animal friends from a preserve to my residence, I have found that Lucius will do it for me.

The first time I confronted this problem Lucius informed me in his own way that he could help. Actually, I wanted to move Casper and Grace from Francis' preserve in Africa to my residence. I had asked Francis about this and he had agreed. I told the Lions about this and they acted very excited. They had never been out of the preserve that they had been born in. I began to make arrangements with a local transporter to send them to Atlanta by ship. The trip was to take over three weeks and I hoped that they would not get seasick. I was traveling openly so it was known who I am and Lucius was visible just above and behind me. The transport man was temporarily called away on another matter so I sat there in his garden drinking some tea.

Lucius moved directly in front of me. I thought that it was a summons to go somewhere. When he did not speak, I asked. "What? Lucius, what is it?"

"Keeper, I can move the animals for you," he responded.

What a marvelous idea. Why had I not thought of it? After all, Francis travels with animals and his angel opens a portal for them.

"Great, Lucius," I said. "I don't know why I did not ask you in the first place."

"That is quite all right, Keeper," he answered. "You and I have not encountered this before."

When the transporter returned, I thanked him and apologized. "You see, sir," I said. "I had failed to ask my angel here if he could do it. But he can. So sorry, I will be glad to recommend you to other mortals."

He was polite, but I could tell that he was a little angry about me getting his hopes up about the opportunity of serving the Keeper. That would probably increase his business. I really should be more careful.

[N.D.] As it worked out, I ended up by returning to the residence with Casper and Grace, a pair of ostriches named Bwana and Binti which is Swahili for Mister and Miss, a gorgeous Parrot named Bertrum who talks almost as good as Francis' friend, Arthur, a pair of Zebra named Horace and Herminie, a hippopotamus named Pounder, and the tiny black and white monkey that I held when I first met Francis' named, Kidogo, which means 'small.' He is grown now but he will never be very large. Francis had named the monkey and the other animals had been named by the mortal game helpers which Francis keeps at that preserve. When we arrived without warning in the middle of the lawn in my front garden, it was quite a surprise to my staff.

"Everyone just stay calm," I shouted. "There is no reason to get excited." My librarian's little highland terrier named Gordon came running at full speed half barking and half trying to form some words. The animals who had arrived with me were still recovering from their first instantaneous journey and, as it turned out, they had never met a highland terrier. They were all just about to bolt when I commanded, "Hold it! Freeze. Every animal just stay where you are!" They all did as I ordered. "Gordon, that means you as well!" I bellowed. Gordon stopped. "Sit," I said. Gordon sat and the new arrivals looked at me with a look of great thankfulness. We took a few minutes for them all to get acquainted and I talked to my head gardener Jimmy about where to house them all. It was not too long before I redesigned my garden to accommodate animal visitors from all over.

"A highland terrier?" Bertrum said. "Where do they come from, Keeper?" Then he cocked his head expecting an answer from me.

"Uh, Scotland, I believe, Bertrum."

"Yes, yes, of course," Gordon managed to say. It was part growl and part speaking. Terriers don't take well to speech even during the Reign.

All in all I have to give my gardener Jimmy credit for being both creative and patient with my new found love of animals. However, after about a week he came to the library for me quite disturbed.

"Sir, Keeper, really I must . . .," he began.

"What is it, Jimmy?"

"The Hippo, er, Pounder. He has ruined our small pond. He has eaten the water lilies, flowers and all, and he has made a mud bath out of half of the pond. What am I to do, sir?"

"Now, Jimmy, please calm down. I am afraid that is Pounder's nature. As a matter of fact, we will probably have to enlarge the pond and put up with the muddiness."

"But I thought you enjoyed the lilies," he said.

"I do, and so does my staff. We will put in a smaller pond in the back for the lilies and enlarge the front one for Pounder. That is his native habitat, you know? A pond."

"How will we keep him out of the new pond?" Jimmy asked.

"I will ask him to stay out. He is a nice fellow; he will cooperate," I said.

"Oh, it's that simple then?" Jimmy asked.

"Of course, let's go talk to Pounder now."

We went to the front pond where I must admit that the Hippo had made a glorious mess.

"Pounder," I called.

The big animal surfaced in the water where before only his eyes could be seen breaking the surface.

"Siiiiir?" he said in a deep bass tone.

"Can you come here?" I asked pointing to the shoreline.

He came directly to us and started to emerge from the water. I motioned for him to stay with his massive legs still in the water.

"Pounder, we are going to enlarge this pond for you," I said.

"Goooood," was his answer. Then, "I caaaaan heeelp."

"Yes, fine," I said. I presumed that he would act as a mighty earth mover. But I left poor Jimmy to discover that.

"Now I want you to work with Jimmy here on this," I said.

"Yeeees, Jiiimy. Niiiice maaaan," he said. Jimmy seemed surprised but pleased.

"Now, Pounder," I said. "We are going to build another pond around behind my house," I pointed. "It is for flowers. I am asking you to not go there. Will you help us with that?"

"Yeeeeess, Keeeeeper," he answered.

"Does he really understand?" Jimmy asked.

"What are you going to do for me now?" I asked the Hippo.

"Nooooo swimmmm iiin oooootheeer pooond," he answered.

"There, you see, Jimmy," I said. "Everything will be fine." Jimmy seemed to be convinced.

"If you would like for me to help communicate with these, I would be glad to," Bertrum said to Jimmy. I had not noticed him follow us from the house. He was riding on the back of the terrier. They had become great friends. Bertrum would much rather ride than take the effort to fly.

"Uh, yea, great," Jimmy said a little surprised to be approached by a Parrot.

Bertrum shouted something to Pounder in another language. The Hippo rose up out of the water and shook his head vigorously. We didn't ask about this.

[N.D.] This afternoon during my tea break in the rear garden Bwana and Binti approached me. It seems that they like to race. They shifted from one long leg to the other as they stood in front of me. They started to speak, but it just came out as a series of shrieks. Then Bertrum flew in and landed on Binti's back. This got my attention as

Bertrum is usually too lazy to fly and I have never seen him on the back of another bird, even the ostriches. Bwana and Bertrum exchanged a series of peeps and squeaks, then Berturm said something to Binti and she moved closer to me so that the parrot was practically in my face.

"They have a concern, sir," Bertrum said politely.

"And that is . . .?" I said.

"They like to race. Actually they need to race, you know, race and run."

"I have noticed that," I answered.

"They have set up a sort of a course around the residence, but they frequently step on some flowers or ruin one thing or another. So, they have stopped running as much."

"So, what do they want?" I asked.

"Well, if it does not offend you," Bertrum went on cautiously. "They would like to know if they can run outside the residence grounds, and if you could bring some more of their kind here to run with them. They, realize, Keeper, that they are asking for a lot and if it is not possible they . . . "

I interrupted at this point. "No, that is not too much," I said.

The ostriches jumped around and clucked excitedly and Bertrum almost fell off of Binti's back.

"Aawwwk! Steady now, steady!" Bertrum shouted. They calmed down a little.

"I'll tell you what," I said. "I will send for two more couples and we will lay out a great circling path for them to run on."

This time Binti was careful not to throw Bertrum in her excitement.

Jimmy was not thrilled with his new assignment, but he got the path laid out and I fixed it with the local civil administrator so that the community was ready to see 'the ostrich races' on a daily basis. The only complication we have had is that the local children and pets love to join in the race. So far no mortals have been injured and it is a great thrill to the community. Of course, the ostriches always win so that does not count. The runner up is considered to be the winner of the race. It is usually an especially fast young man and sometimes one of the faster pet dogs. My residence is pretty much of a menagerie, but everyone seems to enjoy it and no one better than I.

10.17.759 C.R. Today I had a most unusual report come to me and I have had to refer it to the Dais. It is a little known fact that Elaine has her own small Dais not far from Henry Sawyer's. She occasionally uses it to deal with matters within Buckhead. There are even a few under rulers for her there. I decided to take this matter directly to Elaine. One of my jackals, yes I brought in two pairs of jackals to my menagerie, sat muttering at my front door for quite a while. Lucius shooed him away several times, but he just kept coming back. Finally my cook brought it to my attention. I went out to see the animal. At first she seemed surprised that I had actually come. Then she said in her usual whiny yammering tone, "It's jus not right, eggs-cellen-see. Jus not right."

"What's not right?" I asked as I squatted down by her.

"They hurt tham, eggs-cellen-see. They hurt tham." Suddenly she was joined by her mate who had been waiting in the bushes.

"Tha cow-herds, Keeeepr," he said. "They hurt the pettts."

I was beginning to catch on.

"Izz it nut aginst the coode?" the male asked.

"What are your names" I asked. "I'm sorry I have forgotten."

"I em Jeth," the female said. "He em Raa ."

"Alright Ra, Jeth, you are telling me that some mortal is abusing some of the pet animal friends near here?"

"Yaz, yaz,' they both answered.

"Lucius, get Bertrum," I said. In a few seconds Lucius was back with the parrot who was quite shaken by his ride. Lucius had traveled the angel corridor to get the bird and then flashed immediately back to my side.

"Awaaaaakk!" Bertrum said shaking his head as though to clear his thoughts.

"Is he all right, Lucius"

"Yes, Keeper."

"Why did you bring him back that way?"

"It is my way, Keeper. Did I do wrong?" Lucius asked.

"No, no, of course not," I answered. I was not quite accustomed to dealing with so broad a range of creatures.

With the parrot's help I pieced together the entire story. It seems that there is a group of young men with a few young women in Buckhead that although not in open rebellion do not have enough to do and they started tormenting some of the pet dogs and even some cats. At first it was simple enough, hiding their food or making them beg for it. Then they started hurting the animals and seem to get some sort of perverted satisfaction out of that. Some of the animals have been partially crippled and one has apparently lost the vision in one eye as a result of this treatment. Since the local animal pets are not improved by the Immortal Francis, they can not express themselves like the members of my menagerie can.

The jackals have taken some tours of the community and have somehow been 'told' about this treatment. The male, Raa, was afraid to approach me but Jeth just could not hold back. When Raa saw that I was willing to listen, he came out of hiding.

"So, Elaine, that is the entire story," I said as I stood before her Dais with a jackal on either side of me and Bertrum on my shoulder.

"Ken, you were right to come to me. But I would have met you at your residence," Elaine said.

"Well, since this is an official matter, I thought that I should present it officially, mistress," I said.

"I can deal with that," she answered smiling. "It is against the Imperial code to abuse any created being. And we, the princes, think that it is terrible."

"Now, tell them to tell us through the parrot, it will be more efficient that way, where and when this activity can be observed and we will put a stop to it," Elaine instructed.

Bertrum spoke quickly to the jackals and reported to us in clear language. It seems that this activity occurs at irregular times and they could not pin point a time and place to catch these pet abusers. Then Bertrum told us that all four jackals would go into the community and send us word through some of my own sparrows. The sparrows would report to the parrot who would inform me and Lucius and Lucius would get Elaine or one of her under governors and we would flash directly to the scene. That sounded rather round about to me and to Elaine but we agreed to try it. They cautioned us that it would most likely be in the early evening hours.

[N.D.] It was only two days before the whole string of contacts worked perfectly. Elaine and Lucius and I were on the scene in no time. Two dogs, barely more than puppies where being mercilessly gouged with sticks. Our appearance was quite startling there in that dirty alley. Of course, they stopped their activity immediately and the young woman even started stroking one of the pets very lovingly. As soon as we arrived, Raa and Jeth emerged from the shadows. When these young people saw the jackals, they were obviously frightened. The jackals made good use of this by growling deeply and narrowing their eyes to look as threatening as possible.

Elaine saw their fear and said, "Perhaps I should just let these jackals have their way."

"No, mistress, no, please. We did not really mean any harm," the young woman said.

"But you have. You have hurt these animal friends and others," I said angrily.

One young man recognized me. "Keeper, Excellency, we did not start out to hurt them, please."

"Nevertheless you did," I said. I could barely hold my temper. I approached the two puppies and scratched them behind the ears. They received it with joy and seemed forgiving towards everyone as they are so prone to do.

Elaine spoke directly to the puppies and the jackals. "Go get every animal who has been harmed by these mortals." She snapped her fingers and a dozen of her angels appeared. These mortals cowered in fear. Elaine continued, "If they can not come on their own, bring them," she commanded the angels. Then she snapped her fingers again and we were all at her Dais. Within half an hour every abused animal and every abuser stood before her.

Elaine touched and repaired every animal. They were all very affectionate and seemed most thankful. She sentenced all the youths to community service and threatened them with harsh judgments if they failed in their duties. The terms of their punishments were left open and they were commanded to appear before her every month. Her patrol would see to that. Then she had the guardians, some might call them owners, of these animal friends brought before her and charged them to better care for them. They were duly impressed and I expect that they will not forget this. Then she went to the Metropolitan and asked him to issue a public directive that no animal friends were to be abused.

12.02.765 C.R. I have decided to open shelters for needy animal friends everywhere and to send spies far and near to uncover instances of abuse. I have decided that birds will probably be the best spies. Bertrum now has three assistants to help take the reports from these birds. I have also had Lucius coordinate with the angel patrols in this project. The Immortal Francis is quite pleased and has given his full support.

[N.D.] Last night at about three A.M. Lucius woke me. I was very fast asleep and it must have taken him some time as he is always very gentle when awakening anyone in the family. In my dreams I remember feeling like someone was washing my face with a very soft damp washcloth like mother used to do. It was Lucius stroking me face with his 'hands.' When I opened my eyes, he was very close.

"Uh. Lucius. What is it?" I asked.

"Keeper, Chloe has been attacked in London during a speech," he said softly.

I was instantly awake. "Where is the Legate?" I asked.

"She will arrive here momentarily," the angel answered.

I jumped up and got dressed. As I was tying my shoes, Elaine appeared in my room.

"Ken, my dear boy," she said. She came directly towards me. I had been giving myself a hard time for using Chloe so much at speaking engagements. She was so good at it and loved doing it. She was probably the most recognized of any of the fifteen of us for her public appearances. She always represented me exactly and never gave the appearance of having any office herself even though she was my Assistant for public affairs. I was blaming myself for her hurt and wondering how bad it was or whether Elaine or another prince would fix everything. Elaine touched my head and I immediately felt calmer.

"This is not your fault," she said immediately.

"What is there to know, mistress?" I asked.

"She was speaking at an early morning rally in London, talking about the history of the Reign and where we are now in it when someone threw a large knife at her, a knife designed for throwing, it pierced her exactly through the heart." I blanched white.

"Easy, easy now, Ken. The prince of Chelsea, Mary Pearl, has removed the blade and effected some healing. Do not be concerned. Are you ready?"

"Yes, mistress." We were in London. The crowd was being held back by the mortal police. Chloe was sitting on the platform that she had been speaking from. She looked at me and smiled. She still looked shaken and pale. Several Immortals where holding her in an upright position. Elaine had brought her full escort as Legate in order to purposely make a large impression, and together with the various other escorts the sky was thick with angels. The Metropolitan of London was there. They were all fussing over my dear sister. The culprit was being held just in front of the stage, a makeshift Dais, by two angels. He was angry and snarling. I talked to Chloe for a few minutes and she still seemed to have a hard time catching her breath. The Immortal who had helped her, Prince Mary Pearl, seemed a little concerned. After a few minutes Elaine motioned for me to join the Metropolitan's examination of the culprit. I listened.

The Metropolitan of London is one Alfred Hotchkins. He is big and burly and still speaks with his mortal accent. The man who attacked my sister freely acknowledged his guilt and did not ask for mercy.

"Recommendations?" the Metropolitan asked of me. "She is your sister, Keeper."

"Put him out of his misery," I said angrily.

To my surprise he did just that instantly. He barely pointed with his finger and the man dropped dead. Some mortals removed the body. Later I wished that I had taken this more seriously. Could the man have been reformed? What was his motive? I learned not to speak hastily when ask for an opinion on judgment from an Imperial Prince.

Elaine and I took Chloe back to her London residence, but she was not quite right.

"Elaine, what is it?" I asked. "Is there something that you can do?"

"Possibly. But I don't think that I am to do it," she answered.

"Then what?" I asked.

"We don't know everything always," she answered. "You think and meditate on it for a while. Meanwhile let her rest, that will probably help."

I agreed.

"Ken," Chloe called to me just before she dropped to sleep.

I hurried to her side. She still had that same sweet smile. "Why? Who was he?"

"I didn't ask," I answered. She looked at me quizzically. I encouraged her to rest. She would have forgiven the man and tried to rehabilitate him. I hoped she wouldn't ask anymore.

08.17.777 C.R. Chloe did not improve any over the next week and a half. She did not complain, but I felt responsible. Elaine was gone to the other side. I finally decided that I had to go to the Emperor himself on the matter. I went to the Metropolitan Alfred Hotchkins and he arranged an audience.

I expected enormous crowds and a long wait before I could speak to the Emperor. This was not the case. I arrived in a beautiful room overlooking the capital with only Lucius to keep me company. I sat in a nice chair near a window and Lucius hovered contentedly. After about ten or fifteen minutes Lucius dropped to the floor and bowed deeply. I still did not see or hear anything, but I got down on my knees and faced the doors opposite the windows. I would never ignore a clue from Lucius. In a moment the doors actually opened and the Emperor walked in by himself. The doors shut behind him. I looked down then I stole a glance as he approached. He walked casually but purposefully like he had nothing to do, but whatever he did do would be full of authority. His robe was white and plain. As he approached, I looked down again. Then I saw his feet in his golden sandals. I saw the scars on the top of his feet between the bones. I felt his hand under my chin raising my face to his. He was smiling and I was overwhelmed. Here was the epitome of love. Here was peace. Here was eternity in the flesh. Here was the Emperor. We looked at each other for a minute or so. The room vanished from my consciousness. It felt like I understood everything, everything about Chloe and me and about the whole world itself although I could not explain a thing. Finally, he sat on a chair and motioned for me to sit facing him. Then he spoke.

"Ken, son of Amanda."

"Yes, Majesty." That was all I could say.

I felt personally recognized. He said my name. He said mother's name, her real name. I felt that he knew me; he knew us; he knew everything that we ever thought or did. He was in no hurry. I wanted to choose my words carefully. Finally, I managed to say,

"My sister, Chloe, Majesty . . . "

"She is not completely well." He said.

"No, Sire."

"What do you want me to do?"

What an incredible question from the Lord of all.

Then it struck me. I remembered Marco.

"Just say the word, Sire, and she will be well and strong."

"You have learned well, young Ken. She is well and strong. Come, walk with me now," the Emperor said.

I did not doubt for one second that Chloe was wonderfully fine back in London from that second on. I walked for over an hour with the Emperor in his private gardens and I have never been the same since.

Chloe has spoken for me many times now since her restoration and she never experiences any fear.

[N.D.] I was reading over some of Joan's journals this morning when Bertrum flew into the library and landed on his perch that I keep for him there.

"Awk! Abuse Keeper. Abuse," he said as he moved from side to side on his perch as he does when he is very upset.

"Where, Bertrum?" I asked.

"Borneo, Keeper. They beat the donkeys without mercy," he answered.

"Are the donkeys there pulling vehicles for them?" I asked.

"Yes, Keeper. But they pull as hard as they can until they are exhausted. Why beat them?" he asked.

"There is no reason for that," I said. "Lucius!"

Lucius was at my side and we were gone. Lucius knew when to bring a small contingent of Francis' patrol, so we arrived at a silver mine in Borneo with four patrol angels, myself, Lucius, Bertrum and Alan, my gamekeeper.

Bertrum had taken to this kind of travel right off, but Alan did not. Perhaps it was because Bertrum was accustomed to flying. I wanted Alan with me on this mission, but I also knew that while he was recovering from the trip, the offenders would certainly stop their abuse of my animal friends and possibly even make a run for it. I wanted to catch them in the act, so I told Lucius to take us to a place nearby where we could observe and I took my binoculars with me. At this request Lucius departed for a few seconds and returned. I knew that he was checking out the situation without mortals because he could be in a place without appearing. If we were with him, he would have to place us immediately as we could not become invisible or wait in the 'in between' during the trip.

"Ready, Keeper," Lucius announced. "I have chosen a place just up the hill where you can look down on them." He glanced briefly at my binoculars. I never asked how Lucius knew exactly where Bertrum was talking about as the coordination between the animals and the angels is usually pretty good. We emerged at this place just up the hill and I assured Alan that he was still alive and uninjured. As I watched, I saw the cruelty that Bertrum's 'agents' had reported. There were several parrots screeching at the men from the trees. Probably part of Bertrum's network. I did not have to watch for long before I was anxious to get down there; these small animals were suffering terribly. There were four teams of six donkeys each just outside the mine entrance.

"Are there any more in the mine?" I asked Lucius.

"Yes, Keeper. Two teams," he answered. "But they can come out here."

"Good. Take us down there," I said. Alan begged to run down and meet us there. I wish he would learn to travel with the angels. We appeared right next to the teams in front of the mine. They were all quite startled.

"Do you know the punishment for mistreating these animals?" I asked.

They all looked dumbstruck.

"Sir, we, that is, they . . ." one man, apparently a foreman, stuttered.

"No excuses," I said. They were all looking at the angels. Bertrum had taken his perch on my shoulder. From there he squawked to the surrounding parrots who answered in kind.

"He says he has witnesses," I said nodding towards my shoulder. "You have been mistreating these small loyal burden bearers."

"He? You mean that bird?" the foreman asked.

"Yes, that bird," I answered.

Before I could continue, Bertrum spoke. "You are a cruel and unfeeling man," he said.

All the men looked surprised. "Did you teach him to say that?" the foreman asked.

"No. He says what he thinks," I answered.

"Oh, get serious," the foreman said. He looked at the other men and they all laughed.

"You won't laugh when the Keeper is through with you," Bertrum said.

"The Keeper?" the foreman said. His face turned very serious.

"Sir, are you the Keeper, er, Keith?" he asked.

"Ken, Ken is my name," I answered. "And I am the Keeper. And this parrot is of the improved variety. And these are real angels from the patrol of the Immortal Francis. And you are all in deep trouble."

They all turned very sober and hung their heads.

"Since I am not an Immortal, I can not judge you," I said. "But I am sending for Francis," I nodded to Lucius and one of the patrol angels left. "We will wait right here until he comes."

After a few minutes the foreman spoke, "Sir, my men are thirsty. Can they get a drink?" he asked.

"No," I said. "But they can release the animals and take them to water."

They released the donkeys leaving their whips on the ground where they had dropped them. By then the other two teams had emerged from the mine and had been quickly informed by the foreman. After all the animals had a drink, the men started to drink from the troughs.

"Stop," I said. "No drinking of any kind."

"But, Sir, that is cruel," the foreman said.

"You should certainly know about that," I answered him.

Francis arrived with another larger escort in a few minutes. The foreman got down on his knees and the other men followed. Francis inspected each of the little burros stroking them softly and speaking softly into each of their ears. Then he turned to the men.

"Why?" he asked.

The foreman answered. "Excellency, unless we apply the whip they will not work. Our employer requires so many tons of ore a day. We have no choice."

"I do not believe you," Francis said. "A little gentle urging and they will pull your wagons. They are glad for the work."

Silence.

"And your employer? Where is he?" Francis asked.

"At the home office," the foreman said.

Francis instructed some of his escort and they vanished to return in a minute with a well dressed man who was obviously quite frightened.

"You are over these men?" Francis asked.

"Yes, Excellency," the man answered.

"Did you know that they beat the animals?" Francis asked.

The man looked surprised. "Excellency?"

"Yes, they abuse these animals. Do you know the Imperial code?" Francis asked.

The man seemed befuddled.

"Then listen clearly and I shall tell you all that you need to know before I lay punishment upon you," Francis said.

"Firstly, it is against the code for you to treat these animals with cruelty. Secondly, I am Francis the friend of all animals and I have the authority of an Over-Lord-At-Large in these matters. Thirdly, this will not be allowed to continue."

Still a stunned silence. By this time the local Over-Lord and his escort had arrived. He and Francis embraced and talked briefly. There was no doubt as to their unity. The local Over-Lord nodded to Francis and stepped back. All of these men were now assembled in front of them.

"This is what will happen," Francis announced. "First, these animals are taken from you along with the reserves in that pen." At this several angels approached the animals and disappeared with them. "They were taken to my reserve for sick or injured animals in Brazil."

"You," Francis pointed to the executive, "will be fined heavily for your lack of action in this matter." An amount was announced which received a severe wince from the man. It obviously hit him where it hurt.

"You men," Francis pointed to the foreman and the drivers, "will pull these carts yourselves for 30 days for 12 hours a day. No animal help will be allowed. The company will just have to bear this loss and replace the animals as well. And you will not slacken in your efforts or worse will happen to you."

"But Excellency," the foreman complained. "These carts are very heavy."

"I know," Francis answered, "as you are about to find out. And you mister executive, these particular animals will never be returned to you. They are honorably retired."

Again a wince from the company man. Silence prevailed among the other men for some time. Finally, the biggest of the drivers spoke.

"Sir, Excellency," he said.

Francis nodded.

"Is there, can there be any other punishment for us? Some of us may not survive this work."

"Death. Now." Francis said flatly.

By now the seriousness of the situation was firmly established. I paid my respects to the local Over-Lord, and I was back at my residence in Atlanta.

04.12.786 C.R. The twins, my sisters Jan and Jean, continue to be an embarrassment to me. I keep getting reports of their inappropriate behavior through mortal channels. People would usually draw me aside and say something like, "I don't want to bother you about this, Keeper, but I felt that it was my duty to let you know. Your sisters, the twins Jan and Jean, well, . . . they, you might say, overdo it from time to time."

When I would ask for more details, they would say, "Well, sir, it is primarily drink and men. They have no discretion. I am so sorry for your sake."

Then they would repeat reports from one city or another. The Keeper's office is well established and known throughout the world by now, and because they are my sisters, they are given a lot of leniency by the mortal authorities and by people in general. They are smart enough to stay clear of any Immortal Dais'. I knew that they were rudderless, but I did not know what to do. Elaine suggested that I have Lucius bring them home and even offered to talk to them with me. One evening soon after Elaine's offer, I instructed Lucius.

"I want you to go and collect my sisters, Jan and Jean," I said. "Find them, wherever they are and whatever they are doing, and bring them immediately to me. Do not give them any time to clean up or change their appearances. Just snatch them up and bring them here in front of me in this room."

Lucius seemed to meditate for a short time, no doubt communicating with his network and then blinked away.

I had already sent for Chloe and Jason and Anne to join me for moral support. Anne was, as usual, in the library. Chloe and Jason had to be brought back from Holland where they had been speaking.

"What! Brother?" was all that Jan could manage when they arrived. She was furious. Jean looked more ashamed than anything, she was the milder of the two. They were both dressed in identical skimpy dresses except for the color; Jan's was pink and Jean's was yellow. Chloe and Jason and Anne and I stood. Lucius hovered just over where he had dropped them. I glanced at Lucius. The twins saw this and looked his way as well. Jan calmed down considerably. It never ceases to amaze me how a wrong-doing mortal's attitude will change at the sight of an angel.

"What is it, brother?" Jan asked more softly.

"Yea, what?" Jean echoed quietly.

"What were they doing?" I asked Lucius.

They knew that the angel would not lie; they had been raised with him. They also knew that he would absolutely obey the Keeper. They both lowered their heads and stared at the floor.

They were with some men, Keeper," Lucius said.

"Doing what?" I asked.

"Mostly drinking," Lucius answered. "But the situation was going bad very quickly."

"I can imagine," I said. "Like turning into an orgy!"

As I shouted the last word, they dropped to their knees. "What am I going to do with you two?" I asked.

"We don't know, brother," they murmured in unison.

Chloe and Jason and Anne and I sat down. We all sat in silence for a few minutes. Chloe got up and went over to the twins and sat on the floor with them. She raised their faces and kissed them both on the forehead; they started to cry and Chloe cried with them and held them. Before long Anne was into it as well. Jason and I looked at each other and waited. Perhaps the love of their sisters would help. I did not know. After all this calmed down, I sent the twins to their room under restrictions. They could not leave the residence grounds without my permission. They knew better than to try to slip past Lucius. They seemed sorry for things this night, but I did not expect this to last long.

I saw the twins around the residence for the next few days and they would smile weakly when we passed. There was still no lasting solution.

"I could bring charges against them before you officially," I said to Elaine one afternoon in my study.

"Yes, you could," she answered. "And I would put them under supervision."

"Together?" I asked.

"No, I don't think so," Elaine answered. "I would separate them as part of the punishment, each with their own supervising angel. They would need jobs somewhere. Not hard labor but something unpleasant. Perhaps just as farm workers here in Georgia until they showed some signs of change."

"What should the charge be?" I asked.

"You are the head of the family now. It can be disrespect for the family head, tarnishing your good name or even illicit sexual actions. I am sure that we could come up with plenty of evidence against them."

"Ugh! What a choice," I said. "To either let them run rampant or this." I thought for a while. "And if I punish the twins, I have to wonder what young Roger is doing."

"Roger is more discrete," Elaine said.

"What do you know?" I asked.

"That is he more discrete. You don't need to be burdened with any more," she said. I nodded in agreement. If Roger was being discrete, then that was enough, for now.

"Why did mother and father want so many children?" I thought out loud.

"Because they loved each other very much and they loved children," Elaine said. "Twelve out of fifteen are productive and loving people. That's actually pretty good for mortals, you know."

"Yes, I guess so, mistress. I guess so."
Elaine departed and I decided to give the girls a few more days.

[N.D.] Today I noticed the twins romping with a baby giraffe, one of Twigga's offspring. The twins had on jeans and shirts but they were still identified by the scarf holding up the pony tail; Jan's was pink and Jean's was yellow. As I watched, I thought that they aren't really bad girls. They just have no sense of calling in life and so they drift to the lowest forms of entertainment with men; at least they have never been reported in any form of perversion. They just drink and sleep around a lot.

[N.D.] Today my gamekeeper Alan came to me with an idea.

"Good morning, Keeper," he began.

"Alan, how are all the animals?" I asked.

"Fine, Keeper, just fine. The hippos keep overrunning their boundaries. It is hard for them. But we speak to them again and they are all right for another month or two."

"I have full confidence in you, Alan."

"Thank you, Keeper. I am honored. Keeper, I came about, . . . well, I have a suggestion concerning your twin sisters."

"Really? What is it?" I asked. He had my attention.

"They seem to really like the animals. They have started helping with the residence animals and I could find full time jobs for them if you so desire."

I could have kissed the man. But he would have gone into shock. I calmed down and managed a better response. "Yes, fine, Alan. Anything that would give them a sense of purpose would be a great help. Thank you. Please proceed."

"Yes, good. I will get back to you later, Keeper," Alan said and he departed hurriedly.

[N.D.] It has been almost five weeks since my conversation with Alan about the twins and today Jan approached me for permission to leave the residence grounds. At first I thought, 'here it comes, she wants to party some more.'

"To go to the preserve of the Immortal Francis in Africa," she said. "Jean and I. We can be of some help there." She looked at me quite innocently.

"Let me think about it for a few days," I said.

"Yes. Brother," she replied. No argument. No attitude. Perhaps she was improving.

I inquired of Alan how the twins were doing and he said that they were working out fine. He said that recently they had stayed up two nights looking over a zebra and an leopard who were having a hard time giving birth. When the colt and the kitten were finally born, they cared for them for days and for the mothers. They seemed to be very involved in their work. I commended them to the supervision of Francis' people who assured me that I would be informed if they wandered from their work. Things seem to be going quite well with the twins now.

[N.D.] Today my sister Pamela came to me with what was to be a surprising complaint.

"Brother, I do dearly love your animal friends, but May's children should receive at least equal consideration from you," she said.

I was shocked. I thought that May's children were receiving all that they needed. I had put Pam in charge of the children's centers that were started by the great Keeper May and she had taken to the task right away. I rarely heard anything from her and all praised her work and dedication to the task. I was pleased that I had known where to put her to work and I felt that she was very satisfied with her work.

"How are the children slighted?" I asked.

"There are still too many in each home," Pam answered. "And I need more mortal help in caring for them. There are more and more of them every month."

"I did not realize this," I said. "Of course, I will help. But why do you think there are more of them every month? Are more children being neglected? If so, this should be taken to the highest level."

"There are more being neglected, Ken. There are more irresponsible people having children and not caring for them than ever before," Pam told me.

'During the glorious Reign?' I thought. This can not be. What should be done about it? We asked to see Elaine immediately.

"There certainly should be something done about this," Elaine said. "This is unacceptable behavior during the Reign. The Emperor has always been the friend of children. Something will be done and it will be severe and effective. I am going to talk to the Chancellor right away."

[N.D.] An Imperial decree has been issued and summary judgment promised to anyone who conceives children and does not take care of them. I don't know why this was not caught earlier. Surely it was not merely waiting until Pam made a issue of it; at least I don't think so. But I have learned not to question the timing of justice in the Reign. How ever it comes out, I must presume that the timing and the end result are under the ultimate control of the Emperor and his governors.

The decree unfortunately did not do much for the children already in the homes. Most of their parents had already died due to their unsavory practices or as the result of judgment for other crimes. I have issued a public request for help and the response has been most encouraging. Pam says that she now has all the helpers that she needs and that loving adoptions are now more frequent than before.

[N.D.] As I talked to Pam and Jason today, I again assured her that I did not intend for my animal friends to be treated any better than the children. Jason is my assistant for public liaison and he is a great help in this matter.

"Oh, I know, brother," Pam said. "You have so many things to do. Jason has been a dear in this. We also have a suggestion."

"Suggest," I said.

Pam looked to Jason.

"Ah, it is merely this, brother," Jason began. "We think it would be wonderful if we could combine the care of the children with the care of the animals." He paused and I waited.

So he continued. "You see, we think that they could get a lot from each other. Many of the animals have a very good calming effect on the children, especially the furry ones. But some of the other do as well. It mostly depends on the child. And the children need to get their minds off of themselves. They need someone to care for so that they can learn responsibility. They have not had a lot of care or much responsibility. So, if the children could help take care of the animals and the animals could help to comfort and calm the children, we think that it would be a great combination."

"Well, many of our people have pet animals," I said.

"Yes, brother, they do. But they are the healthy families. Pam's children, er, May's that is, don't have that kind of a background. Yet, they also need pets, or animal companions, and they need to learn how to take care of them."

"I see," I said. "That sounds like a wonderful idea. How would we proceed?"

"Well," Jason answered. "That is where we would need your backing. We can work and 'sell' the idea, but the animals caretakers and the child caretakers would have to cooperate in this. We would need the full authority of your office and perhaps some Immortal authority as well. At first this might look complicated and difficult to many, but we believe that the benefits would far out weigh any problems."

"You two have convinced me," I said. "Let's get started."

"Great," they chimed in unison.

"Also, brother," Jason added, "the twins could help a lot here, too."

"Do you two think they are ready for that?" I asked.

"Oh yes," Pam said. "They would be a great help and they would get a lot out of it as well."

The twins were thrilled to be asked to help.

07.22.808 C.R. I am in my 79th year. As I look back on my term as Keeper, I often wish that I could have done more. The animals are my great comfort. I have seen many generations of them come and go. I am always amazed at their nobility. I am very thankful for the work of the Immortal Francis. He has done so much for his animal friends. My siblings have all done well as the children and brothers and sisters of the Keeper. Some of them are already gone. My daughter Merle will succeed me. The Emperor be praised!

Kathryn

875 – 948 C.R.

3.12.876 C.R.   My name is Sarah. I am the grand daughter of Merle, the daughter of Kathryn, and the sister of Elizabeth. I am of the Annatic line but I am not invested myself; I am not the Keeper. This is my private journal. My sister Elizabeth is the Keeper Heiress. She is two years older than I am. She is gone much with her duties. I am her secretary. I publish her works and do some research. She is not very good at research, but she is very good with the public. Our mother, Kathryn, uses Elizabeth a lot with the more routine public matters as she herself is so interested in eradicating rebellion among the mortals of the empire.

[N.D.]   The joy of my life is my young nephew Tim. He will be 15th Keeper and his life shall probably span over the 1,000th year of the Emperor's Glorious Reign. My sister Elizabeth was older than myself and destined to be the Keeper. She died giving birth to Timmy and it fell to me to mother him and raise him. My mother Kathryn is still very active as the Keeper and she has distributed the tasks that Elizabeth was doing among three or four assistants. It does not bother me that I am not the Keeper Heiress and that I am not to be the Keeper. I am very happy to be Timmy's mother.

Mother had very few motherly tendencies when Liz and I were young and in her old age she is even less inclined. She likes Timmy well enough, but she does not want to be his "granny." When Timmy first began to talk, I told him I was "aunt Sarah" and he picked up on that rather quickly. Since he never knew his mother, he has never missed her. I am his mother to him. My mother Kathryn is seldom around as she is truly a traveling Keeper. She loves to travel and she does so at every opportunity or excuse. I once jokingly remarked that she was going to wear Lucius out with her travels but she quickly retorted that angels don't wear out. On one occasion when Timmy was still quite small, Kathryn dropped in to see us and Timmy pointed and exclaimed, "Aunt Kathryn."

"No, this is your grandmother," I corrected.

"Oh, let him call me 'Aunt Kathryn'" mother said. "I certainly don't want to be anybody's grandmother." With that the dye was cast. Tim will always call her 'Aunt Kathryn.'

[N.D.] Mother uses more makeup than she should and her wardrobe looks like it should belong to a much younger woman. I honestly believe that she is jealous of Elaine for her immortality.

[N.D.] One day while mother was on an official trip Lucius arrived back at the residence without her.

"Where is my mother?" I asked him.

"She is still in Latvia," he responded.

"And you are here," I said.

"I am not required," Lucius said. I almost sensed a small bit of grief in his voice, but this must have been in my mind as angels do not have emotions.

A few days later mother arrived home with another angel by the name of Bright. He is of the Vicar rank and quite intimidating. I remembered reading something in the journals about him, so I looked and found it in the journals of Mandie. He scared her as well. Mother is not scared of Vicar Bright. I think he is scared of her. It seems that he is temporarily assigned to her to help quell rebellion. I can see how he would have a chilling effect on rebels. Since he can also do anything that Lucius can do, Mother has no need for Lucius.

[N.D.] Since it now appears that Lucius will not be recalled, he has always served the Keeper, I am making good use of him and I am glad to have him around to help with Tim. Tim will grow up close to the angel and they should do well together when he is invested.

[N.D.] Vicar Bright is, of course, several ranks higher than Lucius. I forget the exact sequence in the angelic ranks so I had to look in the journals of Merle. Yes, there it is. From the top down; Seraphs, Cherubs, Worshippers, Princes, Vicars, Chiefs, Archangels, Heralds, Angels. They are all angels but Lucius is from the rank named simply angels, or the bottom echelon. So this new scary angel is a Vicar, he is four entire ranks above Lucius and of the kind hardly ever seen in our world. Elaine told Mandie that he was designed to 'unnerve' mortals. That is true. I am never glad to see this angel. I am always glad to see Lucius. Also, this one is from something called 'Imperial Security.' Mother in her zeal to stamp out all mortal rebellion in the empire evidently needs the help of this high angel and his legion. Although from what I hear, the harder she tries the more the rebels abound.

[N.D.] "I do not understand it," mother said over tea one afternoon.
"Don't understand what, mother?" I asked.
"Why? Why do they continue to rebel?" She shook her head. I let her go on. Once she starts on something that interests her she needs little encouragement.
"There is absolutely no chance of winning! None whatsoever. The Emperor's power is absolute. And they have no real complaints. You and I and many others have read the Journals. Life is good for mortals on this world. Very good. Why do they do it? There must be a root reason."

"I believe I've found that, mother." I said. She looked up from her tea. I was casually stirring mine.

"Good. Excellent. You are a good researcher, Sarah. What is your conclusion?" she asked.

I was thankful for the complement.

"Mother, I believe it is part and parcel of the human condition." I began. She did not interrupt; so I continued.

"From what I have read in the Journals, and you say that I am a good researcher, the main point of this Glorious Reign is to give the Emperor his due and to prove that mankind can not rule itself, that even individuals can not rule themselves."

"Didn't the mortal ages before this Reign prove that?" she asked.

"Not really. At least, I do not believe so."

"Why not?"

"Because the evil prince was loose during that time and free to lead everyone astray. Most rebellion was blamed on him."

"You have a point there, daughter," mother said. "You have researched the Journals."

"So now, rebellion has to come from the hearts of men and women," I said. "And the Emperor has his due."

"The Emperor's due?" mother asked.

"He is due, as a man, a millennium of obedience even if it has to be forced. Meanwhile, he and the Father and the Presence have proven that the evil prince, who is now bound away, is not the wellspring of all evil and rebellion. Mortal mankind is capable of quite a bit of that on their own. It is continually being proven," I finished.

"So mortal mankind is proven rebellious and the Emperor is proven righteous and just and we must all play our parts," Kathryn said in a resigned tone.

"Yes," I said.

We both shook our heads in agreement.

"I go to play my part," Kathryn said. "You take care of the residence, the library and little Timmy and keep in touch. Send Lucius if you need me. Where is that Vicar now? Bright!" Her angel of impending doom appeared. "Bright, we go now!" she said. And they were off to fight rebellion.

5.15.939 C.R. Reports came in from all over. Just as soon as one rebellious group or another got organized and started to express themselves, the Keeper Kathryn and the dreaded Vicar Angel Bright would appear and put the whole thing down. People would be executed at the nearby Immortal Dais and things would calm down in that area for a while. Still overall things seem to be getting worse. I am glad that mother has to deal with all this and not me.

6.11.940 C.R. Mother seems to be getting more and more discouraged with her work. I do not know exactly when she appointed herself the enforcer in the Empire. I don't know if she knows when; it just seemed to grow upon her. She does not catch every instance of rebellion. Many of them are caught by Imperial Security. There are more angels active these days like Vicar Bright. They are either Vicars or Chiefs in rank. I do not know why the rebellion is getting worse. It seems like the more merciful the Emperor is the worse it gets. And, conversely, the heavier the crack down the worse it gets. I still hold to my position that it is part of the human condition, but how long will it go on? It is the year 938 C.R. Tim is eight years old. Ten more years until he can assume the duties of the Keeper. Mother is very tired.

10.17.941 C.R. I, Kathryn, am the Keeper and Primate, the fourteenth in line from mother Anna. I take up in this family journal where my daughter Sarah left off. The year is 941 C.R. My daughter Sarah has died. Tim is

11 years old and he is devastated. Sarah was, for all practical purposes, his mother since his mother, my daughter Elizabeth, died giving birth to him. I will try to stay at the residence more, at least for a while, until his grief begins to subside.

11.3.941 C.R. I am very tired in my efforts to quell the continual rebellion against the Emperor. I know that the Angelic Imperial Security and the Immortal Princes can maintain control without my help. The rebels never have a chance from the very beginning of their rebellion. But I keep hoping that as one of the leading mortals on the earth that I can talk some sense into them before they are caught and charged with treason against the Emperor. I go to the areas where I believe a rebellion is fermenting. These places are varied and spread around the world. Elaine and the other Immortals do not seem to be concerned. Tim can assume this office in another seven years and I will be glad to lay it down if I am still alive. It is now only 59 years and the Emperor will have reigned on earth for a thousand years. Many believe including myself because Sarah was firmly convinced, that something great, even cataclysmic, will happen at that time. I am not sure what that will be.

[N.D.] In my desperation and discouragement I have asked for a special conference with Elaine. She will either come to the residence or send for me when she is ready.

[N.D.] It is now three days since I sent Lucius to ask Elaine for a conference. I have temporarily released Vicar Bright back into direct service for the Viceroy Cepata. That is where he came from. I happened upon him years ago in my work and I petitioned the Viceroy for permission to work with him and permission was granted.

[N.D.] It is now five days since I asked to talk to Elaine. I am sending Lucius to inquire again.

[N.D.] On the sixth day after my first request Elaine arrived suddenly in my front garden with a minimal escort.

"Kathryn, my dear, I am so sorry it took me so long to get here," she immediately said.

"I thought I had offended, Excellency," I said.

"Excellency? You are upset with me. We were at a great feast on the other side and I was totally unaware of what was going on here. Lucius was not allowed to approach me until yesterday. So, now I am here. Can we sit together?"

It seems that the Immortals are always feasting with the Emperor. What can they have to feast about so often? I must admit that I do not understand. But, after all, that is not my place. We went into my receiving room. Lucius and Elaine's angel captain accompanied us. I came straight to the point.

"Elaine, I need an audience with the Emperor," I said.

"My, the Emperor," she replied. "Is there anything that I can do?"

"Not this time. I feel that I can not go on unless I can see him," I replied flatly.

"All right. I will put in the request and come directly to you when it is granted," she said.

I thanked her and, of course, she wanted to see Timmy. We brought him in and we talked for a while. He is growing up to be quite a young man.

[N.D.] It has now been two weeks since I requested to see the Emperor and still no response. I dare not send Lucius another time as Elaine made it quite clear that she would come as soon as she knew something.

[N.D.] It has now been four weeks since I requested to see the Emperor. I am leaving Tim in the care of his new governess, a young woman from the staff named Miriam that he is very fond of. He seems to prefer her company to mine or anyone else's. I have decided to visit the Dais of the Viceroy John hoping that it will take my mind off this delay in seeing the Emperor. There is something about being around John that lifts my spirits. It is as close to the Emperor as I can get right now. My office allows me to visit a Viceroy without an invitation. I have never been given a standing invitation to visit the Capital. Sarah, when she was alive, pushed me to ask the Chancellor for a standing invitation, but I have always held that if they wanted me to have one, they would have taken the initiative and given it to me. Lucius will go with me and he can easily inquire at the angelic Legion's Vault for information. Imperial audiences are kept posted there on a daily basis.

[N.D.] Each time I see John the Beloved I get a new lease on life. He is literally brimming with love. He was sitting on his Dais at Patmos when I arrived. The angelic canopy seemed unusually loud this morning. I wanted to cover my ears with my hands but I thought that might be taken as disrespectful for the Viceroy as they were surely just as loud as he wanted them to be. Why are they always singing? John rose and greeted me warmly and with a long hug, longer than usual, but this time it could have been even longer and I would not have minded. I am not a 'huggy' person so I was surprised at my reaction.

"Here, Keeper Kathryn, sit by me," he said motioning to the empty prince's seat directly to his right.

I hesitated.

"That's all right," he said. "Mephibosheth is off to China for a while. He won't mind if you sit in his seat."

I sat down very gingerly at first as though I was afraid of breaking the chair. That is highly unlikely as it is made of some sort of reinforced gold. But I had never heard of or seen a mortal in an Immortal prince's seat. But this was the Viceroy John, only the Emperor could overrule him and that has not been know to happen since the beginning of the reign. I am not sure who the Immortal Mephibosheth is.

"Kathryn, dear, you look tired," John said.

"I am, Excellency," I said. "I am sorry to come to your court so tired."

"That is quite all right, Kathryn," he said taking my hand. "Perhaps we can do something to revive you. Has your work been very tiring of late?"

"Yes sir. Very tiring in deed."

"Well, we shall get you up and going again," he said. I did not know if I wanted to be got up and going but I managed a weak smile.

Just then a patrol appeared and some mortal wrong doers where brought before him. I wanted to leave and just walk in the Viceroy's gardens but I had not been excused so I stayed through the entire session.

This particular mortal looked like hundreds that I have seen lately, a stumpy little man with four days growth of beard and plain clothes and a rebellious look in his eye. I was interested to see what kind of treatment he would get from John. He was accused of treason, of course. Just another one who believed that self rule was the only fair kind in this world. Out of fear he knelt before the Viceroy. Five of his cohorts knelt behind their leader.

"The Over-Lord of Scandinavia sends you to me," John began. "Why are you a special case? You name is?"

"Sven," the man replied.

I thought there are only a million Svens in Scandinavia. So far this man does not look or sound very special.

"I suppose it is because I was once very loyal to the Emperor," the man offered.

"So, you weren't always a rebel," the Viceroy said.

"No. I mean, no sir. I was a champion in my country for the Imperial way. I even got a medal from that very same Over-Lord. I suppose that is why he hesitates to judge me now, Excellency."

"I see. And what has caused you to change?" John asked.

"I forgot," the man said. He waited for a response.

John looked him intently in the eyes. He looked back and did not blink. This seemed to go on for a very long time. John looking and the man looking back. Of course, no one hurries an Immortal prince at his own Dais. So I sat very still in my newfound chair of honor. I was horrified that the Viceroy might ask for my opinion, but he did not. Then John did something even more strange. He slid off of his seat and knelt before the kneeling offender while never breaking eye contact. Tears started to form in Sven's eyes. They brimmed to overflowing and then started to roll down his cheeks. He started to sob softly. Then the sobbing increased. The Viceroy embraced him and held him as he cried. The man collapsed seemingly under the weight of his burden and then the Viceroy sat back on his heels and cradled the man's head and shoulders in his arms and held him close to his chest. I have never seen anything like it. This man was reduced to molten wax by the mere presence of the apostle of love.

Several more Immortal princes arrived at the Dais and I started to stand to vacate the chair as I did not feel that I would recognize the Prince Mephibosheth by sight. But one of them signaled for me to keep my seat. All the Princes present, some male and some female in appearance, were absorbed in what was happening here. One of them motioned for the other offenders to be taken away. They mostly had perplexed looks on their faces. I don't know where they were taken or whatever became of them. The entire focus was on Sven.

Finally, the Viceroy wiped the man's tears with his own sleeve again and helped him to sit upright. John resumed his seat and the man got to his knees again in front of him.

"Now, my dear man," the Viceroy began. "What shall we do with you? You have done bad deeds. What should your punishment be?"

"I am worthy of death, Excellency," the man said. He looked straight at the Viceroy. There was not a trace of fear.

"Yes, you are," the Viceroy responded softly as he reached towards the little table at his side for his scepter. It was a Viceroy's scepter, no larger than most with only the small distinctive cross on the top. Still the man showed no fear. He kept his eyes only on John. The Viceroy laid his scepter in his lap. Sven glanced briefly at the scepter. Then he looked just a little perplexed.

"No, you shall not get off that easy, Sven," John said. "You name your punishment."

"Me, Excellency?"

"Yes, you heard me." John was smiling now.

There was a long pause as the man thought. He looked away for the first time in a long while. He looked at the floor. Then finally he spoke.

"I could go back and talk to all my old contacts and tell them that love is better than rebellion. I could count my life as forfeit so that if they kill me I would be no worse off than I am now. I could start groups that study the mercy and wisdom of the Emperor. You know, things like that." Then he was quiet.

"Go then, Sven." The Viceroy rose and pulled the man up with him. He picked up his scepter and touched the man lightly on both shoulders with it. "You have your mission. Tell all that the Emperor is just and merciful. Tell all your message of love."

"Yes, Excellency. I will. Thank you. Thank you many times over," Sven said as he backed away from the Viceroy. He almost backed into an angel just before he and the angel vanished, apparently back to Scandinavia.

All at the Dais erupted in spontaneous applause. I too had forgotten. I had forgotten how it was to be at the Dais of the Viceroy of love. I was considerably refreshed but still somewhat tired. I sat in that chair most of the day until John rose to retire and the night judge took over. His name is Mephibosheth. He returned just as we were preparing to leave. From what I could make out he is a special friend of the Chancellor. I wish I knew the writings as well as Sarah did.

[N.D.] I had just about given up hope of seeing the Emperor. But my time at John's court has made the time pass easier. Now word has come. I do not know if I will be in private with Him or whether he will be displeased with me. I still do not have the strength to care. Tomorrow we go, Elaine and myself.

[N.D.] We arrived at the Temple immediately. Elaine had her full escort and I had Lucius. The angels immediately joined the Imperial Canopy. We were rushed into the Temple by thousands of Immortals and mortals who were entering in great excitement. I had been included in a General audience. My heart sank. The Temple was quickly filled to overflowing. Mortals and Immortals sat mixed together. At the first great strains of music which came from somewhere above and behind us everybody stood. The procession entered from the rear, hundreds of Immortals in Imperial robes with scepters and banners. It was magnificent. Finally, the two Viceroys entered side by side and then there was a break in the procession and in the music. Slowly the strains of a very old song began to rise. All the Immortals were joining in. It was familiar to me from the collected songs of Merle. The words began, "All people that on earth do dwell . . ." The words had been written by the Chancellor during his mortality. Soon all, mortals, angels, Immortals including all ranks of princes, were singing as loud as they could. It was deafening and magnificent. The Emperor finally entered. He wore only his simple white robe and walked purposely but almost casually up the two thousand yard center aisle. He was smiling as usual. A luminous golden light surrounded Him. I wept uncontrollably as did many others. What a moment! All my problems and cares and tiredness melted away. The Emperor sat on his simple throne facing all of us and flanked by the Chancellor, the Master of the Feast, both Viceroys, and most of the Over Lords. There were a group of very high ranking angels over the throne; I believe they were Seraphs. He sat and we sang. As loud as we were singing, the angelic Canopy almost drowned us out. We sang for more than an hour to Him and to Him alone. He smiled constantly.

Then He began to show his glory. I had never seen this before, but when it began, I knew what was going to happen. He stood and held out His hands as if to bless us all. Then the light began to brighten around Him. It brightened until it was an intense white light. The light came from every part of his body. It got so bright that you could not exactly make out his form; he was just a mass of light in the midst of the brightness. With all the brightness you could still look at Him; the light did not hurt your eyes, even the eyes of us mortals. We all looked until the sheer brightness of the light filled the room so that all you could see was light. It is like the opposite of darkness. In total darkness you can not see any objects or shapes because the darkness engulfs everything. In His brightness the light swallows up everything. Finally, in this brightness we were all either kneeling or lying on the floor because we could not stand in this glory. In the Emperor there is no room for any darkness. I do not know how long this lasted. It seemed like minutes and it seemed like hours. Finally, I was aware of some slight stirrings around me and I opened my eyes and got to my feet. People were getting up all around me. It was still pretty quiet. The Emperor was still sitting on his throne. He was looking around at the people. The canopy of angels above us was quiet. This quietness pervaded everything. I could have stayed that way for ever.

The Chancellor was motioning for people to sit. In a few minutes Viceroy John said, "resume your seats." We obeyed. Awards were given to dozens of mortals most of whom fainted when they approached His Imperial Majesty. They were transported back to their seats by angels where their family and friends could help them sit up until they regained their composure.

Then it happened. The Chancellor David called my name. "The Keeper Kathryn will approach," he said.

I was in a state of shock. Elaine took my arm and guided me up the stairs to stand before Him.

"Kathryn, I give you a gift of love," the Emperor said. He reached out and placed his hand gently on my head. This time I saw the scar. I did not pass out. Again I felt an enormous peace and I believed that this time it would stay with me always. I looked into his eyes. The next thing I remember Elaine and I were back in our seats and I had a purple ribbon around my neck with a gold medallion on it. In the Emperor's own language it simply said 'Love.'

[N.D.] My life is transformed. I have nothing but love for everyone. I speak on it everywhere. Timmy loves to be with me. He tells me he loves me all the time. The love never weakens. I feel 30 years younger.

Reign II

[N.D.] I have come to the conclusion that it is upon me in my older years to more clearly explore the life of our mother, Anna, to study the kind of person that she was, to see her motives and her strengths. Why was she, of all the mortals alive in her time, chosen to begin the line as Keeper. I will get as much information out of Elaine as I can but I know her and she will expect me to first do my homework. Also, I want to study and explain how the office of Keeper developed over the centuries. I will turn most of the routine chores of my office over to Tim. It will be good practice for him as he gets ready to assume the office after I am gone. I have asked Elaine to designate Tim as Keeper Heir and she has graciously agreed.

4.12.945 C.R. After some 8 months of studying the ancient writings and the journals I am amazed at how well things have worked out under Elaine's supervision. She is a very skillful guide. Most of her charges have grown into the job quite naturally and she seems to know just when to give advice and counsel and when to hold her peace. I have a few questions for her beginning with mother Anna. Since I believe I have done my research, I intend to start questioning her at our regular biweekly meetings. She usually comes to my residence for these meetings. When she comes, that means that she is not pushed for time. If she calls me to her residence, the meeting is usually short and to the point. I will save my questions for when she comes to me.

[N.D.] "So Elaine," I began, "you knew that Anna would be interested in researching your mortal times when you brought her to the court of Henry Sawyer?"
"Yes." She answered very quickly.
"You remember those days clearly? I mean, I know you are Immortal but I can not imagine remembering back that far. Your memory is not like ours? It is perfect?"

"My memory is pretty good. But I was just there yesterday," Elaine said.

"It seems like just yesterday. That is amazing," I said.

"No dear, I really was there yesterday," Elaine said.

"You were behind the veil yesterday. You told me that," I insisted.

"Yes," she walked to me and touched my cheek with her hand. "You can go places from there, places on worlds and places in time."

As the meaning of this began to sink in, I was dumbfounded.

"You travel in time as you wish?" I heard myself saying.

"Not as I wish," Elaine answered. She sat down near me. "It is strictly regulated. We need permission from the highest level each time we do it."

"Permission from the Emperor?"

"From Him or the Time Warden," she answered. That was a new term for me. I had never heard it or run across it in the journals.

"Who is the Time Warden?" I asked.

"You don't know him. He is a Cherub."

"An angel?" "

"Yes, a very high ranking one."

"And you do this from the other side" I asked.

"Yes. It is difficult to explain," she said.

"Why have you let me know this when you never revealed it to any of my predecessors?" I asked.

"They never pursued your line of study. I knew when you started this line of investigation that you would start to notice that things often went well for me and for my plans. You would assume some sort of intervention from above my office and abilities even as an Immortal, even as Imperial Legate."

I nodded.

"And, well, and there is also your place in the line, this time in the Reign. We are nearing a change."

There was silence for a while. She waited for me to process this information. She spoke again.

"Also, Kathryn, you are mature for a Keeper, for a mortal. I almost revealed this to Joan. She was mature in her old age, but I delayed too long and she died."

"You did not know she was going to die?" I asked.

"No. We are not omniscient. Only the Emperor . ."

I interrupted, "I mean, you did not go ahead and see?"

"No. For one thing we have to have a good reason to use the time portal, and we can not go forward, only backward."

"I see, only backward. Do you know why that is?"

"Not really. There is a block forward. I don't know if it occurs naturally or if it is added for control purposes. There are a lot of things we are still learning. We are never done learning."

"Does that frustrate you as it does us?" I asked.

"Occasionally, but when it does, we know to spend more time with the Emperor. The regular feasts usually suffice. I know that our Immortal state looks very godlike to you mortals. We are Immortal but we are still creatures; we are created beings. Only the Emperor, his Father and the Presence are God. We continue to wonder at their creativity."

I wanted to get back to the time travel issue but one of Elaine's angels indicated that she was needed in Montevideo and she had to leave. I would get back to that next time, and next time my questions would be a little different.

[N.D.] "When you 'go back' and see, let's say, Anna or May, does your visit ever appear, ah, 'odd' to them?" I asked at our next meeting.

"How to you mean 'odd'?" Elaine asked.

"I mean, does it seem out of place or different?"

"No, it is just like any other visit. They don't know where or when I have just come from. We spend a lot of time beyond the veil and mortals expect that. When we can not be located, mortals just presume that we are where they can not go. And this is true. Mortals are used to not getting responses. Even the Keeper does not question when Lucius does not find me or bring back an answer. They learn very young to just wait as there is usually a reason beyond their control when we are not available."

"It's no wonder that we can't understand you." I said. "You said something about the time in which I live when we last talked."

"Yes, Tim will be the last Keeper," Elaine answered.

I had become accustomed to shocking statements from Elaine of late. She continued.

"I believe that I do not have to tell you to keep these subjects only in your private journals," Elaine said.

"Yes, I presumed that. I would probably only spread confusion among the people," I said.

"Very wise, Kathryn."

"So help me to understand, if you will," I said pressing my luck a bit. She did not respond so I continued.

"Say, I ask you a question about Anna or her time and you don't know or don't remember well enough to answer – just for the sake of my education. You go to the other side. You have to go to the Capital portal?"

"I have to be on the other side," she said.

"Over mortal history some have tried to go back in time," I commented.

"You can't get there from here," Elaine said. "Only from the other side."

"O.K. Then you get permission to go through the time portal and go back to visit Anna. Does permission take long?"

"No. The Warden knows the mind of the Emperor. He was created for this."

"I see. So you go back and to her eyes you merely step into her space as if you came from somewhere on the other side or on earth."

"That's right. I did come from the other side."

"Oh, yes, you did. Then you find out what you need and then leave." I thought for a minute. "What if you change something, something that will affect the future, Anna's future?"

"We are careful not to disturb the timeline. That is the most important thing. When we go back, we are not to disturb the timeline."

"What if you did, say, by accident or something?"

"The Emperor would have to fix it."

'That also is handy,' I thought. I also thought, 'why do we live our lives generation after generation? Ultimate control is apparently possible.'

"None of us know everything," Elaine interrupted my thoughts in that way of hers that seemed to know my thinking, "we just rejoice in life and leave the hard stuff to the Emperor."

I liked that. There was a time when I wouldn't have. But now it sounded good to my ears. I returned to my list. I had memorized it and I was determined to continue while Elaine was willing. "So there would be nothing at all that would clue a mortal that you are appearing from another time?" I asked.

"If I appeared without an escort," she said. "But mostly they don't question that."

"No, they wouldn't. And you sometimes do appear without one, even now."

"There is more than one reason for that," she continued. "Mostly, it is as we wish it. But when we travel back, the angels do not go."

"I see." It seemed that every question created three more questions.

"I would like to be able to explain what being on the other side is like to you, Kathryn," Elaine said. "Have you ever been in a play?"

"Yes. When I was in school."

"Do you remember the difference between being on stage and being back stage, behind the scenes?"

"Yes."

"Well, that's the best way I can explain it. Being here in this world is like being on stage; being on the other side is sort of like being back stage. All the secret slits in the curtain, all the secret doors and secret trap doors are obvious back there. The door to time is there too, and the mansion where we live with the Emperor."

I thought for a while and Elaine was quiet. I decided to stop at least for now. But from now on I would always wonder more about just what Elaine was doing.

"There were even times when I was a mortal that I stepped outside of time," Elaine suddenly added.

I wished that she had not. I was almost overloaded. But this was too good to pass up. "Really? When? How?"

"When we were mortal, the Presence dwelt within us," she reminded me. That brought to my mind a whole raft of questions which I was not prepared to ask now.

Elaine continued, "When we would talk to the Emperor through the Presence, we called it 'praying', or if we adored the Emperor through the Presence especially, we called this 'worship'; we often stepped outside of time and we rarely noticed it."

"But sometimes you did?" I asked.

"Sometimes, afterward, after the talking or the adoring, we would notice that much time had passed and we would remark that it seemed like hardly any time had passed for us. Then our souls had been beyond the veil."

"That must have been wonderful," I said.

"It kept us going," Elaine answered.

"But that does not happen to mortals now during the Reign?" I asked.

"No, the Presence is not inside mortals during the reign. The Emperor is visible," she said.

It was a lot to absorb. I would certainly never go public with it. Some mortals might think I had gone mad.

1.30.946 C.R.   I can no longer ignore my responsibly. I must start training Tim and taking him with me when I travel. As a matter of fact, I need to plan some trips with Tim in mind. There are some places that I can show him and some mortals and Immortals that I can introduce him to that will help him when it is his time to take over. There is no use of him needing to learn the ropes the hard way like I had to. Don't get me wrong, my mother, Merle the Keeper, was a wonderful woman. She loved me and I knew it and she was very devoted to her mission to get mortals to worship the Emperor. But it was not her nature to take the time to show me the intricacies of the Keeper's office. It may not be my nature either, but I want to help Tim get ready for it all. It is already clear that he will not have an easy time of it. I know several Immortals who are unique even for Immortals. They are people of unusual wisdom that Tim can consult secretly, if necessary, who can guide him through things that most mortals could not even imagine.

[N.D.] There are a group of Immortals around the Emperor most of whom do not have any official position or title within the Empire. But they are close to Him and they come and go frequently from the Capital and the other side as they will. It is not that most Immortals do not have the ability to do this, but many of them pick one place or the other and just stay there. Some of them prefer to live in this world, many in their own old mortal communities. Many of them prefer to stay on the other side and rarely if ever come to our world. Many of them have duties in the court on the other side or in this world.

This small group that come and go and know so much are known as the Signets because they are each like a ring on the Emperor's hand. Elaine first told me about them several years ago. They move for Him and for the Empire without straying from His heart or will. They represent Him only in the sense that they resemble Him in their character and not because they have a title or office of any kind. I am sure that I do not know all of them. They all do know each other both on this side and the other side of the veil. They lived in many different times as mortals. If there was a lack of respect in their time for the Emperor in any place or community, they seem determined now to have homage paid to the Emperor as if it were a debt. They are all of one mind and they can not be diverted from their task.

The first one that I shall take Tim to meet is a man who has been wrongly accused of being sad and somber. This is the farthest from the truth. He was mortal in the sixteenth century and immigrated to the new world. His people were known as 'puritans.' His name is Josiah Pemberton. He stays most of the time in Boston and is frequently found at the Dais of the Metropolitan there. He has no position at this court and no regular seat. However, when he shows up at the Dais one of the junior members of the court invariably gets up and offers their seat to Josiah. He thanks them and takes the seat. Sometimes there are several who offer their seat and Josiah seems to be able to remember where he sat in the past and takes the seat that should be next in line. The newly displaced Prince either stands or vanishes for the time being. They rarely sit or get on the ground unless the Emperor arrives and then they all dive for the grass before Him. Josiah will be an excellent Immortal for Tim. Tim can ask him any thing and Josiah will be a great help. I want Tim to have all the help he can use. I have a feeling that his time as Keeper may be the hardest of all, more difficult than any of us have had it. May the Presence help him mightily.

03.11.974 C.R. *Grandmother was right. The rebellion and straying from the Emperor is worse than ever. But I am sure that He has a plan. He always does. Tim, K. & P.*

www.ingramcontent.com/pod-product-compliance
Lightning Source LLC
Chambersburg PA
CBHW031216020726
47499CB00002B/604